DATE DUE			
JA 04 '12			
MAR 0 ? 2013			
SEP 3 0 2013			

PRAIRIE STORM

*Also by Catherine Palmer
in Large Print:*

Prairie Fire
Prairie Rose

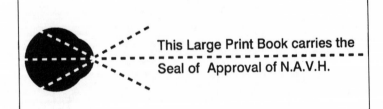

PRAIRIE STORM

A Town Called Hope # 3

Catherine Palmer

Thorndike Press • Waterville, Maine

Library of Congress Cataloging-in-Publication Data

Palmer, Catherine, 1956–
   Prairie storm / Catherine Palmer.
      p. cm.
   ISBN 0-7862-3820-8 (lg. print : hc : alk. paper)
   1. Evangelists — Fiction. 2. Orphans — Fiction. 3. Large
type books. I. Title.
PS3566.A495 P74 2002
   813'.54—dc21   2001058199

For my earthly father,
Harold Thomas Cummins,
whose gentle love helped lead me
to my heavenly Father

My thanks to those whose vision and diligence helped bring the town called Hope to life: Tim Palmer, Ron Beers, Ken Petersen, Rebekah Nesbitt, and the whole HeartQuest team. My special thanks to Kathy Olson for her insightful editing and constructive suggestions as I wrote this series. Bless you all.

The Lord is slow to get angry, but his power is great, and he never lets the guilty go unpunished. He displays his power in the whirlwind and the storm. The billowing clouds are the dust beneath his feet.

— Nahum 1:3, NLT

You have not come to a physical mountain, to a place of flaming fire, darkness, gloom, and whirlwind. . . . You have come to the assembly of God's firstborn children, whose names are written in heaven. You have come to God himself.

— Hebrews 12:18, 23, NLT

CHAPTER 1

Hope, Kansas
June 1866

A sudden, high-pitched cry caught Lily Nolan's attention. She sucked in a breath. A baby? Somewhere in the growing darkness, a baby was crying. Lily pushed aside the tent flap and stepped outside, listening. There it came again! Weak but insistent, the wail curled into the marrow of Lily's bones.

Abigail, she thought. *Oh, my darling Abby!*

No. That wasn't possible, was it? Abby was gone, buried in a little wooden box at the edge of Topeka. But whose baby was crying? Why didn't the mother rock the child?

Lily's body contracted and began to ache in response to the baby's cries. Could the voice be Abby's, calling to her mother from the spirit world? Beatrice had tried to assure Lily that the baby was an angel now, a soul drifting in the great unseen, a messenger who would come to her with hope and comfort from beyond. But this cry sounded so real. And so near.

Lily stepped out into the tall prairie grass. In the distance she could see the town of Hope, Kansas — little more than a mercantile, a smithy, a newly built church, and a few shabby soddies. Women wearing homespun dresses, men in tattered trousers, and barefoot children moved down dirt paths toward the main road. Seeking entertainment or hoping for a cure for some unnamed trouble, they came to the traveling show, just as such people did in every town across the country.

Clutching the velvet cape of her fortune-teller's costume closer about her, Lily concentrated on Beatrice's speech. "Are you sad and blue?" the woman called. "Does your heart ache, your blood race, your liver leap, and your stomach churn? Is your hair limp? Do your feet hurt? Are your fingers stiff? Whatever ails you, come and find the answers to your troubles!"

Lily knew it would be a while before "Madame Zahara" started peddling elixir, and even longer before she would send customers to the tent to have their fortunes told. With the cry of the baby haunting her, Lily gathered up her skirts and set off through the grass. If she could find the child's mother and gain permission to hold the infant for a few moments — maybe even kiss the soft cheek or sing a little lullaby — perhaps then she could stop aching so for Abby. Maybe she could find reason to go on.

Just a week ago, while the traveling show was camped on the outskirts of Topeka, an epidemic of diphtheria had swept through the city. With it came the nightmare of fever, listlessness, and the panicked struggle for breath. Though diphtheria was known as a childhood illness, the strain that tore through Topeka grew especially virulent and soon began to claim adults. Scores had died, young and old alike.

Lily pressed her knuckles against her lips to hold back a sob. After two days of unbearable suffering, her precious Abigail had slipped away forever. Before long Lily's husband had also succumbed — Ted Nolan, the dashing but lazy fellow she had married to escape her sanctimonious and abusive father. Hours after the women had buried Ted, diphtheria claimed the traveling show's manager, Jakov Kasmarzik. In a panic, Beatrice had loaded as much of the show's gear as she could into one of their two wagons and headed west, with Lily barely able to function in her grief. Now the two women were trying to fill all the roles of the traveling show, hoping to earn their way to California. Or at least that was Beatrice's plan. Lily had no intention of going to California, but she didn't think Beatrice

11

needed to know that yet.

"Would you take a look at that gaudy wagon, Caitrin," commented a woman strolling with her three companions just ahead of Lily. She wore her rich brown hair piled on her head, and the bulge beneath her dress gave evidence that soon she would bear a child. "Dr. Kasmarzik's Traveling Show," she read from the sign painted on the wagon where Madame Zahara proclaimed her message. "Fine Theater, Singing, Juggling! Featuring Dr. Kasmarzik's Patented Elixir. Cures Guaranteed!"

"Aye, Rosie," the other woman in the group chimed in, "and my own father was a leprechaun."

With a giggle, the one called Rosie read from the sign Beatrice had put up, its black canvas painted with silver stars: "Madame Zahara — Fortunes Told! Palms, Tea Leaves, and Tarot Cards Read! Now that sounds interesting. I've always wanted to visit a traveling show. What do you think, Seth? Could we stop at the show before we go and listen to the preacher?"

Lily frowned at the woman's mention of the traveling preacher who was running a stiff competition for Dr. Kasmarzik's Traveling Show. Who did the fellow think he was, this Reverend Elijah Book, scaring off business and ruining her chances of a good evening's income? Lily could see him, outlined by the golds and pinks of the setting sun, as he raised his hands to beckon the gathering crowd. No wonder the women came, dragging their husbands behind them. The preacher was as good-looking a fellow as Lily had ever seen.

Straight and tall, with deeply tanned skin and piercing blue eyes, he towered over his congregation like a stately cottonwood tree. Rather than a fine silk top hat, the preacher wore a brown Stetson that perched just above his dark brows and straight slash of a nose. In a blue chambray shirt, worn denim trousers, and scuffed leather boots, he looked like he ought to be rounding up strays on a Texas cattle ranch. But there he stood, waving his big black Bible and barking out Scripture like John the Baptist himself.

Lily glared at him. Three or four months more with the traveling show and she would have enough money for a train ticket to Philadelphia. Though she had fled her pious father almost two years before and had vowed never to return, now Lily was determined to journey back to the big brownstone that once had been her home. The consequences would be severe, she knew, but her future with the show held no hope at all.

Lily heard the woman's husband, Seth, give a grunt of disgust. "This little town has had enough troubles without a bunch of ne'er-do-wells looking to skin the locals."

"Aye," the Irishwoman agreed. "These sorts of people wander through Ireland in bright caravans, selling useless potions and swindling innocents of their hard-earned coins. The doctors are bad, and the fortune-tellers are worse. But 'tis the actors who cause all the bawdy revelry."

Behind them Lily bristled. It was true that Dr. Kasmarzik's potion, which sold for ten cents a bottle, was nothing more than a mixture of corn syrup, vinegar, peppermint oil, and a dash of turpentine. But her acting had never caused one moment of bawdiness. She performed selections from Shakespeare and the poets of Europe. She played the melodeon and sang arias from the great operas. Educated at the finest school for young ladies in Philadelphia, she brought culture and dignity to Dr. Kasmarzik's show. If customers did sometimes get out of hand, it certainly wasn't due to her performances.

"I've seen whole villages run amok when the traveling caravans passed through," the flame-haired Caitrin continued. "Husbands neglect their chores, and their wives form long lines at the fortune-teller's wagon.

Children roam about neglected and hungry. On top of all that, the members of the traveling shows usually manage to steal anything left unattended."

Of all the gall, Lily thought, clenching her teeth. How dare these provincial prairie hens accuse her of thievery! She considered passing around them, but they continued on in the direction of the baby's cries, so she followed.

The preacher had managed to draw a bigger crowd than Madame Zahara, Lily realized. At thirty-five, Beatrice Waldowski cast a commanding presence in her flowing robes, long raven hair, crimson lips, and sultry brown eyes outlined in black kohl. Lily was never sure whether it was Madame Zahara's mystic predictions or the intimidating woman herself who struck awe in the hearts of the most rough-hewn customers. Whatever it was brought them back night after night to spend their coins at her table.

But now she had stiff competition. The preacher had spread open his Bible in his big hand and was holding it out toward the people like a plate of tempting hors d'oeuvres. The evening breeze riffled the thin pages, lifting and turning them one at a time, but the preacher didn't seem to notice. He just kept right on talking, reciting the story of

15

Nicodemus's visit to Jesus in the middle of the night.

Lily shook her head. How many times had she heard *that* sermon? She could probably preach it with as much accuracy as she could recite Jakov Kasmarzik's opening act for the traveling show. Before long the preacher would announce those familiar words, "For God so loved the world —"

Ha, Lily thought. If God loved the world so much, why had he allowed her father to beat her black and blue while her mother stood by wringing her hands and doing nothing? Why had God let Ted and Jakov die of diphtheria? Why had he snatched away helpless little Abigail? For that matter, why was God permitting that poor baby in the distance to go on crying unattended? Couldn't any of these pious Crawthumpers hear the child's sobs? To her, the baby's wails sounded as loud and demanding as the clanging bells of a fire wagon.

"Do you suppose Madame Zahara really can tell a person what's going to happen, Caitie?" The woman named Rosie paused to look back at the tent where Lily's table was set up. "Do you think she might know whether I'm bearing a boy or a girl?"

When the two couples halted at the edge of the crowd, Lily tried to move around them,

16

but they were blocking her path. The preacher had packed the people as close around him as oysters in a can. Rooted to the ground, the crowd gaped upward as the man expounded on his text.

"You'll not set foot near that wagon, Rosie," Caitrin said in a loud whisper. "Sure you recall the very words of Scripture about such deviltry."

"I do not. I've been to church all my life, and I don't recall anyone ever saying it was wrong to visit a fortune-teller."

"It's in the middle of Deuteronomy, Rosie," Seth drawled. "I remember reading it that time you made me search for the verse about foundlings."

"I declare," Rosie muttered. "One of these days Deuteronomy is going to do me in."

Lily searched for another way through the crowd as Caitrin pulled a small Bible from her pocket and scanned the pages. "Here 'tis. 'There shall not be found among you any one that maketh his son or his daughter to pass through the fire,' " she read in a low voice, " 'or that useth divination, or an observer of times, or an enchanter, or a witch, or a charmer, or a consulter with familiar spirits, or a wizard, or a necromancer. For all that do these things are an abomination unto the Lord.' "

"Well, for Pete's sakey," Rosie whispered. "I had no idea."

Lily pinched her lips and tapped the woman on the shoulder. "Excuse me," she said. "Could you step aside, ma'am? I'm trying to find that crying baby."

Brown eyes focused on Lily, roving from her white blond hair down the purple velvet cape to the tips of her scuffed brown boots. "Oh, have you lost your baby?"

Lily swallowed as the question stabbed through her. "Oh," she breathed. "Yes, I've lost . . . lost my baby. My Abigail."

"I can hear her crying," Rosie whispered. "Where did you leave your child?"

"I don't . . . don't know where she is." Lily shook her head. That wasn't what she meant to say. She knew Abigail was buried in the little box. The wooden box. "I need my baby. I can't . . . I can't stop hearing the cries."

"We'll find your daughter," Rosie said, taking Lily's hand. "Come on, Caitrin. Let's help this poor woman look for her baby. In the crush of people, the dear child could get hurt. Seth, you and Jack stay right here. We'll be back in a minute."

"I hear the wee one now," Caitrin said, in a strong Irish lilt. " 'Tis on the other side beyond the Reverend Book. Let's go around the crowd."

Lily tried to force down the tears that

welled unexpectedly in her eyes as the two women began to move her toward the sound she had been following. She wanted to tell them it wasn't Abigail, that her baby was dead, that this was some other woman's child. But the preacher's voice rang too loudly, hammering every word into the silence like a nail into a coffin.

" 'Except a man be born again, he cannot see the kingdom of God!' " he thundered. Lily huddled down between Rosie and Caitrin as they pressed her through the throng. " 'How can a man be born when he is old? can he enter the second time into his mother's womb, and be born?' "

No, Lily thought. Abby was dead, and she could never be born a second time. Only once would that precious newborn be laid on her mother's exhausted body. Only once would Lily feel the gentle pressure of the baby's weight in her arms, the nuzzle of a pink cheek, the grip of tiny fingers. Abby was lost. Lost forever.

"I've found her!" Rosie cried, dragging Lily toward a leather saddlebag hanging on the side of a horse that had been hobbled near the road. Within the pouch, something pushed, wriggled, and flailed as a cacophony of desperate cries drifted into the evening air. "Here's your baby!"

"Abigail?" Lily whispered, approaching the bag. Her heart faltered as she laid her hand on the soft leather. At her touch, the wailing ceased. But this couldn't be Abby. There must be another mother nearby. Some woman had left her baby in this bag. But why?

"Goodness gracious," Rosie said, "why did you put your daughter into a saddlebag? That's no place for a baby."

"No, I —" The baby began to wail again, cutting off her words.

"Why don't you take the poor little thing out and feed her? I grew up in an orphanage, and I've taken care of many a baby. I can almost bet your sweet Abigail is wet and hungry."

Hardly able to make herself breathe, Lily drew open the leather pouch and slipped her hands around the warm, damp little body. Oh, Abigail! The baby felt just like Abby . . . only smaller . . . newer. She lifted the squirming bundle out of the bag and tucked it against her neck. The child's soft lips immediately began to root hungrily.

"Aw, she's precious!" Rosie cried. "But she looks like she's half starved. You'd better feed her."

"Aye, sit here on this blanket," Caitrin spoke up, guiding Lily to a square of brightly woven wool stripes spread beneath a spindly tree. "Is this your camp? Here, I'll put the pillow behind your back. There now, little Abigail is so hungry she can hardly bear it. Sure she's all wrinkled up like a newborn! How old is she?"

Lily couldn't make herself speak. The kicking baby clung to her, sobbing in anguish as she tucked it beneath the purple cape. Where was the child's mother? She was the one who should be feeding this baby.

"Do you need help with your buttons?" Rosie asked, kneeling on the blanket.

"No, I can . . . I can do this." Lily couldn't hold back her tears as she performed the familiar motions of slipping apart the row of buttons, untying her camisole ribbon, and nestling the baby close. The moment the child began to nurse, all crying ceased, and the tiny legs curled into a ball.

"Abigail was famished!" Rosie said with a laugh. "Goodness, I don't believe she'd been fed for hours."

"Whisht, Rosie," Caitrin murmured. "The lady's still weeping, can't you see? There now, madam, you've got your baby once again. The wee thing will forget all about her hunger in a moment, and the pair of you can have a good night's rest."

Lily tried to stop crying. Truly she did. But as the baby drank milk meant for little Abby, her pain and longing only intensified. All around her, the world drifted away — the two caring women, the rough blanket, even the preacher, whose voice droned like the hum of a lazy bee. The baby's fingers were splayed across the bodice of Lily's dress, and she knew they were not Abby's fingers. The tiny head wreathed in a cloud of dark curls bore no resemblance to Abby with her golden wisps. The face was smaller, the cheeks sunken, the skin wrinkled. Abigail had been plump and round, at four months the picture of health. This was not Abby.

"She's still crying," Rosie whispered to Caitrin. "I hate to leave her alone like this."

The Irishwoman glanced over her shoulder. "The preaching's nearly finished for the evening, so it is. Sure we'd best get back to our men." She laid a hand on Lily's arm. "Are you all right? I know you're not from one of the homesteads around Hope, so you must have come traveling our way. Perhaps Rosie and I could have a look in the crowd for your husband."

"My husband is dead," Lily whispered as she cupped the baby's tiny head. The child was still nursing as though every drop of milk must be drained into her tiny, shrunken stomach. Lily shifted the baby into her other arm, and the child began to suckle again.

"Three days ago. He's buried near Topeka. My daughter lies beside him."

"Your daughter?"

Lily brushed her damp cheek. "I buried her in a wooden box."

"Oh, dear," Rosie said. "I'm so sorry. No wonder you're upset — a husband and a daughter both gone. I couldn't imagine how any woman could forget where she'd put her baby, but now I see you've been through a terrible trial. If I lost Seth and Chipper, I'd be just wild with grief. I couldn't bear it. Oh, honey, do you and little Abigail need a place to sleep tonight? I hate to think of you out here on the prairie with nothing but a blanket and that old horse. Seth and I have a great big house, lots of space, and we'd be glad to put you and your daughter up for the night."

Lily could feel that the baby had finally drifted off to sleep, warm and content at last. "No, no, you don't understand," she murmured, drawing the tiny form out from beneath the purple cape and gazing down at the child's blissful face. "This is . . . this is going to be all right. In a moment, I'll leave."

"Leave?" Caitrin exclaimed. "But 'tis almost fully dark now. You're a nursing mother and a *frainey* one at that. Sure you can't be tramping down the road in the middle of the night."

23

"Hey!" The preacher's voice pealed out like a clap of thunder. "What's going on here?"

Lily's head snapped up. Just beyond the blanket stood the two men who had accompanied Rosie and Caitrin. Between them, his boots planted a pace apart on the prairie grass, towered the preacher. He swept off his Stetson, took a step toward the women, and punched the air with his forefinger.

"Look here, lady," he snarled at Lily. "I don't know who you are or what you're up to, but you'd better hand over my baby. I've been given two jobs to do in this world. One of them is to preach the gospel. And the other is to take care of Samuel."

"Samuel?" Rosie and Caitrin said in unison. *"Samuel?"*

CHAPTER 2

"Yes, Samuel. That's my baby." Elijah stuffed his hat back onto his head and took another step toward the pretty blond-haired woman in the purple cape. What was going on here? "Who're you?"

She looked up at him with big blue eyes and tearstained cheeks. "Lily Nolan," she said softly, holding Samuel out in her arms. "I'm sorry."

"Well, I reckon so." He knelt on one knee and took the baby. The instant his big hands closed around the damp little bundle, Samuel's eyes shot open and he let out a squall that could have shattered glass. Eli's heart sank. "Aw, don't start that again, fella. Come on, now, young'un, buck up."

He drew the baby close and awkwardly rocked him from side to side. Just like always, it didn't do a bit of good. The baby kept on hollering, his little fists pumping the air in a rage.

"Please," the woman said, reaching out. Before Eli could react, she took the baby, turned him sideways, and tucked him into the crook of Eli's elbow. "This is the way to hold your son," she said, "and put your hand under his bottom."

"He's wet!"

"He certainly is. Where's his mother? She ought to have changed and fed him hours ago. It's no wonder this baby's been crying his head off. He's miserable. He wants his mother."

"We thought *you* were his mother, Mrs. Nolan," the woman beside her said.

"What's going on here, Rosie?" Seth Hunter asked.

"This woman told Caitrin and me that she'd lost her husband and her daughter in Topeka three days ago. She said she could hear Abigail crying, and when we found this baby in the saddlebag, she started feeding him."

"You fed Samuel?" Eli demanded of the blond woman. He looked down at the baby, who had settled into a drowsy daze. As a matter of fact, this was the first time Sam had been quiet since Eli could remember. A miracle. "What did you feed him?"

"She nursed him," the other woman said. "She told us the baby was her daughter, Abigail."

"No . . . no, I didn't." Lily gathered her skirts and stood. "I said I had lost my baby.

And I have. I've lost Abigail. Sometimes I think I hear her crying, but then I remember that she . . . that Abby is dead. My baby is gone . . . she's dead . . ."

Clapping her hand over her mouth, she fled. Eli frowned. A dead husband and a lost baby. A complete stranger nursing Sam.

But the baby was quiet. Quiet for the first time ever. Sleeping.

"Whoa, lady!" Eli bellowed. "Hold your horses there."

When she didn't stop, he took off after her. Samuel jerked awake and went to wailing again, but Eli had gotten so used to the ruckus he hardly noticed as he loped through the tall prairie grass. *God,* his heart cried out, *show me what to do here! You gave me this child, and I don't want him to die. Maybe you sent along this gal, too. Please make her stop running away.*

Her purple cape billowing behind, the woman jogged on as if she had no idea where she was going. Eli easily caught up to her, snagged her elbow, and swung her around. To his dismay, he saw that tears were streaming down her cheeks.

"Ma'am," he said over Sam's screams, "listen, I didn't aim to scare you. You don't need to be afraid of me. I'm just a preacher, and not much of one at that. Look, I don't know a thing about babies, feeding them or holding them or anything, and I'm real sorry to hear about your husband and your young'un passing on. Fact is, I appreciate you taking care of Samuel here."

"What?" She wiped her cheek with the heel of her hand. "Where's your wife?"

"I don't have a wife. I'm not married."

"You're not marr— oh, give me that child."

She took the screaming baby out of his arms, rearranged the wrinkled blanket, and tucked Samuel's head against the side of her neck. When she began to sway gently from side to side, the baby gave a big hiccup and fell silent.

"Where is this child's mother?" she demanded in a low voice.

Eli took off his hat and tapped it on his thigh a couple of times. "Dead." He spoke the word under his breath, as if the child could understand its significance. "A few days back when I was down south, inside the border of the Osage Indian reservation, I came upon a wagon on the trail. It had been shot full of arrows. I reckon you know the Osages don't like the way squatters have been moving onto their land and petitioning the government to move the tribe into Oklahoma. Anyhow, I saw right off that the man was already dead and the woman was a goner. She pushed the little fella into my arms and begged me to keep him safe. 'Teach Samuel to love the Lord,' she said, and then she breathed her last."

The swaying stopped. "How long ago?"

"Four days."

"But this baby can't be much more than a week old. What have you been feeding him?"

Eli scratched the back of his neck. "I tried mashed potatoes," he admitted. "He doesn't like them much. He did better on scrambled eggs. I don't have a bottle, and he's not real good with a cup. I manage to get a little water down him now and then. I know he needs milk, but I'm a traveling man —"

"The baby is starving. He'll die without proper nourishment." Her blue eyes flashed. "You'd better find this child some milk, Preacher-man, or you'll have his soul on your conscience."

"Brother Elijah?" Seth Hunter, Jack Cornwall, and the other two women were striding across the prairie toward him. Right after the preaching service that evening, Seth and Jack had approached Eli with an interesting proposition, and he wanted to hear more. But now all he could think of was this woman's prediction of doom.

"Brother Elijah," Seth called again. "I want you to meet my wife, Rose, and this is her friend Caitrin Murphy. Jack Cornwall here is engaged to marry Miss Murphy."

"Elijah Book," he said, giving the women a nod. "Pleased to meet you, ladies."

"Reverend Book," Rose Hunter addressed him. "It's our privilege to have you in Hope."

"I'm not much of a reverend, ma'am. I'm just a cowhand from Amarillo who heard the voice of God calling him to preach. I've been on the trail since March, riding from one place to another and speaking the word of the Lord."

"I've asked Brother Elijah if he would be willing to stay on in Hope for a couple of weeks," Seth told the women. "He could perform the wedding for Jack and Caitrin, and maybe he'd preach us a few sermons in our new church."

"A couple of weeks?" Rose Hunter cried. "Why not permanently? You could become our very own minister, Brother Elijah! You and your wife and son could live here in Hope while you minister to the homesteaders."

"I'm not married, ma'am," Eli said. "Samuel's parents were ambushed on the trail, and God put the boy into my hands to bring up."

"Then he's a foundling like I am!" Rose exclaimed, wonder lighting her pretty face.

"Brother Elijah, this is the answer to your prayers *and* ours," Rose's friend Caitrin said warmly. "Sure you can raise little Samuel in a town filled with loving people who will look after him as though he were our own. And instead of making poor Seth search all over Topeka for a preacher willing to move to Hope, God has sent you to us."

"Now hold on a minute there," Eli put in. "I appreciate the notion, and I know you folks mean well. But the truth is, I'm on my way to China."

"China?" Rose and Caitrin echoed each other again.

"That's right. I told the Lord I'd go wherever he sent me to preach his message of forgiveness and salvation, even across the seas to the farthest lands of the earth."

The woman holding Samuel gave a little grunt of laughter. "And what did God say to your grand offer?" she challenged him. "Look, Preacher-man, I've got to go. You'd better start feeding this baby on something better than mashed potatoes. And change his diaper now and then."

She held Samuel out to Eli. He shook his head and hooked his thumbs in his pockets. "If God sent anyone, I believe it was this lady to Samuel."

"Oh, no. I —"

"You just gave Samuel a taste of manna from heaven. Look at him lying there in your arms. That boy hasn't slept more than a wink since the day I found him. Now his belly's full and warm, and he's got the light of hope in his heart. Would you consider keeping it burning?"

"What are you talking about? I can't stay here. I have a job to do. I've got to earn enough money to get back home."

"Then I'll pay you to feed him."

"You're crazy." She glanced away for a moment, hesitating in spite of herself.

"Just a few days, ma'am. Just to get Sam on his feet."

Scorn flashed in her eyes. "He's a *baby*. He won't be on his feet for months — and it'll take a lot longer than a few days to make him healthy again."

"Please." Eli rolled his hat brim in his hand. "Please help me. Do it for the boy."

She gazed down at the baby in her arms, and Eli sensed her weakening. *God, she's a woman,* he prayed silently, *a tender, loving woman. Open her heart to Samuel. Touch her soul, please, Lord.*

"How much?" she asked, her voice flat. "I can make three dollars a day at my regular job, and that's for just a few hours of work. How many of those tithes and offerings are you willing to turn loose of, Preacher-man?"

Eli's eyes narrowed at the harshness of her

words. Would it even be right to let such a bitter woman tend to the boy? The fact was, he couldn't come close to paying her three dollars a day. True, people often contributed to his ministry when he finished preaching a sermon. But he barely scraped enough money out of his hat to buy himself a little flour and a few mealy potatoes each week. Any extra money he could put aside, he kept in a pouch on his belt — the savings for his passage to China.

"All right," he said, untying the pouch. If God wanted to send him to China, he'd provide the means some other way. "You can take all I've got, ma'am. It's four dollars and fifty cents. That'll keep Samuel going for a day and a half."

He held out the pouch, pleading with God to make the woman take it. It didn't matter that she had a hard heart, or that he ought to get back on his horse and ride to another town to preach, or even that this would clean out his entire missions treasury. What mattered was Samuel. The baby had to live.

"Now hold on a minute there, Brother Elijah," Seth Hunter said. "Let's think the situation through. This woman needs pay. You need this woman. And we need you. Why not let us pay you to be our town preacher? Then you can pay her to feed the baby."

"The fact is, I'm on my way to China," Eli said.

"The fact is, I'm on my way back to Philadelphia," the woman spoke up. "And I don't intend to sit around all summer in a barren little town waiting hand and foot on some good-for-nothing preacher who thinks he can just pick a baby up off the road like an old discarded hat and . . . and feed it mashed potatoes and keep it in a saddlebag, when other people . . . other people's babies die of diphtheria . . . and fever . . . and they have to be buried in little wooden boxes . . . and what do you know about God anyway, Preacherman?" She had started crying again, heavy tears dripping onto Samuel's blanket. "You don't deserve this baby. You didn't do anything to earn him. Nothing. You don't have any idea what it means to suffer . . . and . . . and marry someone you don't even love and live in a tent just so that . . . so that you can know the joy of one day holding your own baby . . . your own baby in your arms . . . and loving her . . ."

"There now," Rose Hunter said, slipping her arm around the sobbing woman. "Of course Brother Elijah doesn't know the terrible pain you've suffered. All he knows is that he cares for this little baby, and he needs your help."

"Won't you help?" Caitrin asked her. "Do it to honor the memory of your little Abigail. Do it for Samuel."

Stricken, Eli stared at the woman holding the child God had given him. Who was she? Why did anger bubble out of her like lava, searing everything it touched? She was beautiful, delicate-boned, as fragile as a porcelain teacup. Her golden hair gleamed in the lamplight, and her skin looked as soft as the petals of a white rose. Who had hurt her so deeply that raw pain tinged every word she spoke?

"All I wanted was to hold Abigail again," she was murmuring against Mrs. Hunter's shoulder. "I thought it might be my own baby crying, but then . . . then it was this little . . . this boy with dark hair and wrinkled skin . . . and he's not Abby. . . ."

"No, he's not," Rose Hunter said. "But he's alive, he's hungry for life, and he deserves the chance to grow and learn and become a man someday."

"Sure the best we could do for him here in Hope is feed him sugar water or cow's milk," Caitrin continued, "and you said yourself that he's already far gone. Samuel needs what only you can give him. Please do this."

"Please?" Rose whispered.

Elijah stared at the blond woman as though by sheer willpower he could force her to agree

35

to help. *Care for the baby,* he mentally ordered her. *Care for him as much as I do.*

Growing up out in cattle country, Elijah had had only one person to look out for. Himself. He'd always lived a rootless life, as a child wandering with his father from job to job and then as a young man making his own way as a hired hand on one roundup or another. One night during the past winter, cold and hungry, he had broken into a settler's cabin and stolen everything he could lay his hands on. Including a Bible.

Three days and nights of nothing but reading the words in that book had broken him like a dried-up cottonwood limb. Down on his knees he had begged for God's forgiveness and surrendered his soul to Jesus Christ. He had returned the stolen goods, ridden into the nearest town, found a preacher to guide him, and started walking on the path of a new life.

And he'd realized that the world was not about Elijah Book. It was about other people — people who were hurting, empty, rebellious, and lost. People like this woman in the purple robe. Eli longed to reach out to her and touch her soul with the words of God. But he knew she held Samuel's future in her hands, and one wrong move from him . . . one misspoken word . . . *Please God, unlock her heart. . . .*

"All right," she said, nodding quickly. "All right, I'll do it for a few days. But I have to have money."

"Then I'll take the preaching job," Elijah told Seth Hunter. "Whatever the town can afford to pay for my work, give all the money to this woman."

Shock widened her eyes as she lifted her head to look at him. "Why would you do that? This baby isn't even yours. You don't love him. You don't know how to take care of him. You have no wife, no home, nothing to offer him. Why would you go to all this trouble for a baby you found on the trail like a —"

"Like an old discarded hat?" Eli settled his hat on his head. "The way I see it, ma'am, most folks are just like Sam here. We're lost, abandoned souls on the trail to nowhere. And we're all just about to starve to death. If we let him, God will come along and pick us up, feed us manna from heaven, and make us his own children. And that's the way Sam is my son, even though all I did was find him on the trail and pick him up out of his dying mama's arms."

"A very pretty sermon, Preacher-man," she said, her blue eyes unwavering. "Now where do you plan on holing up with this baby? Or are you going to keep camping on an old wool blanket under that skinny tree over there?"

Whoa, she was one tough little woman, Elijah thought. Hard as a rock and stubborn to boot. But he knew she had a softness somewhere inside her, and he was just going to have to trust God to touch it.

"Brother Elijah, you can live in the new church building," Seth Hunter said. "We built a little room in the back with the aim of starting up a Sunday school some day. You can stash your gear in there and stable your horse over at my place. And as for you, Mrs. —"

"Nolan," the woman said. "Lily Nolan. I won't be needing your charity. I have my own wagon, and I'll keep the baby with me until —"

"Lily?" A wild-looking female in a red Chinese silk robe, with long black hair and eyes smudged all around with black paint, came racing toward the group of people gathered around the baby. "Lily Nolan, where have you been? I sent the crowd to your tent half an hour ago, and they're already swarming around demanding their money back and threatening to tear me apart. What in the name of heaven have you been doing? Whose baby is that?"

"He's mine," Elijah said. "Who're you?"

"I am Madame Zahara." She straightened her shoulders and gave him a half-lidded gaze. "I know you. You're the preacher."

"I sure am."

"You've been luring away our customers the past two nights. Now I see you've put my assistant under your spell."

"Your assistant?" Elijah turned to Lily Nolan. "*You* work at that traveling show?"

"I perform operas and soliloquies," she confirmed.

"And she reads palms, crystal balls, and tarot cards," Madame Zahara added. "With the deaths of both her husband and our leader, Mrs. Nolan and I run the traveling show together. Now, Lily, you've got to get over to the fortune-telling tent and do your job. I've taken in almost two dollars from folks wanting to hear their fortunes, and they're mad as hops waiting for you to show up."

Elijah studied the golden-haired woman, waiting for her response. Would she buckle in to the witch in the red silk gown? Would she choose to return to that sinful, fleshly occupation of *actress?* Or would she take the higher path of sacrifice for her fellowman?

Eli's chest almost hurt with praying that she would give herself to Samuel. But now his gut twisted with doubt about her worthiness for such a high calling. A woman who had chosen a life as a performer with a traveling show — could this Lily Nolan do anybody any good?

"Well?" Madam Zahara snapped. "Give

the fellow his baby, and come on!"

Lily bit her lower lip as her eyes traced over the small shape in her arms. "Not tonight, Beatrice," she said, lifting her head. "The preacher's offered me good wages to feed his baby. You'd better go read the fortunes yourself."

"What?" The woman's dark eyes hardened. "Are you running out on me, Lily? After all I've done for you?"

"I'm not deserting you, Bea," Lily said. "You know I would never do that. We'll stay here a few days and save up my earnings. While I look out for the preacher's baby, you can boil a new batch of potion. It'll be a chance for us to figure out how we're going to manage the show without Ted and Jakov."

"I know how to manage the show. All Jakov ever did was perform the opening act. I created the entertainment. I planned the programs and counted the money. Oh, Lily, I told you I'd take care of you, didn't I? We're partners, the two of us. We'll make it. We'll be fine."

Elijah had the awfulest feeling that Madame Zahara was about to cry, and he didn't think it would be a pretty sight. The woman herself was attractive in a mysterious, exotic sort of way. She had almond-shaped brown eyes, full red lips, and glowing olive skin. Her crimson silk gown was cut too low for any decent man to approve of, and her black hair draped around her shoulders like a luxurious cloak.

But every time she looked at Elijah, a prickle ran right up his spine. He felt pretty sure he recognized that prickle. It warned him of the presence of evil.

"Lily, let's head west like we planned," Madame Zahara said, her painted eyes persuasive. "We'll go on to Manhattan and set up camp. You can recite Ophelia's soliloquy there if you want. I know you've been under such a strain losing little Abby, and this preacher is preying on your kindness. Look at him, Lily. He's no different from the sort of man you've always despised. He's selfish and pious and unloving, and he's out to make all the money he can — and doing it in the name of God."

Lily's blue eyes focused on Elijah, and it was all he could do not to take off running. Truth to tell, he *was* selfish. Always had been. But God was working on him, breaking down the walls he'd built as a boy. And he sometimes was pious. Sure enough, not two minutes ago he had stood there mentally running Mrs. Lily Nolan into the ground for being an actress. What made *him* so perfect? Nothing but the forgiving grace of God the Father.

And unloving . . . well, he never had been too warm around people. He wasn't much for hugging and kissing and all that. Made his back itch.

"I can read your spirit, Preacher," Madame Zahara said, turning her painted eyes on him. "I know what lies within your heart. If I looked into your palm, I could see the roads on which you've traveled. Paths of arrogance and self-importance. You believe you've found the one truth — the single answer to life. But you're wrong. All paths lead to God. Every person has the spark of divine truth within himself, and all we need to do is trust our own heart to touch the holiness inside us."

Elijah listened to her words. They had a ring of truth to them — but they weren't right. He knew there was only one path to God, and that was through Jesus Christ. On that path, he had found peace and comfort and hope. He had found forgiveness and a reason to live. Why was this woman trying to distort the truth?

"Let Lily go," she said, laying a hand on his arm. "Set her free to follow her own destiny. Don't try to control others with your words, Preacher. Let them seek truth and find that spirit in the place where it has always dwelled. In their hearts."

Elijah took off his hat and tapped it on his thigh a couple of times. "Well, ma'am, I appreciate your concern for Mrs. Nolan," he began. "Truly, I do. But the fact is, I've got a starving baby here, and she's got the means to feed him. Now, we've made a deal, this lady and I, and I aim to see that it's honored."

"That proves exactly what I was saying!" Madame Zahara exploded. "You are an arrogant, selfish —"

"I am a man with a hungry baby and nobody to —"

"Excuse me here," Lily Nolan cut in. "*I'm* the one who'll be making the decision. Beatrice, this baby needs a fresh diaper, another feeding, and a good night's sleep. I'm going to see that he gets it. And as for you, Preacher-man, you'd better start cooking up a humdinger of a sermon. It's almost Sunday, and I'll expect to find you over at the church reeling them in and emptying their pockets so you can pay my wages."

Eli swallowed hard as she turned and walked off toward the gaudy wagon of the traveling show. He didn't like Lily Nolan. Didn't like her at all. And sure as shootin', he didn't want her looking after little Samuel one more day than necessary.

"You're such a teensy little fellow," Lily

murmured the next evening as baby Samuel regarded her solemnly. "But you've got big brown eyes and lots of hair. Where'd you get all that hair, huh? I think you're strong enough that we might try to wash it tomorrow. Yes, sir, Mr. Samuel, you need a bath and some warm oil on your skin." Lily had lovingly tended the tiny baby all through the night and today as well. After settling up with the irate customers, Beatrice had been pointedly ignoring Lily and her new little companion.

As Lily stroked the baby's cheek, he turned his head to the side and pressed his mouth against her hand. "I bet you're hungry again, you fuzzy little caterpillar. What has that big ol' preacher been feeding you? Mashed potatoes? And scrambled eggs, too? Glory be, no wonder you're so skinny. Next time he tries a trick like that, you just spit those potatoes right back in his face."

She reflected on the handsome preacher and his bold sermonizing. What a contrast to the frantic look in his blue eyes when he was pleading with her to feed the baby he'd found. Truth to tell, she would gladly care for little Samuel and never take a penny. But she had enjoyed watching the man squirm.

She sensed he was just like her father — held in high regard by the townsfolk, while they knew nothing of his true nature. She could picture her father marching into church with his head held high and his huge walrus mustache gleaming with wax. The grand gentleman, conductor of the Greater New England Symphony and minister of music at the First United Church of St. George, cut an imposing figure as he stood before the congregation and sang hymns in his melodic baritone.

No one knew, of course, that this same man could use his voice to subjugate his wife until she was sobbing in humiliation. The huge hands that held a baton with such finesse could slam a child to the floor or swing a leather belt across a little girl's bare flesh until it split open and began to bleed. The man who sang that "God is love; his mercy brightens all the path in which we rove" could turn on his family with hatred, rage, and unforgiving fury with a speed that rivaled the sudden flash of summer lightning.

Always fearful, yet somehow always unprepared for her father's wrath, Lily would crouch on the floor and cover her head until the storm of his anger had passed. And while he punished his daughter for the demons that lived in his own soul, she would journey to a secret place inside herself and listen to the sweet music in her heart.

"Forget me not, forget me never," she sang softly as she cradled the nursing Samuel. "Till yonder sun shall set forever."

Only after she had escaped her father, only in the sanctuary of the traveling show, had Lily ventured to sing aloud. Like a miracle, music had bubbled forth from her voice — arias, ballads, even meaningless jingles she had heard among her schoolmates. Beatrice had encouraged Lily to add singing and drama to the show, and as she performed, the young woman began to feel alive for the first time in her life.

"I gave my love a cherry that had no stone," she sang to the drowsy baby.

"I gave my love a chicken that had no bone.
I gave my love a ring that had no end.
I gave my love a baby with no cryin'."

Then with Abigail, Lily finally had known true love. Oh, Abby! Her baby's precious face formed in her memory. Deep blue eyes, downy golden hair, a sweet toothless smile. In the sea of misery, mistakes, and futility that Lily's life had become, Abby had been the only ray of hope. Gazing into that angelic face, a lonely woman could forget her father's rage-twisted features, her husband's wandering eyes, even her own desperate race down a darkened path with no end.

For the hundredth time, Lily's mind rebelled at the idea that the child was dead. Her heart refused to believe she would never again kiss that petal-soft cheek. Even her body had refused to acknowledge that the child no longer needed nourishment. Swollen, aching, tender, Lily hugged the orphaned Samuel close as she continued singing.

"A cherry when it's blooming, it has no
    stone,
A chicken when it's pipping, it has no
    bone.
A ring when it's rolling, it has no end.
A baby when it's sleeping, there's no
    cryin'."

"No cryin'," a rich voice echoed the final three notes. "Amen and amen."

A tiny female face with skin as dark and shriveled as a prune peered through an opening in the wagon's canvas covering. Gasping in shock, Lily clutched the baby tightly. When the old woman's bright brown eyes took in the sight of the nursing woman and contented child, a wide smile spread across her face.

"Mercy, mercy, mercy. Don't this beat all?" A gnarled hand with clawlike fingers reached out and gave the baby a pat. "Howdy-do."

"Hello," Lily said warily. "Do I know you?"

"Not yet, but you will. I'm Margaret Hanks. Folks round here call me Mother Margaret."

Lily stared in confusion. What business did this woman have snooping around in other people's wagons? Samuel had almost dropped off to sleep, and Lily herself was exhausted.

"Excuse me, ma'am," she began, "but I'm —"

"Oh, I know you, sure enough. You're the lady come to look after the baby. Folks is talkin' about it all over town, and I come out to see you for myself. When I heard you in here singin' like an angel, I knew God hisself done sent you. Mercy, mercy, mercy, child, and bless your heart."

Lily couldn't hide her smile, though she couldn't understand why her heart warmed so quickly to this odd little stranger. "I don't mind," she said softly. "I lost my own baby."

"I heard that, too. Child, I lost three of my fourteen, and my heart ain't never healed from the pain of it. Listen to Mother Margaret, now; why don't you and that baby come on over to our house and take supper with us? We got fried chicken and greens. Cherry cobbler, too. You eat with us, and then you stay the night in one of our beds. We'll make you a place with us, yes ma'am, and may the Lord be praised for his almighty wisdom. Amen and amen."

CHAPTER 3

Lily cradled the baby and willed herself to remain seated. Why did the old woman's words inspire such a sense of assurance and calm? How could a stranger know what a hot meal and a warm bed would mean to a grief-stricken traveler? And what had propelled this Mother Margaret across the prairie in the darkness?

"I know it don't seem usual," the woman said, "and maybe you wouldn't want to visit with folk who used to be slaves —"

"No," Lily said quickly. "It's not that. But you don't know me. You know nothing about me."

"Aw, sure I do. God sent you along here to help us out. Now you plannin' to come eat some of Mother Margaret's cherry cobbler or not?"

Lily's stomach tightened at the enticing thought. With her body depleted and this new baby so ravenous, Lily couldn't deny her own need. "All right. I'll come with you," she said. "And I thank you for welcoming me."

"Mercy, mercy, mercy," the old woman clucked as Lily made her way out of the wagon. "You're as welcome in Hope as any-body else. Look at the Hanks family! Two months back, my boy, his wife, and I followed the Cornwall family out here to Kansas. Hankses been in the Cornwall family for gen-erations, don't you know. We was their slaves, of course, and now we're freed folks. Yes, ma'am, free as the wind. But the fact is, we respect the Cornwalls, and they always done us good. My Ben built us a fine house over yonder near the Cornwall smithy."

Lily tried to concentrate as she carried the baby through the tall grass. "I don't know the Cornwalls."

"You met Mister Jack earlier. He's a big tall fellow, lives with his mammy and his little sister, Lucy. The Cornwalls is as happy as fleas in a doghouse these days. It just took a little doin' for everybody in town to get used to them."

"Did the Cornwalls cause some kind of trouble here?"

"Hoo, you done said it, gal. But that's all in the past. Ben helps Mister Jack at the smithy, and Eva takes in laundry and mendin'. Me, I look after Miss Lucy when she's feeling bad. We're as much a part of things round here as quills on a goose." She paused. "Now, who's this a-comin'? She's got eyes that would chill a side of beef."

51

"Lily?" Beatrice Waldowski raced toward them. "Lily, where are you going?"

"Beatrice!" Lily stopped. "I didn't realize you were still about. It's very late."

"Have you gone mad?" Beatrice wore yet another version of her Madame Zahara outfit. "Of course I'm up. I've been reading palms and tarot cards in the tent. We have customers, you know. We have commitments. What are you doing?"

"I'm . . . I'm going with Mrs. Hanks." Lily swallowed, realizing how foolish she must appear to her friend. "She invited me for dinner, and I —"

"Dinner? Do you even know this woman? Oh, Lily!" Beatrice clasped the younger woman tightly and spoke against her ear. "I'm so frightened for you. You're not acting like yourself — taking in this baby and then wandering off with a stranger. Losing Abigail has distracted you and upset your spiritual balance. I'm frightened for you. Come with me, Lil. Come back to the wagon now. We'll pack up and leave in the morning, and I promise I'll take you far away from all this."

"Now just a cotton-pickin' minute," Mother Margaret spoke up, swelling to her full five-foot height. Her clawed finger shot upward and wagged in Beatrice's face. "Miss Lily is comin' to my house for supper, sure enough.

You can come too, if you want, but don't you go turnin' this poor woman away from my door. Not now. Not when she needs me."

"Lily doesn't need you," Beatrice snapped. "She doesn't even know you."

"It's all right, Bea." Lily held up a hand. "Mother Margaret has offered me a meal. Why don't you join us?"

One eyebrow arched as Beatrice took in the small black woman. "I'd rather dine in hell."

She turned to leave, then swung back around. "And, Lily, don't think I'll let you go so easily. You're all I have. You're my dearest friend. I won't let your grief and these conniving people tear us apart."

Lily watched in dismay as Beatrice marched toward the wagon. It was true — they were close friends and had been comrades through many hardships. Beatrice Waldowski had believed in Lily when no one else would. Beatrice had helped Ted Nolan covertly marry and then spirit away the forlorn young woman who had appeared at their show night after night in Philadelphia. Elopement, escape, freedom. Beatrice had promised Lily a new life, and she had delivered.

True, they'd often gone hungry and unwashed. The show had been run out of many towns. No one but Beatrice had really appreciated Lily's soliloquies and arias. And then there had been Ted — a vain man, a drifter, a womanizer. But he hadn't beaten Lily, as her own father had, and he had given her Abigail. Beautiful Abigail.

"Hoo, I'm glad she's gone," Mother Margaret said. "That woman flat gave me the willies."

"Beatrice is my friend. She may appear harsh at times, but she has a kind heart."

"Uh-huh." The old woman sounded unconvinced. "Let me tell you about some kind folks. You see them lights a long way off, child? That's the home of Rosie and Seth Hunter. They've got a little boy named Chipper, and they're gonna have a new baby come autumn. Down the middle of town is the mercantile. Miss Caitrin Murphy lives in the soddy nearby, and she's fixin' to marry Mister Jack. The Cornwalls built them a place near the smithy, and my boy Ben put our house on the other side. Come on, now; I can smell that cobbler."

Reluctant to stray so far from her friend, Lily moved slowly up the road toward the smithy. Where would she be without Beatrice Waldowski? She'd be back in the brick house in Philadelphia, living under the thumb of her father and probably preparing for marriage. No doubt her parents would expect her to marry a man like Reverend Hardcastle's son, who was planning to take his father's place in the pulpit of St. George. Lily groaned. The last thing she wanted to do was marry a preacher.

"Mrs. Hanks?" Elijah Book stepped out of the small frame house and held up a lantern. "Did you find her?"

Lily stopped in her tracks. "What are *you* doing here? Is this some kind of a trick?"

"Brother Elijah is eatin' supper with us, same as you," Mother Margaret said as she headed for the front door. "Folks has got to feed the preacher, don't you know. It's mannerly."

Unbudging, Lily watched the tall man approach. He took off his hat, clearly as ill at ease as she. "Mrs. Nolan," he began, his blue eyes intense in the lantern light. "I was hoping you'd come to the Hankses' home."

"Why? Don't you trust me to take care of Samuel in my own wagon?"

He shifted from one foot to the other. "Well . . . as a matter of fact, it does make me a little uncomfortable."

"Because I'm an actress."

"But that doesn't mean I want you to stop feeding Samuel. Sam needs your help. I just thought maybe if you'd be willing to stay here with the Hanks family for a few days —"

"Do you mean to tell me you sent that poor

old woman all the way across the prairie to rescue this baby?"

"No, it's not like that. Mrs. Hanks suggested it. I was over here visiting with the family, and I got to talking about the wagon and how maybe you'd like someplace quieter. I know you live in a traveling show, and that means —"

"What does it mean, buster?" Lily took a step toward him. "That wagon is my home, and Beatrice is one of the kindest people I've ever known. She took me in, and she gave me food and a bed and honest work — and don't you ever, *ever* —"

"I'm just thinking of Samuel."

"You're thinking of your own high-and-mighty reputation!" she snapped. "You want to make sure nothing around you looks too bad or too shameful because then it would reflect poorly on you. I'd wager you took in this baby just to prove to everybody how righteous and holy you are. 'Oh, the poor traveling preacher with his little orphan baby,' everybody will say. 'How sweet, how kind! Why, let's feed that preacher some dinner. Let's flock all around him like hungry little chickens. Let's give him our money.' "

"Now, listen here, ma'am," Elijah growled, his forefinger jabbing toward her. "I accepted that baby because God gave him to me. You think I'd be crazy enough to *want* to haul a squallin' kid around with me? I can't sleep, I can't think, I can't even pray with him hollering his head off every minute of the day and night. But I'm going to give that boy all I've got as long as I live because he's my responsibility, and I don't care what anybody thinks about it. Especially you."

As he spoke, Elijah advanced on her. Shoulders squared and head thrust forward, he was menacing, terrifying. "And as for the notion that I take folks' money," he barked, "I'll have you know I was supposed to go to China, but I gave all my money to you. That's where the money's gone — to you!"

Lily couldn't listen. She had to hide. Had to find that place inside herself where she could escape the anger.

"And if you think I'm so righteous and holy," he went on, "well, I'll tell you a thing or two about that. Not too long ago, I was just where you are. I was roaming around, doing whatever felt good to me, living my life just the way I liked it. I know how an actress in a traveling show lives. I know the kinds of things you do to earn money. . . ."

He was coming now. Closer and closer, he was coming. And soon, very soon, it would begin. Lily sank to her knees and covered the baby with her body. Both hands over her head, she squeezed her eyes shut and began to listen to the music inside herself. Golden melodies poured through her heart and filled her mind. The music lifted her up and away from his words, taking her far from the fear, the rage, the pain.

"Miz Nolan?" his voice asked.

She shrank from his touch, willing the music to keep her alive. Silver harmonies. Crystal notes.

"Are you all right, ma'am?" He was crouching in the grass beside her, his big hand gently laid on her arm. "I didn't aim to scare you. I'll admit I was a little frustrated, but . . . are you OK under there? You can come out. I won't do a thing, I swear."

Lily lowered her hands and lifted her head. It wasn't her father after all. It was Elijah Book. The preacher gazed at her with blue eyes full of concern. His Stetson had tumbled to the ground. A lock of hair had fallen over his forehead.

"You can keep Samuel in your wagon if you want," he said in a low voice. "I'm sorry. I'm sure sorry I scared you."

Unable to stop trembling, Lily straightened and held out the baby. "Take him. I can't do this."

"Please. I need you." He slid his hand down her arm and touched her fingers.

"Don't be afraid of me. I would never hurt you."

"Mercy, mercy, mercy!" Mother Margaret's small feet appeared at the edge of Lily's vision. "What you two doin' down in the grass? I went in to check on the chicken, and next thing I know, you done disappeared. Everything all right?"

"Yes," Elijah Book said, his eyes locked on Lily's face. "It's going to be all right."

"Lemme see what you got there, Brother Elijah," Mother Margaret said as she and her family joined their guests outside on the front porch after the sumptuous meal. "You got the biggest, fattest Bible I ever did see. And what is that other book?"

Elijah showed the old woman the Holy Bible he had purchased right after his call to preach the gospel. He had traded his life's savings for the leather-bound volume, and he considered it a treasure. But the small hymnal he now placed in Mother Margaret's hand ran a close second. His mother had once owned the slender book of music, and she had sung the hymns to him as he sat on her lap. Elijah had found it in her trunk many years after her death. Even before he came to understand the message in the Bible, he had read those songs again and again. Their words had lit his path.

"That's my hymnbook," he said. "I can't carry a tune in a bucket, but I know every song by heart."

The old woman turned through the worn pages one by one. Her son, Ben, leaned over and examined the book with his mother. Elijah pushed back in his chair, hooked one boot over the other, and locked his hands behind his head. He could see Lily Nolan three chairs down on the porch, rocking the baby and humming some little tune. Maybe this was going to work out all right after all, though he never would have believed it.

That woman sure brought out the worst in him. She seemed to know exactly how to pull the anger right up out of his chest. Before he could stop himself he had been hollering at her, shouting in her face, and scaring the living daylights out of her. He'd never felt such shame in his life as when he saw her cowering in the grass, her arms over her head and her body sheltering the baby. As though he would hit her!

Sure, in his old saloon days, Elijah had been a rough and rowdy fellow, but he'd never touched a woman with a harsh hand. Now that he was walking in Christ's footsteps, he'd surrendered his old notion of "an eye for an eye, and a tooth for a tooth." He was working hard on turning the other cheek.

"This songbook ought to go to somebody who can use it right," Mother Margaret said. "Here, Miss Lily, you take it."

Elijah sat up straight. Lily stopped rocking the baby. Everyone in the gathering turned to the preacher as if awaiting his response. Ben Hanks, a strapping man with arms like tree limbs, gazed at him with soulful brown eyes. His wife, Eva, looked up from her darning. Mother Margaret just grinned as she held out the precious hymnbook.

"Miss Lily," she said, "you have the voice of an angel. Take this book, and keep it. You sing the baby every song in there, and he'll grow up right."

"Mother Margaret," Lily said, "the hymnbook belongs to the preacher."

"He don't need it. Can't carry a tune in a bucket; he said so himself. Take it, girl. And sing us somethin', would you? Sing the first song in the book. What's it called? You know, I can't read worth beans. Can't even sign my name."

Lily took the hymnbook and opened it. Elijah swallowed. That was his *mother's* book, his only memento of her. He didn't want some no-account actress — he caught himself and took a deep breath.

"Holy, holy, holy!" Lily began to sing.

61

"Lord God Almighty!
Early in the morning our song shall rise
  to Thee;
Holy, holy, holy! merciful and mighty!
God in three Persons, blessed Trinity!"

"Mmm," Mother Margaret said. "Ain't that the prettiest voice you ever heard, Ben?"

"Yes'm," her son agreed.

"Sounded like a funeral dirge to me," put in his wife.

"Eva!"

"Well, it did. Miss Lily, sing the verse about the darkness. Here we are out under the stars, and I can just feel the presence of the Lord. Sing it, Miss Lily. Sing it with joy."

Elijah studied the young woman as she gripped the hymnbook. Her fingers skeletal, Lily seemed mesmerized by the book. She swallowed twice, as though the words must be forced out of her throat.

"Holy, holy, holy!"

Her voice began slowly, and then grew stronger as she sang. High, clear, perfect — each word formed on her tongue. Every note sounded like the ringing of a single crystal bell.

"Though the darkness hide Thee,
Though the eye of sinful man Thy glory
    may not see;
Only Thou art holy — there is none
    beside Thee,
Perfect in pow'r, in love and purity."

"Thank you, Jesus!" Mother Margaret exclaimed. "Love and purity. Yes, sir, that about says it all. The Lord of love is in my heart — holy, holy, holy. And he is pure! Amen!"

"Amen," chorused Ben and Eva.

Elijah eyed his mother's hymnbook, his chest tight and his heart dark. He didn't want Lily Nolan to have the book. It wasn't hers. A woman like her didn't deserve such a gift.

"Oh, Miss Lily, you have a voice that can rival the tongues of angels," Mother Margaret said. "You need that book. Take it with you, and sing to everybody far and wide. Sing to that baby God gave you. Sing to the preacher. Sing to God hisself!"

Lily lifted Samuel to her shoulder and began to pat his back. "I know plenty of songs by heart," she said. "I don't need Mr. Book's hymnal."

"It did belong to my mother," Elijah said, leaning forward.

"Belong?" the old woman said. "Nothing

63

belongs to nobody but God. Everything we got is here on loan from the Almighty. This house, that songbook, even that young'un over there. You better start listenin' to the Spirit of the Lord, Brother Elijah. Don't act on your own will, now. You listen. Listen good."

Elijah stared at his mother's hymnbook and tried to listen to the Holy Spirit. But all he could think about was the afternoon he had discovered the book in a trunk and had realized that his own mother's hands had touched its pages. She had died when Eli was only four or five years old, and he mourned her to this day. She had sung to him out of the book, held him in her arms and sung hymn after hymn. . . .

He lifted his focus to the young woman cradling baby Samuel. *Nothing belongs to nobody but God,* Mother Margaret had said. She was right. The child had been given to him by God. Even this woman had been sent to him by God. He had to believe that. Hard and bitter as she was, Lily Nolan needed the words in that hymnbook more than Elijah needed a physical memento of his mother.

"You keep it," he said to Lily. "Sing to Samuel."

"That's right," Mother Margaret intoned.

"Well," he said, standing, "I reckon I'd better get going."

Eli settled his Stetson on his head and picked up his Bible. After thanking the Hanks family for their welcome, he walked toward the rocking chair. Lily Nolan was a vision out of a fine oil painting. Her golden hair glowed like a halo of holiness around her head. Her pale blue gown swept to her feet, and her slender arms enfolded the sleeping baby. With skin the color of fresh milk and eyes like a pair of bright bluebonnets, she could warm the heart of any man.

Lord, why does she have to be an actress in a traveling show? Elijah prayed silently as he approached her. *Why does she have a sharp tongue and a stiff spine? Why can't she be the kind of woman I asked you to send into my life?* Elijah longed for the gentle touch of a righteous woman whose eyes and heart were committed to the Lord. He envisioned someone sweet and pure. Why couldn't God have sent someone like that to tend Samuel?

"Mrs. Nolan," he said, "I'll be over at the church, in case the baby needs anything. You could send Ben Hanks to fetch me."

She gave the baby a pat. "You'll be preparing sermons, I guess. Make them good. I need the money."

He recoiled from the cynicism in her words. "Maybe you'd like to suggest a subject?"

"Hellfire and damnation, I should think.

65

Isn't that what you preachers like to talk about the most? How about the thirty-second chapter of Deuteronomy as a text? 'For a fire is kindled in mine anger, and shall burn unto the lowest hell, and shall consume the earth with her increase, and set on fire the foundations of the mountains —' "

"Mrs. Nolan —"

"Or maybe something from Psalms? How about this, from Psalm 55?" She lifted her chin, narrowed her eyes, and recited in a venomous voice, " 'Let death seize upon them, and let them go down quick into hell: for wickedness is in their dwellings, and among them.' "

Elijah shook his head in confusion. The woman knew the Scriptures better than he did. And yet her pain and anger were overwhelming. How could someone who had taken the Word of the Lord into her heart be so empty of his holy presence?

"I guess I could preach about hell," he said. "But I'd rather preach on the love and forgiveness of the God who sent his own Son to die for us."

"Hell is much more effective." She gave him a frigid smile. "If you haven't learned this lesson yet, Preacher-man, you soon will: fear is a great motivator. Humiliate, shame, and terrify a person if you really want to get something from him."

"Not if you want his love. Or hers." Eli bent down and ran his fingertips over the baby's velvety forehead. "Good night, Samuel. Good night, Mrs. Nolan."

He turned to leave, but her words stopped him cold.

"Love?" she said. "What would you know about love? You didn't even kiss your baby good night."

Eli squeezed his fists together in anger at her taunting words. Kiss a baby? What for? He was a man, and Sam was just a little pup — asleep, at that. Who would know the difference? Eli's own father had never kissed him. Not once.

Lily's voice was more gentle when she spoke again. "Please come and kiss your baby, Reverend Book."

Eli turned and walked back to her side. His father had never kissed him — and Eli had never felt his father's love. In fact, he hadn't understood what love was until Christ came into his life. If the woman Christ had sent was instructing him to kiss Samuel, then he'd do it.

Hunkering down on one knee, Eli set one hand on each arm of the rocking chair and bent over. He gave the baby a swift peck on the forehead and then drew back. "There," he said. "Done."

"Very good, Reverend Book. A truly loving gesture."

He frowned at her. "You kiss him then."

"All right," she said. As she gazed at the sleeping baby, her face transformed. Her blue eyes grew soft, her lips tilted into a smile, and her voice gentled. "Sweet Samuel," she whispered, "precious baby. Sleep softly, little one. Rest in comfort and hope. I love you, Samuel. I love you so much."

A tear slid from her eye as she pressed her lips to the baby's cheek. Then she kissed his little forehead. And then each of his eyes.

Elijah could hardly breathe. As though blinders had been stripped from his eyes, he saw Lily Nolan for the first time. This *was* the kind of woman he had begged God to send him. She was so soft, so tender, so perfect. He could hardly keep from taking her in his arms and holding her.

It wasn't the baby he longed to kiss. It was the woman.

Her spirit seemed to beckon him. She was fragile and vulnerable, so wounded she had built walls of bitterness around her gentle heart. He absorbed her trembling pink lips and tearstained cheeks. How could he break down those walls? How could he reach the soul inside? Had God sent her to him for this reason? *Lord, help me know what to do!*

"You'd better go on back to your church now, Preacher-man," Lily said, her walls rising stronger and higher as she faced him. "And take your baby with you. My place is in the traveling show, and I'll sleep in my own wagon tonight. I'll find Sam in the morning and feed him."

When Eli didn't move, she held out the tiny bundle. "Go on now," she said. "And here's your hymnbook."

Uncomfortable as ever at the notion of holding the fragile baby, Elijah tucked his Bible under one arm. Though Lily's voice had grown cold, he felt the warmth of her hands as he lifted Samuel from her. "You keep that hymnal," he murmured. "You sing better than any gal I ever heard."

Before she could cut him again, Eli pressed the baby against his chest and set off across the prairie. The moment the child felt the movement of the man's footsteps, he jerked awake and began to whimper.

"Aw, Sam, don't start that now," Eli mumbled as the baby let out a howl that could rival a coyote's. "We're not going to get a wink of sleep, and I have to come up with a sermon good enough to change the heart of Mrs. Lily Nolan."

"I've been consulting the cards," Beatrice

said as she handed Lily a bowl of hot oatmeal made from the last crumbs in their storage bin. "I was up half the night, Lil, and I just couldn't get over how powerfully the cards spoke to me. It was a deeply spiritual experience, and I can't wait to tell you what I learned."

Lily stifled a yawn as she lifted a spoonful of oatmeal. She had been up half the night, too, and her wakefulness had nothing to do with consulting the spirits. Even from inside the church, Samuel's screaming, fussing, whimpering, and sobbing had been audible for hours. It had been all she could do to keep from crawling out of the wagon and racing to get him. When she dozed at all, she dreamed of Abigail crying out for her mother.

"The cards have told me there's a great future in store for us," Beatrice was saying. "Even though it seems impossible to believe, the deaths of Jakov and Ted are a part of the great plan. You see, you and I couldn't go forward on the path we're to take if we had continued in the shackles of those men. This is *our* time, Lily. Our destiny!"

Lily set the empty bowl aside and began folding the diapers she had just washed. Who could think about destiny? Who could see a path ahead? For Lily there was only this moment. She had to live through this day, surviving each hour, enduring each minute without Abigail.

"We're going to build an opera house," Beatrice announced.

Glancing at her, Lily placed a clean diaper on the stack. "A what?"

"An opera house! To make money!" The older woman seized Lily's shoulders. "It came to me in a vision. We'll go back to Topeka —"

"Topeka?" The image of Abby's makeshift grave inserted itself in Lily's mind. "I don't want to go to Topeka."

"But this is perfect. Do you remember those men who visited the show the first three nights before the diphtheria struck? Those two rich fellows who liked your singing so well? They're partners, and they own a saloon in Topeka. The Crescent Moon, it's called. You and I are going to go straight over to those men and ask them to back us in a venture to build an opera house right here in Hope, Kansas."

"Here?" Lily tried to picture a fancy theater with festoons and bright lights sitting out in the middle of the prairie.

"Hope is the crossroads of the East and the West. I saw it in the cards, Lil. Wagons travel over that pontoon bridge day and night. If we build our opera house beside the main road,

71

we'll be bursting at the seams with customers. You'll sing and do your acts. I'll read fortunes, sell elixir, and manage the money. I'll bet those rich Topeka fellows know a fair number of talented men and women who would love to perform with us. We'll book touring shows, and we'll even let the townsfolk use the place for a meeting hall. They'll support our business, I just know they will. It'll draw all kinds of people here to spend their money. This'll be a regular boomtown in no time at all."

Lily drew a shawl around her shoulders and regarded her friend. "I need to go and feed the baby, Bea," she said softly. "We'll talk about the opera house later."

"There'll be no *later*." Bea's lips hardened. "I can feel the forces pulling on you, Lily. Don't surrender to that preacher's whims. You know what he's like. You know that kind of man. He'll use you. He'll wear you out and dry you up. He'll drain the very life out of you, if he can. Please, Lil, I'm trying to save you. Come with me to Topeka."

"Oh, Bea," Lily said with a sigh.

"When you see how those men are going to treat us, you'll forget all about that preacher and his scrawny little kid. We'll buy ourselves some new dresses. We'll go out to eat in fancy restaurants and sleep in a fine hotel. Elijah

Book will be long gone by the time we get back to Hope." She clasped Lily's hand. "This is your chance to shine!"

Lily closed her eyes and thought for a moment. When she had first run away with the traveling show, the dream of one day performing in a real opera beckoned her with glory, fame, and riches. With each mile of the hard road and each day in her loveless marriage, her dream faded. Hope vanished. All she knew now was that she had escaped her father. Nothing more.

And then Abby had been born. A baby.

"You go to Topeka, Beatrice," Lily said. "I'm going to stay here and take care of Samuel."

Bea's nostrils flared. "I hope you're joking."

"I'm not. I'm needed here. You can talk to the men in Topeka without me. When you come back —"

"*If* I come back."

A stab of fear ran through Lily's heart. "You will come back, won't you?"

"Maybe." Bea shrugged. "The cards have shown me I'll build an opera house somewhere. But if you don't come with me, you might lose me forever."

Lily swallowed. To be left alone . . . abandoned . . . "I guess I could go to Topeka.

You'd need me to sing in the opera house."

"You sing very well, Lily, but I can always find another singer. This is your chance to be part of the dream."

Silence filtered through Lily's heart as she pondered her choice. Why did the future always look so black, so uncertain? Why did she have no direction in life? Where should she turn?

She studied the diapers. And then her eye fell on the hymnbook. *"God sent you along here to help us out,"* Mother Margaret had told her. *"Sing to everybody far and wide. Sing to that baby God gave you. Sing to the preacher. Sing to God hisself!"*

Lily didn't know who God was, but she did know Mother Margaret. Something about that tiny old woman filled Lily's heart with hope.

"I'm going to stay here," she told Beatrice. "I'm going to take care of Samuel."

"You're crazy!" Beatrice snapped as Lily scooped up the diapers and clambered out of the wagon. "That's not *your* baby. Your baby is dead, Lily. *Dead!* I'm going to Topeka. I'll leave without you! And I'm taking the melodeon!"

Lily halted. That was *her* organ. When she had left her house in Philadelphia, she had taken enough money from her father's vault to buy the small instrument. She had selected it herself, and it had accompanied her in every performance. Beatrice had no right to the melodeon.

On the other hand, Lily felt a certainty — a mixture of dread and anticipation — that Beatrice Waldowski would be back.

CHAPTER 4

Eli stood inside the empty church building, the baby wriggling fitfully on his blanket inside a small produce box on the floor. Through bleary eyes, the preacher squinted at the gaudy show wagon in the distance and prayed that Lily Nolan would hurry. He hadn't slept more than half an hour the whole night. Samuel had hollered and howled. He'd messed his britches three or four times — Eli had lost count. And he wouldn't eat a thing. It seemed that once the baby had tasted mother's milk again, he wouldn't settle for anything else.

Eli had been sorely tempted to go to the traveling-show wagon and rouse Mrs. Nolan to feed Samuel. But he knew that he'd frightened and insulted her at the Hankses' house the night before. And both he and Sam had paid for his carelessness.

And so Elijah had counted the hours until dawn, his sermon ideas lost somewhere in the haze of his sleep-deprived mind. As Eli stood waiting for the congregation to arrive, Sam began to wail. Then Eli noticed that the show wagon was starting to pull away from the campsite onto the main road.

What? Lily was leaving?

Eli groaned. Why had he expected more of her? Obviously the actress was a gypsy at heart, unable to commit to home and family, unwilling to labor at decent work, unfeeling and hard-hearted. Now what was he going to do?

"Hoo, that is one loud baby you got there, Brother Elijah." He turned to see Mother Margaret stepping into the church. Clad in a bright yellow dress tied with a crisp white apron, she was a ray of sunshine. Her dark eyes sparkled with joy. "You're liable to scare off more than the devil this mornin'."

Eli raked his fingers through his hair and mustered a smile. "Mornin', Mrs. Hanks. I reckon it is pretty loud in here, thanks to my buddy Sam. I don't imagine we're going to draw much of a crowd."

"Where's Miss Lily?"

"Heading out." He shrugged in the direction of the window. "The wagon is rolling toward Topeka right now."

"Mercy, mercy, mercy." Mother Margaret leaned over the sill and stared into the distance. "I do declare, I thought better of that pretty little gal. I was hopin' she'd caught a glimpse of heaven last night, but I guess the

Lord's gonna have to knock her upside the head to get her attention. She's runnin' from him like a cat with its tail afire."

Eli nodded. "I reckon you're right, Mother Margaret. Something sure set her against God — and it was probably me."

"Don't blame yourself. The Lord has a good plan for each person's life. But the devil makes plans, too, don't you know? His schemes are low-down and wicked, and he'll try all kinds of sneaky tricks to keep people off the straight and narrow."

"Amen to that."

"Now, you better give that baby to me, Brother Elijah, and I'll see if I can get something into his belly while you preach your sermon. Mercy, he's a skinny thing. Puts up quite a fuss for bein' so weak and scrawny."

Eli studied the old woman as she hunched over the flailing bundle of damp blankets that had become his greatest burden. If he'd known what trouble a baby could bring, Eli wondered, would he have rescued Sam from his dying mother's arms?

Yes.

For some reason he couldn't explain, he had known God meant him to take the baby. He knew, even now, that he was supposed to care for Samuel. *But, Lord, have mercy on my weary bones,* he lifted up in prayer. *And please send help!*

"Yonder comes your flock, Brother Elijah," Mother Margaret said as she gave the baby a firm pat on his back. "What you plannin' to preach on today?"

Eli let out a deep breath. "I don't know," he said. "I have no idea."

With a sympathetic smile from the old lady to bolster him, Eli strode to the front of the church where he'd left his Bible. Before the baby entered his life, he had spent hours searching the Scripture for God's messages to the people. Eli loved to pray, silent and listening, in the early hours just after dawn. He pondered his own life and the lives of so many other sinners for subjects on which he could expound.

And when he finally delivered his sermons, God's Word seemed to pour through him. Women wept. Men fell to their knees in repentance. And the Holy Spirit went to work changing the hearts of sinners and renewing the vows of believers. Eli had never been so sure of anything as his call to preach the gospel of Jesus Christ.

And then he'd found that baby.

"Mornin', Preacher," someone greeted him as folks began filing into the new church building. Each family carried in a bench or two, and some hauled in chairs and stools. Eli recognized Ben and Eva Hanks from dinner the night before. And here came Jack Cornwall with the pretty red-haired Caitrin Murphy he intended to marry. Seth Hunter stepped inside, his round-bellied Rosie on one arm, their son on the other.

Next came a family of freckle-faced, green-eyed folks with more carrottopped children than a body could count. Following them, a big, tall man with shaggy blond hair gave the preacher an awkward bow before sitting on a chair that looked like it might splinter under his weight. There were others, too, so many Eli lost track as he thumbed through his Bible for an appropriate passage.

"Who vill lead singing today?" the shaggy blond man asked in a thick German accent. "Ve got new preacher, goot church, happy day. Who can sing?"

"Casimir Laski usually leads us," someone called. "But he's gone to Manhattan for supplies."

"All right, then, I'll do it." A skinny, bandy-legged fellow with bright red hair got to his feet. When he spoke again, his words danced with a light Irish lilt. "I'm Jimmy O'Toole, so I am, and I'll have you know I've not set foot inside a church for fifteen years. Sure I thought the whole lot of you were

Crawthumpers who didn't have a grain of sense in your heads. I wouldn't allow the church to be built on my land, and I resisted the very notion of a preacher movin' into town."

"Aye, Jimmy," his plump wife said, "so you did."

"But as everyone knows, now I'm a changed man. Once I was walkin' so far from heaven that I nearly got myself burned up. Now I have the grace of forgiveness, and I'm a thankful man to set myself before you."

"And to Jack Cornwall we owe our gratitude," his wife added.

"We'll sing the first hymn to the tune of 'Llanfyllin'," Jimmy went on. " 'Tis a Welsh air, but we'll forgive it that."

At that comment, his wife gave him a not-so-subtle elbow to the ribs. Unfazed, the skinny man lifted his voice in a hauntingly beautiful song, which the others joined him in singing.

> "Sometimes a light surprises
> The Christian while he sings;
> It is the Lord who rises
> With healing in his wings.
> When comforts are declining
> He grants the soul again
> A season of clear shining,
> To cheer it after rain."

Eli gulped as the song ended and the chorus of voices died down. *He* didn't have a season of clear shining. In fact, the waters of his future looked muddier than ever. He'd given away all his China mission money, Lily Nolan had run off, he didn't know what to do with his wailing baby, and now he was stuck for a sermon topic. *Lord, help me!*

Standing before the congregation, he turned to the middle of his Bible and prayed that a good psalm would jump right off the page. He read the first words his eye fell on — and realized to his chagrin that he'd landed in Hosea.

" 'Hear the word of the Lord, ye children of Israel,' " he read. " 'For the Lord hath a controversy with the inhabitants of the land, because there is no truth, nor mercy, nor knowledge of God in the land. By swearing, and lying, and killing, and stealing, and committing adultery, they break out, and blood toucheth blood.' "

Oh, great. He'd preached plenty of sermons admonishing the wicked — in fact, the topic moved him deeply. But he didn't think a guilt-and-repentance message was a great way to introduce a preacher to his new congregation.

Eli looked out at the sea of expectant faces, tried to figure out what to say next, and went back to reading. " 'Therefore shall the land mourn, and every one that dwelleth therein shall languish, with the beasts of the field, and with the fowls of heaven; yea, the fishes of the sea also shall be taken away.' "

He could feel the heat prickling up his back and onto his neck. This wasn't getting any better. Did he really want to do just what Lily had said and preach a sermon on the wrath of God? Eli fished in his pocket for his handkerchief to mop his brow, realized he'd tied it onto Samuel for a diaper in the middle of the night, and shut his Bible. *Oh, Lord, speak through me,* he prayed. *Say what you want to say, Father, because I'm up the creek without a paddle.*

He summoned his wits the best he could and began. "Do you want your land to mourn? Do you intend to languish here on the prairie? No? Then turn from your sin. Repent! Walk away from your evil — your lies, your swearing, your thieving, and your murder. Beg forgiveness of the Father!" He hammered his fist on the wooden podium. "Fall down on your knees and pray to be spared from the wrath of almighty God!"

At that, one of the little redheaded O'Toole children burst into tears. Dismayed, Eli watched the child's mother trying to comfort her daughter, and he prayed again for divine assistance. Not hearing any heavenly messages, he said the first thing that came to mind.

"Weep! Weep and wail for the sin that besets you. You enjoy your evil deeds. You argue, fight, and squabble among yourselves. You gossip and slander and lie. Repent now, I say! The hour of the Lord is at hand. He sees your wickedness. He knows even the smallest sin in your heart. You cannot escape!"

As Eli continued to expound on the wages of sin, a huge dog wandered into the church building. Tail thumping one bench after another, the mutt carried a meaty bone in his big chops as he meandered over to the Hunter family.

"Stubby!" the Hunter boy cried out. "What're you doin' in church?"

The crowd broke into muffled laughter as the dog flopped onto the floor and began gnawing his bone. But not even the loud crunching and slurping were enough to cheer the O'Toole girl, who continued to sob as though the world were coming to an end. At a loss for what to say next, Eli opened his Bible again. He glanced at the page and realized he was holding the book upside down.

When he lifted his focus to yet another disturbance at the back of the room, he recognized Lily Nolan silhouetted in the open doorway. Hands on her hips, she scanned the crowd in search of Samuel. Eli's spirits soared.

She didn't leave! She's here!

He swallowed a victory whoop. *Preach, Eli,* he heard the voice inside his heart. *Preach the Word of the Lord.*

But what had he been saying?

"You cannot escape," he repeated his last words. "You cannot escape God's wrath —"

He met Lily's bright blue eyes.

"And you cannot escape his love," he went on. "God hates sin — that much is true. But he loves you. He loves you more than you can ever imagine. All through the Bible, time after time, God showed his love for his people. But the greatest gift of love God gave us is his Son."

The dog dropped his bone, let out a loud groan of canine satisfaction, and stretched himself across the floor, tail thudding contentedly. Mrs. O'Toole stood up and carried her crying daughter out of the building. A rooster flapped up onto a windowsill and surveyed the crowd, his red feathers glossy in the sunshine. Lily's lips twitched in amusement.

"Most of you folks have heard about the baby God gave me," Eli continued, determined to ignore the interruptions. He didn't often mention his own life in sermons, but somehow he didn't feel much like he was preaching right now. He felt as though he were talking to Lily Nolan.

"Now little Samuel is my son," he said, "and I'm about as partial to him as any papa could be. Sure, he kept me up all last night with his hootin' and hollerin'. And I have no doubt he's messed more diapers than any baby on God's green earth."

At this, the crowd chuckled. Lily crossed her arms and leaned against the door frame, watching. Her dress was the color of new lilacs in the springtime, and she looked as wholesome as fresh milk. Eli's heart ached at the memory of the bitterness that rose so quickly to her tongue.

"The fact is," he said, "I'm not much fit to be a papa. I didn't ask for the job, and I don't have a wife to help me out. But God gave Samuel to me, and I love the boy. I love him more than I've ever loved anybody. Do you think I'd ever give him up? Do you think I'd turn him loose in a crowd that hated him? Do you think I'd ever let anybody hurt my son?"

He stepped away from the rough-hewn pulpit and faced his congregation. "Never," he said. "But I'm not God. 'For God so loved the world, that he gave his only begotten Son, that whosoever believeth in him should not perish, but have everlasting life.' God sent Jesus Christ among us — and we ridiculed him, tormented him, beat him, and finally killed him. God loves us so much he didn't want us to have to endure the punishment we deserve."

When he lifted his focus to the back of the room again, Eli realized that Lily had slipped away. His heart burning, he continued to speak as though she were still there. The rooster fluttered down from the windowsill and hopped over to inspect the dog bone. An elderly woman had a fit of coughing. Two children went to sleep. Eli didn't care. Maybe someone in this room needed to know about the amazing gift of God's love, and that was all that mattered.

The Word of the Lord was a flaming sword inside him — a sharp-edged, soul-cleansing, heart-piercing, all-protecting blade — and he had been commanded to wield it. Elijah Book was God's soldier, and for his Lord he would battle to the death all sin and wickedness.

"What a fine sermon, Reverend," Lily said when she spotted the long-legged preacher making his way down to the creek bank, where she sat nursing his baby. "And how many souls did you save from the fires of everlasting damnation?"

She saw him pause a moment, and she knew her words had wounded. Why did she feel such a need to strike out at the man? What brought on this compelling urge to hurt him? He'd done nothing against her. In fact, he had offered her good pay, searched out a place for her to stay, given her this chance to hold a baby once again. Though her heart ached with grief for her precious Abigail, she could not deny the pleasure she felt when little Samuel snuggled close against her, his eyes shut in peaceful slumber.

"I've never saved anybody, Mrs. Nolan," Elijah said, covering the last few feet toward her. "I just tell folks what God says in the Bible. He's the one who does the saving."

"Ah," she said, "how humble of you."

Biting her lip in dismay at the ease with which bitter words slipped from her tongue, Lily watched Elijah step onto the jumble of stones where she sat. Without meeting her eyes, he hunkered down and selected a flat rock. He picked it up and tossed it into the creek.

"You bring out the worst in me, Mrs. Nolan," he said finally. "Every time you talk, I get so angry I could just spit."

"The feeling is mutual, Mr. Book."

"Why is that?" He turned his blue eyes on her. "Are you upset because I found a baby and you lost yours?"

Lily swallowed. She hadn't expected him to be so direct. The men she had known in Philadelphia treated her with amused detachment. She had been a pretty prize to display at the symphony, a refined accessory at society's elite balls, an object for potential matrimony. But not a real woman. Not a package of emotions, dreams, hopes, sorrows, and joys worth opening and exploring. Yet this irritating preacher waded straight into her pain and demanded to understand it.

"It's none of your business how I feel or what I think," she said. She peered under the white shawl that covered the nursing baby and realized that Samuel had grown drowsy and was drifting to sleep. "I'm nothing to you. And you're nothing to me."

He flipped another stone into the creek. "Wrong. You mean a lot to me, Mrs. Nolan. Whether you like it or not."

Lily stared at the gurgling water to keep her eyes from Elijah Book. He was lying. She had never been important to anyone. Only Beatrice Waldowski had found value in Lily. And then it was for the services the younger woman could perform. Lily's singing, her acting, her participation in the shows gave Lily worth. Of course, with the preacher it was no different. She was keeping his baby alive. That was all.

"You matter most because you're a special lady," Elijah said. His deep voice took on the same intensity she had heard during the most heartfelt words of his sermons. "God made you different from everybody else. You're pretty — prettier than most, though I'm not much of a judge of that kind of thing. You can sing. I'm not too good in that area, either, but Mother Margaret said you have a voice that can join with the angels. She's right, too. And you have a tender spirit inside. I see it when you look at Samuel. It's your heart that matters most to me."

"And to God. Isn't that what you're leading up to, Mr. Book?" She cast him a sidelong glance. "You're after my soul. If you can feed your baby and rope my soul into heaven, you can add a few more stars to your saintly crown. Well, I have news for you. I won't be one of your missionary projects. I've sat in church a hundred thousand times, read every Bible verse and memorized half of them, and there's nothing you can say or do to convince me that your precious religion has anything to offer. I like my life just the way it is."

"Then why didn't you head out with your friend?"

Lily stiffened. "Why should I? Beatrice is coming back here. I'm sure of it. The only reason I stayed is for the money. Last night

Bea read a wonderful future for us, and she's on her way to Topeka to follow the plan in the cards."

"A stack of paper cards told her what your future would hold?"

"What's wrong with seeking truth in the tarot cards? You look for answers in the stack of papers between those leather Bible covers. There's not much difference between my cards and your book, except that the cards are a lot more accurate than a God nobody can see or hear."

"Maybe you never looked or listened."

Lily scowled. She didn't want to discuss religion with Elijah Book. As a matter of fact, she didn't want to discuss anything with the man. He made her uncomfortable. Look at him sitting there in his indigo trousers and homespun white shirt, his thick black Bible propped on his thigh, and his chin lifted as though he had the world by the tail.

How did he make his words sound so sincere? Why was he so confident in his faith? What made the man glow with assurance every time his resonant voice spoke?

"Anyhow," Elijah went on as though the conflict between them meant nothing. "I was telling you why you're important to me, Mrs. Nolan. It's not only because I could see right off what a special kind of woman you are, but it's also because of Samuel. I realize you're looking after my son because I'm paying you, but the fact is, you're keeping him alive. I meant what I said this morning. I do love him."

"Oh, please, Mr. Book. You picked him up off the trail, and you've hired me to feed him. Where's the love in that? He might as well be a puppy."

Elijah watched the gurgling water for a long moment. "Maybe I need someone to teach me how to love my son better. Will you do it?"

She looked up in surprise. "I can't *teach* you how to love. It's a natural thing."

"Not for me. I've never been real good with people."

"Then how can you think you're going to succeed as a pastor here in Hope? Oh, preaching is one thing. It's easy enough to wander around the countryside spouting Bible verses and warning people to repent of their sins. It's quite another thing to really know those same people — and to love them still. If you take on the responsibility of a church, Mr. Book, you can't just preach your clever sermons. And it'll be a lot more than deacons' meetings and committees and Sunday school picnics. You'll be called on to tend the sick and dying, and to comfort their despairing families. You'll be asked to heal troubled marriages and tame rebellious children and charm doddering old ladies who can't remember their own names. You'll be wakened in the middle of the night, called away from your dinner, interrupted in your bathtub —"

"Mrs. Nolan, is your father a preacher?"

Lily gave a harsh laugh. "My father is the devil."

"Whoa," Elijah murmured. "What makes you say that?"

"My life is my own business, Mr. Book," she said. "You stay out of it, or I'll set this baby at your feet and walk away."

Unwilling to let him read the emotion welling up inside her, Lily turned her back on the man. Elijah Book knew nothing about the path she had walked. And he never would.

"I can't seem to put two words together without making you angry," he said. "But you're right about one thing. I don't know beans about being a pastor. I was brought up on the cattle trail, and I never had much of a home. The only folks I spent time with were the trail hands — hardworking, hard-drinking, hard-talking fellows. In those days, my job was to keep an eye on the livestock. Flip over a cow and brand it, bob its ears, keep the wolves and coyotes from eating it, and drive it to market. There's not much room for love in that line of work."

"I guess not," Lily said, wishing the man would go away and leave her in peace. For some reason, ever since she'd had her baby, she couldn't control her tears. Abby's death had only made the situation worse. She didn't want this preacher to see her crying. Especially since nothing she said to wound him seemed to drive him away.

"When I saw you with Sam last night," he was saying, "I figured out right away that you knew some things I didn't. And I'm talking about more than how to put on a diaper. Mrs. Nolan, do you think you could teach me how to take care of Sam the way I ought? Not just when he's a baby, but as he grows. I want to raise him right. I want to love him."

"Then talk to him," she murmured. "And listen. Hold him close. Touch him. Comfort him when he cries. Kiss him. Take care of his needs. And bring a little fun to his life. That's all."

She brushed away a stray tear and blotted her finger on her skirt. What was it with men? Her father, a man she had struggled so hard to please, had been unable to love his only child. But Lily had loved Abigail so easily. So very easily.

"I'd offer you my handkerchief, but I had to use it for a diaper on Sam last night." Somehow Elijah had moved to within a foot of Lily

94

and the baby. "Talk, listen, comfort, and have fun. Clean diapers and good food. That's all there is to it?"

"And touch," she said softly. "Don't forget to touch him."

He reached out to one of the baby's bare feet. Lily observed him as he set the little foot in his palm and ran his fingertip across the tiny toes. "They look like kernels of new corn," he said in a low voice. "You know how you shuck a cob sometimes, and you see those little white nubbins? That's what his toes look like. Nubbins."

He bent over, his head nearly touching hers, and examined the baby's foot. The preacher had good hands, Lily noticed. They had seen hard work and plenty of sun. But the nails were strong and clean, and the fingers conveyed a sense of power even as they gently explored the baby's tiny toes.

The man smelled nice, too. The fragrance of fresh soap mingled with the scent of his sunbaked leather hat and worn boots. He had rolled the cuffs of his sleeves halfway to his elbows, and she could see the mat of dark gold hair that covered his arms. If she dared to trust his words — and she didn't — she might believe that he was the simple man he claimed to be. She might accept that he truly cared about the baby, truly believed in God, and truly wanted to learn to love people. But it would take more than his pretty words to convince her. It was how a man lived that made the difference.

"You reckon I could hold him?" the preacher asked. "Of course, if he's still feeding —"

"He's not nursing." She slipped the baby from beneath the shawl. "Circle your arms, Mr. Book. Nestle his head in the crook of your elbow. Tuck your hand under him. There."

Elijah sat unmoving, as stiff as a statue, staring at the dozing child. "I'm scared I'm going to drop him or crush him or something."

"He's all right. You're doing fine."

"Hey, Nubbin," he cooed. "How ya doin' there, buddy? Look at his eyelashes. They're so long."

"He's pretty."

"Nah, he looks like one of those old potatoes you find at the bottom of the bin in the chuck wagon. Wrinkled and splotchy and all shriveled up."

"He's not well."

"I'm afraid that's my fault."

"You didn't kill his mother," she said. Then she looked up at him. "Did you?"

He looked up, his blue eyes flashing. "No,"

he whispered. "Why would you ask something like that?"

Lily met his gaze. "Why not? All I know about you is what you've chosen to tell. You say you're a preacher who found a baby in a wagon. Maybe that's true. Maybe not."

"Why would I lie?"

"Why not?"

"I don't have anything to hide. I told you who I am, where I've been, what I've done. You've hardly told me anything."

"And I don't intend to," she said, starting to rise.

"Look here, Lily Nolan." He caught her arm and pulled her back down beside him. "God put the two of us together, whether you want to believe that or not. I need you. Samuel needs you. And even though you'll argue yourself blue in the face about this — you need me."

"No, I —"

"I'll treat you right. I'll never lie to you. I won't hurt you or cheat you or play games with you. I'm just Elijah Book, that's all, and what you see is what I am. Now, you can fight me and try to drive me away. Or you can work alongside me. I'm asking you for peace. I'm asking you to be my partner. Will you do that?"

Lily drew back from Elijah, her heart hammering. "If I become your partner," she said, "I'll have to let you in. And I'll never let anyone in."

As she walked up the creek bank toward town, she could feel his eyes following her. A sparrow swooped down and perched on the end of a bowed blade of bluestem grass. Lily tugged her white shawl tightly around her shoulders and began to rebuild the sagging walls that fortified her heart. She could not afford to let Elijah Book come too close. Though he claimed to know nothing of love, he somehow reached out to her, touched her, held her, and caressed the wounded edges of her soul. She could not let him in. She would not.

CHAPTER 5

As Elijah carried his son back up the creek bank toward the church, he recognized Seth Hunter standing outside the building. The man held a large woven basket topped by a bright, red-checkered cloth. "How about some lunch?" Seth called.

Eli grinned. "You read my mind, Brother."

"Rosie had a roast in the oven all morning, and we intended to invite you to eat at our house. But you got away."

"I went looking for Sam."

"How's he doing?"

"Half his breakfast is on my shoulder," Eli said. "I guess it's not a good idea to jiggle a baby right after he eats."

Seth laughed. "I'm fixing to learn all about that. My wife is due come autumn, and this will be the first baby I've helped with."

"I thought you had a son. The little fellow with the big dog?"

"Chipper was born to my first wife while I was away at war. Mary died before I could get back to her."

Eli tried to think what to say. He wasn't accustomed to hearing another man's personal matters. But he supposed that for a minister, it came with the territory.

"I've never been married," he mumbled. "Uh . . . and I'm sure sorry about your first wife."

"Well, God sent Rosie to me last spring. That was a miracle, if there ever was one."

"He does look after us." Feeling awkward, Eli patted Samuel. For once, the child was quiet.

"I sure would hate it if anything happened to Rosie," Seth said. "You know . . . while she's laboring over the baby."

Eli shook his head. "That can be bad. Boy howdy, it sure is trouble on a woman to give birth. My own mother died in childbirth when I was just five years old. She labored for three days. It was awful, all of it. The baby never did come, and finally my mama passed on. I don't believe my papa ever got over the grief of losing her."

Observing the farmer's stunned expression, Eli suddenly realized he hadn't said one word the man needed to hear. As a matter of fact, he'd only added to Hunter's fears. Eli's spirits sank. He didn't have any sense of how to comfort or reassure a person. Women did die in childbirth. They died often.

Lily Nolan had told him a pastor had to

tend the sick and the dying. During the worst moments in their lives, the people of Hope would look to Eli for answers. He didn't even know how to begin.

"But — uh," he fumbled, "I'm sure Mrs. Hunter will be fine." *Lord,* he breathed, *help me out here.* "There's bound to be a good doctor around these parts."

"No," Seth said. "We don't have a doctor in Hope."

"No doctor."

"If you believe there's a God in heaven," Lily Nolan said, joining them, "then you'll remember he keeps his eye on everyone — even the sparrows. I couldn't help overhearing you, Mr. Hunter, and as I'd just noticed a sparrow near the creek, I thought I'd remind you of those verses in Matthew: 'Are not two sparrows sold for a farthing? and one of them shall not fall on the ground without your Father. . . . Fear ye not therefore, ye are of more value than many sparrows.' "

Eli gaped at the woman.

"Reverend Book," she went on, "why don't you reassure Mr. Hunter that the God you trust with your eternal soul considers the lives of Mrs. Hunter and her baby important?"

Seth and Eli looked at each other. Eli swallowed. "Mrs. Nolan is right," he said. "God doesn't promise to protect us from every bad thing that comes along. But he loves us, and he's right here with us through thick and thin. He listens to our prayers, Mr. Hunter, so every day I'm going to talk to God about your wife. I believe he'll see her through the hard labor ahead. I'm going to have faith that come September you'll welcome a fine, healthy baby into your home."

Seth visibly relaxed. "You'll pray for Rosie?"

"Morning, noon, and night." Remembering Lily's instructions about how to show love, Eli reached out and laid his hand on the other man's shoulder. "You can depend on it, my friend."

"Thank you, Brother Elijah," Seth said. "I'll tell Rosie. She'll be mighty grateful, too."

"You folks pray, too, and we'll even do some looking for a doctor who might want to move to town."

"That would be great." Seth gave Lily a warm smile. "Mrs. Nolan, I've brought along some of Rosie's roast beef. Maybe you'd like to join Brother Elijah for lunch. We're happy to have both of you in Hope, and, Reverend, thanks again."

Eli took the heavy wicker basket in his free hand and gave Seth Hunter a farewell nod as the man started up the road to his own home. Then he turned to Lily. "You were hopping mad at me a few minutes ago. Why did you help me?"

She shrugged. "You were botching it."

"But you told me you don't believe in the Bible."

"I believe in comforting people." She lifted the lunch basket from Eli's arm. "Samuel has spit up all over your shoulder."

"I was jiggling him."

She rolled her eyes. "You're not much good at anything, are you, Mr. Book?"

"I can brand cattle."

With a laugh, she headed to a tree near the church and spread the checkered cloth on a patch of shaded grass. Eli let out a breath. *Lord,* he lifted up, *I don't understand this woman. I don't know what I'm doing in this town. And I can't see where you're leading me. Would you mind letting me in on the plan?*

"I am so hungry," Lily exclaimed, taking mismatched china plates and cutlery from the basket. "Nursing a baby just drains all the strength right out of a woman. Here's some roast for you. I'm surprised the Hunters would have beef. Surely they're trying to build up their flock of cows."

"Herd," Eli said, kneeling across from her. "Cattle run in herds. Sheep run in flocks."

Her blue eyes sparkled. "Maybe you're not as ignorant as I thought."

"Not about livestock, anyhow."

"Have you ever been to school, Mr. Book?"

"Once or twice. My father and I were on the move a lot. I like to read, though. I'll read anything I can lay my hands on. Did you get any schooling?"

"Certainly." She spooned peas onto his plate and set a warm roll beside them. "I am well educated and trained in all the proper social graces."

"Lonely, too."

"I am not." After giving him a withering glance, she set about buttering her roll. "Beatrice Waldowski is my good friend. She'll be back in a few days."

"I guess we'll see about that. She took the wagon, you know." Eli settled the baby on the blanket beside him. "Mind if I pray over this meal?"

"I'll try not to be offended by your beliefs as long as you're not offended by mine."

"Dear Lord," he began, wondering if there would ever come a day when Lily Nolan didn't irritate the living daylights out of him. "We praise you for this beautiful afternoon and for the folks who came to the service this morning. Touch them with your message of hope and salvation. I want to ask for your special protection over Mrs. Hunter and her baby. Please keep them safe, Lord. And, if you would, help me figure out how to manage Sam. Most of all, I want to thank you for sending along Mrs. Nolan. Touch her heart. In the name of Jesus I pray. Amen."

"You forgot to thank God for the food."

Eli lifted his head. "You know this religion business pretty well, don't you?"

"I'm a walking university of religious folde-rol. Ask me anything. Go on."

"All right. Who parted the Red Sea?"

"Moses."

"Who walked on water?"

"Jesus. And don't forget Peter, the poor fellow. He managed a few steps before his faltering faith sent him under." She popped a bite of bread into her mouth. "Those are easy. Ask me something harder, like Who drove a tent peg through the head of Sisera the Canaanite?"

Eli worked a few peas onto his fork. "How can a person know the Bible front to back and not believe it's the Word of God?"

Lily paused. "It was Jael, the wife of Heber the Kenite, who drove the peg through Sisera's head."

"That's not the answer to my question."

"Well, it's all the answer you're going to get from me," she said. "Please pass the butter."

Eli set the small crock near her plate and watched her tear apart a second roll. "You're

105

right that I'm not cut out to be a pastor," he said. "All I know is to preach the gospel and let the Lord do his work in people's souls. I can't comfort the sick and the dying, and I don't know how to reach a woman who's shut her heart up tight." He studied the hand-hewn shingles on the roof of the new church. "The folks here need a real minister — not some ol' Texas cowhand."

Lily tucked a strand of golden hair behind her ear. "Didn't King David start out as a shepherd?"

"Sure, but I'm not educated or tender-hearted or well mannered — none of those things you talked about. I know how to do a day's labor, earn my pay, eat a little chow, and sleep on the ground at night. I'm just a plain workingman."

"Jesus was a carpenter. Paul made tents. Peter fished for a living. You're not in bad company, Reverend Book."

"Right now, I'm in your company, and I can't figure you out."

"Why should you bother? I'm doing my job feeding your baby. Isn't that enough?"

"No." He reached across the checkered cloth and took her hand. "It's not enough for me. I thought about you all last night when I was up with Samuel. Today, when you walked into church and I saw you standing there at the back, I wanted to shout hallelujah. It didn't have a thing to do with the baby. You're not just Sam's nurse. You're a cyclone who's blown through my life and turned everything topsy-turvy. In the space of two days, you've made me boiling mad, lifted my spirits, bailed me out of trouble, challenged my faith in God, and filled my mind to overflowing. In spite of myself, Mrs. Nolan, I care about you."

Her hand was trembling as she slipped it out of his. "Please don't do that, Mr. Book," she said in a thin voice. "Care about these people — your church. Let them into your heart and learn to love them. Then you'll be a pastor."

"And you?"

"Don't care about me. I don't want anything from you except what you can afford to pay me. I have everything I need."

"A person who has everything she needs ought to be happy. You're not happy. You're angry and hurting. There's something inside you that's so sad —"

"No. I've chosen my path. I'm going to make my own way in this world. And I'll do it alone. I don't need the crutch of religion."

"My faith in God is no crutch. When I was trying to get through life without the Lord, I was limping along, stumbling and falling down every two or three steps. I tried to fill the emptiness with work, drink, cards, women — whatever. Nothing satisfied for long. Then I asked Christ to come into my heart, and he healed me better than new. A man doesn't need a crutch when he's whole and complete."

"Well, I'm a whole woman," she said, stacking their dishes. "My strength comes from within myself. I'm my own source of light and power."

Eli touched the sleeping baby's cheek. "I'm impressed. You must be a lot better person than I am, Mrs. Nolan. When I looked at my spirit without God, all I saw was confusion and nothingness. I didn't know which way to turn, and I sure didn't feel any power. Oh, I was strong all right — blustering around one saloon or another, fighting any man who looked at me crossways, running cattle from Abilene to Kansas City. But all my strength was on the outside. I pulled anger and hurt around me like a heavy suit of armor to keep everybody back. Inside, I was as empty as an old tin can."

Lily pursed her lips for a moment. Then she tucked a strand of hair into her bun. "It looks like rain," she said. "I'd better go and speak to Mrs. Hanks about her offer of a place to sleep. None of the other good Christian citizens of

108

Hope have invited me in. I'm not surprised. When you're filled with the holiness of God, you don't want to sully yourself by spending time with a lowly actress from a traveling show."

Without looking at him, she set the dishes into the basket and stood. "You can fetch me when Samuel wakes up," she said. "I'll stay in town until Beatrice comes back from Topeka."

Eli sat on the checkered cloth watching Lily Nolan walk away from him for the second time that day. He thought about all his years on the trail. And he pondered his months on the preaching circuit. One thing seemed sure. God could use him like a cattle driver — spreading the gospel as he herded people into the kingdom of heaven. But Eli wasn't cut out to be a shepherd — guiding, nurturing, and tending a flock of lambs along the rocky paths of life day-by-day.

No sir. Right this minute he ought to go tell Seth Hunter he was quitting his job as pastor of Hope's church, and then he could head for China.

In the distance, Lily Nolan paused outside the door of the Hankses' house. She lifted the corner of her white apron and dabbed her cheek. She was crying, Eli realized. This woman who claimed to be whole, strong, and glowing with inner peace was weeping.

Lord, he prayed, *I want to run from this work you sent my way. But even more than that, I want to do your will. Teach me how to be a shepherd.*

"Mercy, mercy, mercy, girl. That storm is blowin' up fast. I hope we don't get us a cyclone."

Lily noted that Mother Margaret was taking her washing off the line even though the clothes weren't nearly dry. She chuckled at the older woman's now-familiar foibles. Four days in the Hankses' home had given Lily a sense of family she'd never known. Ben's siblings and his and Eva's children had long ago gone to work for other landowners, and the loss was palpable to this day. Often Mother Margaret mentioned a son or daughter, and at each meal Eva prayed for her absent children by name. Though lacking an extended family, the couple had created a warm and loving relationship with Ben's mother. Now they welcomed Lily as though she had always lived there.

"I'd better get that boy of mine to whittle some new clothes-pegs," the old woman said. "We toted these all the way from Missouri, and they're plumb wore out."

Sitting in a rocking chair on the front porch

of the little frame house, Lily watched Mother Margaret drop gray wooden pegs into her apron pockets. For almost a week, clouds had been lingering on the horizon, promising rain but failing to deliver. The day before, in the mercantile, Rosie Hunter had told a terrifying story of a cloud of grasshoppers that had once plagued the town. Caitrin Murphy followed that with the tale of a raging prairie fire whose smoke everyone had mistaken at first for rain clouds.

Lily was beginning to wonder if life on this barren land might be a lot more intimidating than it appeared. These bucolic peasants were turning out to be warriors in disguise, battling the elements for their very lives. Though she was certain her reception at her father's house in Philadelphia would be unpleasant, she felt thankful she'd be returning there before the winter.

"Eva, you better run next door and tell Ben and Mr. Jack to carry their tools inside the smithy," Mother Margaret called. "It's fixin' to rain. I can feel it in my bones."

Eva peered out the screenless window of the house and gave Lily a wink. "I reckon those two men know enough to get their tools out of the rain before they get rusty, Mama."

"Mercy, I hope so."

Lily fingered the tight collar of her dress.

The air hung dank and humid over the grassland, so heavy it was hard to breathe. She wondered what her parents were doing on this day in Philadelphia. No doubt they were attending a literary reading or a political speech. Her father would be preparing selections for the symphony to play during the Independence Day celebrations. Her mother would be agonizing over summer bonnets and gloves. The townhouse would be dark and cool, each table laden with a bouquet of fresh flowers, pungent smells wafting up from the kitchen, a coat of new wax gleaming on the hardwood floors.

How different from this toilsome prairie life. How empty.

Lily pushed up from the rocking chair and strolled across the beaten dirt yard to help Mother Margaret take down the rest of the laundry. Odd that she felt so comfortable in the home of former slaves. But here in Hope, Lily had discovered laughter that came from the belly, music that came from the heart, and food that nourished the soul.

"Sit yourself back down, child," the old woman said. "That preacher will be along here any minute with his squallin' baby. I don't know why he's takin' so long this afternoon anyhow. Seems like he comes a-runnin' to you the minute that little feller makes a sound."

Lily tugged a wooden peg from the line. She was a little concerned herself. Physically uncomfortable with her need to nurse the baby, she couldn't understand why she had seen Elijah only once this day. She had insisted that the baby spend most of the time with his father. After all, she would be leaving soon. But Lily found herself eagerly anticipating the moment when she would hear Samuel's wails drifting toward her from the church. Surely in a moment the preacher would march up to the house, his dark hair windblown and his blue eyes clouded with concern — as though Sam's every whimper spelled trouble with a capital *T*.

Though they hadn't spoken at length since the picnic beside the church, Lily had turned the man's words over in her mind. He might be uneducated and rough-hewn, but Elijah Book was sincere. At least . . . he seemed sincere. She hesitated to trust him too far. He was, after all, a man.

"What time did you nurse that baby?" Mother Margaret asked, dropping the last damp shirt into her basket. "I thought it was around midmornin'. Don't you reckon Sam's hungry by now?"

Lily set her hands on her hips and stared at the church. "Maybe Eva could go over there and check on things."

"Eva's cookin' supper. What's wrong with those two feet you got? Can't they make it across the street?"

"I don't want to bother Reverend Book. He might be resting."

"He's not restin'. That man's been working himself half to death over there. Hammerin' day and night. Plowin' up the ground. Splittin' fence posts. He hasn't done much visitin' of his flock, but he sure is sprucin' up the building."

"I guess I could walk over and check." Lily crossed her arms. "But he might be writing a sermon or something. With the wedding coming up this Saturday —"

"He never writes down a thing he says. Didn't you listen to him last night at prayer meetin'? Why, he just went to tearin' through the Scripture like a hound dog after a coon. One by one, he pulled those verses apart and put 'em back together — and he never looked at nothin' but the Good Book itself."

"I wasn't at the prayer meeting."

"Well, you missed a good'n. I don't know why you thought you needed to stay here at the house and wash your stockin's all secret-like. Everybody in town knows what a pair of lady's stockin's looks like. Mercy me."

Lily picked up the heavy load of laundry and carried it onto the front porch. The clouds looked no closer to town than they had the past three days, but at least Mother Margaret could stop fretting about her clothes getting rained on. The tiny old woman hobbled up the wooden steps and sank onto a chair.

"Go check on that baby, Miz Lily," she wheezed, "before I give myself a heart attack worryin' over him. Go on now. And don't you get caught in the rain."

Lily took a deep breath and started toward the unpainted clapboard church. She didn't want Elijah to think she ever missed Samuel. Or needed the baby. Or looked forward to seeing the two of them. He had to understand that the arrangement between them was just a job.

Taking care of Samuel would earn Lily the money to leave the nomadic life that had cost her a husband and a daughter. Going back to Philadelphia would return her to the shallowness and fear, but at least in the big brownstone townhouse she would have security. Life couldn't promise much more than that anyway.

A deep voice sang from the church's backyard.

"Hallelujah, Thine the glory!
Hallelujah, amen!
Hallelujah, Thine the glory!
Revive us again."

Hands dug into her apron pockets, Lily peered around the side of the building. For a moment, she failed to recognize the sweat-drenched, shirtless man who was digging postholes. Half built, the fence started from the back of the church in a razor-straight line, snapped into a perpendicular angle, stretched across the prairie to another sharp corner, and then set off back toward the church. In Philadelphia, Lily had never given much attention to such mundane things. But she could tell this was a beautiful fence.

The tall, well-formed man digging holes rammed his clamshell shovel into the ground, worked it around, and lifted out a clump of rich Kansas soil. As he lowered the shovel again, he returned to singing.

> "We praise Thee, O God,
> For the Son of Thy love,
> For Jesus who died
> And is now gone above."

Elijah Book was right, Lily thought. He couldn't carry a tune in a bucket. His heartfelt enthusiasm went a long way to make up for the off-key singing, but she cringed as the man plunged into a second verse. Attempting to keep a straight face, she stepped around the side of the church and approached him.

"Hallelujah, Thine the — whoa!" he said, taking a step backward. "I didn't expect you."

She was amazed to see the man flush a shade of deep rose under his tanned skin as he fumbled in his back pocket for a handkerchief. Mopping his forehead, he grabbed his shirt from the last post he had set and tugged it on.

"Good afternoon, Reverend Book," Lily said. He tried to fasten a button and finally gave it up. "I see you've been digging."

"Yeah." He pushed his fingers back through his damp hair. "I'm building a fence for the church."

"Ah," she said. "I thought churches were supposed to welcome people. Who is it you wish to keep out?"

At that he grinned. "Critters. I plan to put a little garden back here, so I don't have to rely on the generosity of the townsfolk for my food. And then — if need be — I can start a cemetery in that southeast corner. There's a little tree, and I thought I'd try turning over the sod and planting some flowers here and there."

"Flowers?"

"Well, sure. When they're grieving, folks like to come and spend some quiet time in a graveyard. Makes them feel better. I thought flowers would perk up the place."

Lily reflected on Abigail's barren grave. The baby had no headstone to mark her short life. No one would ever tend the spot where she lay. She had not even been given a little speech or a prayer — not that Lily thought prayers for the dead did any good. In fact, she hadn't found prayers of any sort to be worth much. God never listened.

"I could put up a stone marker for your baby," Eli said in a low voice. "I could ask Jack Cornwall to carve her name on it."

Surprised, Lily looked into the man's blue eyes. How had he known what she was thinking?

The preacher shoved his handkerchief back into his pocket and shifted from one foot to the other. "I just figured maybe —"

"Thank you," Lily murmured. "I would appreciate a marker in my daughter's memory."

"I'd be privileged to do that." After a pause, he asked, "Did I tell you Sam smiled at me this morning? Well, sort of. Anyhow . . ." He looked up at the church and frowned. "Sam's been awfully quiet."

Lily felt a twinge of dread. "Have you checked him lately?"

"He was sleeping, and I came out here to dig. But that's been a good while ago."

Tossing down the clamshell shovel, Eli

started past Lily on his way to the church. She gathered up her skirts and ran after him. Side by side, they pushed through the narrow door at the back of the building and entered the dimly lit room where the pastor had been staying.

"Sam?" Eli dropped to his knees beside the wooden produce box on the floor. "Hey, Nubbin."

Lily sank down beside him and drew back the blanket. Heat radiated through the damp cotton gown as she lifted the tiny baby into her arms. Limp, listless, the child opened his eyes and gave a little whimper.

"Oh, Elijah!" she cried softly, covering the baby's forehead with her palm. "Samuel's so hot."

"Is he sick?" Eli took the baby and pressed his face against the child's cheek. "He has a fever. Oh, God, help us."

Lily uncurled the baby's tiny hand. "Elijah," she said, "we've got to have help. *Real* help. Let's take him to Mother Margaret."

CHAPTER 6

"Mercy, you got yourself one sick baby there, Brother Elijah." Mother Margaret watched the preacher carry a bucket of cool well water into her house and set it on the floor beside the washbowl.

"Isn't he any better?"

"He took a little milk," Lily said in low voice. "Just before dawn."

Eli knew that she and Mother Margaret had been awake all night, mopping Samuel's feverish body and trying everything they could think of to lower his temperature. He had hovered over the two women, trying to see what they were up to, asking questions, offering suggestions — until finally the older woman had shooed him outside to pray. Trudging back and forth along his fence, Eli had pleaded with God for the child's life. He was angry with himself for neglecting Sam all afternoon. He was dismayed at the absence of medical care in the little town. And he was truly frightened that his baby might die.

"He's going to be all right, isn't he?" Eli asked, kneeling beside the chair where Lily was rocking the baby. "This is probably just a head cold or something, don't you reckon?"

Her depthless blue eyes gave him all the answer he needed. On the frontier, babies often died for one reason or another. Lily had lost her daughter. Eli might lose his son.

"Here you go, Brother Elijah," Eva Hanks said, handing him a cup of steaming liquid. "It's sassafras tea. You need to eat something too. How about one of these biscuits?"

He shook his head. "My stomach feels like a knotted-up lasso. I don't think I can eat a thing."

"Ben has gone to the neighbors around Hope to let folks know about the baby," Eva told him. "Everybody will be praying."

Eli looked at Lily. Could prayer save Samuel? Obviously Lily didn't think so. Her face showed exhaustion and hopelessness. Her eyes were red-rimmed from weeping. She fingered the baby's thin blanket.

"I think he might have diphtheria," she said. "He's so limp and bedraggled."

"No." A chill of dread wrapped around Eli's heart. "Not diphtheria."

"He's still breathing comfortably enough. But I wish we could give him some kind of tonic to break the fever."

"What about that potion you sell in your show? Could you make up some of that?"

She shook her head. "It's useless. There's nothing in the elixir that would help Samuel. I can't think of anything —"

"Castoria." A cheerful redhead stepped into the house and held up a dark blue bottle. Eli recognized her as Caitrin Murphy, the woman whose wedding he was to perform on Sunday. "Sure I've brought Castoria for the wee one. Sheena — that's my sister, so 'tis — she says you must put a plaster on the baby's chest to draw out the infection, and wrap him tightly in blankets to sweat the fever from his body."

Eli grabbed the blue bottle. "How much should we give him?"

"Wait!" Lily said. "How can you be sure this medicine will help? He's so tiny. He can barely take milk."

"Sheena says he must have Castoria," the woman explained. "My sister has five children and one on the way. She knows about these things."

Eli laid his hand across the baby's heated body. "We've got to do something, Lily."

"Let me try to nurse him again first. If he can just get a little stronger, maybe he'll be able to fight the fever."

"I let him get too weak. I fed him mashed potatoes."

"It's all you knew to do. This is not your

fault, Elijah. Abigail was in perfect health when the diphtheria struck Topeka. You mustn't blame yourself."

"But look at the little fellow. He's skinnier than one of those fence rails I've been splitting. What chance does he have?"

"You answer that question," Lily said. "You're the one who believes in a God of healing and protection. Where is your God when children are ill? Where is he when they're struggling to take in their last breaths? Where is he when they're hurting . . . and . . . and unable to defend themselves . . . and helpless . . ."

A tear started down Lily's cheek. Without thinking, Eli reached up and brushed it away with his fingertips. "Don't cry now, Lily," he murmured. "God's eye is on the sparrows, and he's watching Sam. He knows the number of hairs on our baby's head. He's holding Sam in his arms, and he's holding you and me, too. He's here with us, right now, this minute. I can't see the future, but he can, Lily. Why don't you sing for Sam? Sing one of the hymns."

Eli took his mother's hymnal from the table near Lily's chair and opened it. She shook her head as another tear trickled down her cheek. "I can't . . . can't sing," she said.

Eli began.

"Abide with me; fast falls the eventide;
The darkness deepens; Lord, with me
    abide!"

She joined in, her voice choked with emotion.

"When other helpers fail and comforts
    flee,
Help of the helpless, O abide with me."

"Keep on singing, Lily," Eli whispered. "Sing for Sam."

Standing, he followed Miss Murphy and Mother Margaret out onto the porch. Hands clasped, the two women waited with heads bowed. Eli stared across the vast plain and thought about Lily's questions — and more uncertainties crowded in. Where was God? Why did children have to suffer and die? What had Sam done to deserve the fever that raged through his tiny body? What had Abigail done? Did God really care about his people? And if he did, why wouldn't he heal Sam?

Mother Margaret began humming along with Lily's soft voice. "Yes, Lord," she murmured in prayer. "You are the Lord of life. You know the number of my days, short or long. Oh, God, I give them all to you. In health and in sickness, you are my comfort. In peace and in trouble, you are my strength. Lord, you fill my heart. Amen and amen."

Eli clutched the post that supported the porch roof. God would hold them all in his love — through life . . . and death. *But please, Lord,* his soul cried out, *don't let Samuel die!*

Lily's pure voice drifted out from within the frame house.

"Hold Thou Thy cross before my
    closing eyes;
Shine through the gloom and point me
    to the skies;
Heaven's morning breaks, and earth's
    vain shadows flee;
In life, in death, O Lord, abide with me."

Through the rest of that day and the next, tiny Sam battled the unexplained illness that raged through him. Though Lily was exhausted from lack of sleep and from her efforts to feed the listless child, she was touched by the warmth that poured from the townsfolk of Hope. Ben Hanks and Caitrin Murphy, it seemed, had rallied the forces in support of their weakest member.

Caitrin brought a sample of every medicine she stocked in the Hope mercantile. Rosie Hunter, careful for the health of her own unborn child, sent Seth and Chipper to the

Hankses' house with enough food to last a week. Sheena O'Toole bustled into the cabin with a batch of fresh bread and orders to *brauch* the baby. She and Mother Margaret tightly bound Sam's abdomen and then wrapped him so that no fresh air could reach his lungs. After a time, they removed the wrappings, rubbed his little body with vinegar and fat, moved his legs and arms in rhythmic motions, and prayed out loud. Then the wrappings were bound again, and the child lay in deathly silence.

Not only the neighbors close at hand, but everyone in the community reached out to the ailing baby. Violet Hudson, a young widow with many mouths of her own to feed, brought a new quilt to cover Samuel. The Laski family sent vegetables from their abundant garden. A Frenchman named LeBlanc arrived with oil to keep lamps burning all night as the caretakers watched over the baby. Even Rolf Rustemeyer, the big shaggy German, rode his mule into town and stopped by to see the Hankses and drop off a baby rattle he had carved from a piece of wood.

"Why?" Lily asked Elijah as Rolf stood on the porch that evening talking to Ben Hanks and Jack Cornwall. "Why have they brought all these things? They hardly know you, and most of them have never even seen the baby."

Haggard, the preacher studied the tiny child in his arms and shook his head. "Jesus," he said. "These people love Jesus. That's the only explanation I know."

"How futile." With a sigh of disgust, Lily pushed up from her chair and walked to the rough, hand-hewn table. "Look at all this food. What good can it do Sam? None. And neither can their precious Jesus. Some Savior he is. Why isn't Sam feeling any better? It's been two days. He's hardly eaten, and his fever keeps creeping higher. He's wrapped up so tightly he can hardly take in air. Has he even opened his eyes in the last hour?"

"I can feel him breathing. He's still alive."

"Oh, I can't bear this!" she cried out. "I wish Beatrice were here. She could read the tarot cards and tell us what to do. She has a crystal ball that foretells the future, and she knows how to study a person's skull. Phrenology, she calls it. She even has séances."

"You told me that elixir of hers is useless."

"But Beatrice has magical stones that can heal the sick. If she were here, she could put them on Samuel's body. Amethyst and garnet and quartz — they're very powerful, Elijah."

"Did Beatrice's crystals help your daughter?"

"Why must you bring Abigail into this?" She wrung her hands. "At least if Bea were here she could *do* something. That's better than sitting around praying to a God who doesn't listen. I'm tired of the silly prayers everyone is saying. I'm fed up with their trite little messages of hope: 'Oh, Samuel's so sweet that I'm sure God will let him live' or 'Maybe the Lord needs a new little angel in heaven.' That's horrible. It doesn't do any good. We need help here, Elijah. We need to *act*, not just sing and pray. I feel like I'm going mad!"

"You can't bring Abigail back, Lily," Eli said in a low voice. "Trying to force Sam to live won't bring your daughter back to life."

"I know that. Of course I know that. I'm not stupid." She pulled her handkerchief from the pocket of her apron. "But I can't lose two!"

"Mother Margaret lost three."

"She's obviously a much better woman than I am. I'm selfish and greedy. I want life. I want Abigail."

"Lily —"

"What do you know about anything?" she cried, turning on him. "You're so blindly trusting. You think God is protecting you and watching over you all the time. He's not, Elijah! If there is a God, he doesn't care about you. He doesn't care about Sam. You would understand that if you'd ever had to suffer!"

"I've suffered. I lost my mother when I was a boy. You think that didn't hurt me, Lily? You think I didn't hear my daddy crying in the night after he thought I was asleep? I was as helpless then as I am right now. I couldn't bring my mother back, and I can't make Sam well. But there's one thing I can do."

"Pray," she snapped. "Pray, pray, pray."

"I can trust that the God who created me and loved me enough to give the life of *his* Son for me cares about *my* son." He stood and walked toward her, the baby unmoving in his arms. "I can't see God's plans, but I believe they're good ones. My mama's death hurt, but God used it to pull me close to my father. It was the book of hymns you've been singing from that helped lead me to salvation. If Mama hadn't died, do you think I'd have counted her hymnal special? Do you think I'd have read it over and over? Do you think I'd ever have found the path to joy?"

"Joy? You can't tell me you feel joyful right now."

"At this moment, holding this dying baby, I have the greatest joy, the deepest peace, and the purest strength I've ever known." He slipped his arm around her and drew her against his chest. "Oh, Lily, I wish you knew it too. I wish you had hope."

"There is no hope." Desperate and frantic,

she laid her hand on the baby's fevered little head. Abigail had been this ill in the hours before her death, and Lily had been unable to hold her daughter back from the precipice. All the love in the world had not kept Abby from slipping over the edge.

"Mercy, that's a sweet sight," Mother Margaret said, her bright yellow dress aglow in the light of the oil lamp she carried. "The three of you sure do make a pretty picture. Yes, sir. Once we get past this trouble, we're gonna have to fix you up. You belong."

Lily pressed her cheek against Elijah's shoulder, blotting her tears on the comforting homespun cotton fabric of his shirt. What was the old woman saying? Had everyone gone insane?

"But right now, we better head for a doctor," Mother Margaret continued. "We all been a-talkin' on the porch — Ben, Eva, Mr. Seth, Mr. Jack, Mr. Rolf, and me. We decided you need to take that baby to Topeka, Brother Elijah. Ben's hitchin' his mule to Mr. Seth's wagon, and Miz Rosie is sendin' some food down from her house. Miz Lily and I will take turns with the baby while you drive. You reckon you're up to goin' all the way to Topeka, Brother?"

As though a fresh wind had blown through the room, Eli lifted his head and gave the old woman a warm smile. "Sure thing, Mother Margaret. You're coming with us?"

"The Lord knows I'm not much use around here. I been hangin' up laundry and takin' it down wet for almost a week, waitin' for the rain to come. Maybe if I leave, Ben will finally have himself some dry shirts."

"I suspect it'll rain."

The old woman laughed. "You're probably right. Miz Lily, fetch the baby's box, would you? And let's take along some of them pickles Miz Sheena brought over yesterday. Mercy, I never tasted such fine pickles in all my life."

In a fog of sorrow and anxiety, Lily watched Mother Margaret bustle around the room gathering supplies for the sudden journey. Elijah tucked the jar of pickles under his free arm, and then he carried Samuel out the door to the wagon that Ben had pulled up to the porch.

As she gathered up her dresses and stuffed them into a bag, Lily reflected on her return to Topeka. Another long journey. Another sick baby. Could she bear to visit the unmarked grave where Abigail lay? She felt sure of only one thing. While in Topeka, she would search for and find Beatrice Waldowski.

The Lord allowed the rain to fall. Eli

hunched under a sheet of canvas and, through a veil of pouring water, he watched the lights of Topeka grow closer. All night and all day, he had urged the reluctant mule eastward along the muddy road. They had sloshed through swollen creeks and rattled over rickety bridges. Barely stopping to rest and feed the mule, they had pushed onward.

Somehow, Samuel was still alive. Lily and Mother Margaret had taken turns tending the baby as they huddled beneath a makeshift tent on the wagon bed. Flashes of lightning and the crack of thunder had hardly disturbed Sam's fevered sleep. Now and again, the old woman would lean forward and call out some message: "He took a little milk," she would say, or "He's a-coughin' now."

As Eli guided the mule onto the main street of Topeka, he finally realized he could pray no more. He had begged, pleaded, wept, and cried out for mercy from his heavenly Father. He had searched his mind for Scripture of comfort and hope. He had offered the Lord well-reasoned arguments in favor of sparing Sam's life. He had ground his teeth in rage at the thought of the baby's death, and he had offered up every sacrifice he could think of — if only God would save Sam. "I'll go straight to China and preach your Word," he had told the Lord. "I'll stay in Hope and be a pastor all my days." "Africa? Do you want me to go to Africa? I'll do that, if you'll just let Sam live."

Finally he knew he had no choice but to surrender. He could not will the baby back to health. He could not bargain with the Lord. He could only relinquish Sam into the hands of the almighty God who could turn water into wine, make lame men walk, and calm stormy seas. "Thy will be done," Eli finally prayed as the storm of Sam's terrible illness raged around him. He was helpless against it. "Thy will be done on earth as it is in heaven."

Late evening finally brought an end to the downpour that had accompanied the wagon across the prairie. In the city of Topeka, oil lamps glowed in windows, and the aroma of suppers on the stove began to drift from chimneys. Children emerged to splash in puddles. Businessmen picked their way down wooden boardwalks. The humid chill carried the fragrance of fresh rain along with the reek of discarded, rotting food and open drains. Dogs shook themselves in a spray of droplets, while pigs ambled from the shelter of porches to wallow in the mud.

"You reckon we can find a doctor this late in the evenin'?" Mother Margaret said from under the tent. "I'm afraid they's all shut down, and besides that, it's Sunday."

Eli pushed aside the sopping canvas. He had been scheduled to perform a wedding ceremony this afternoon, but the thought of his obligation had barely crossed his mind. Jack Cornwall and Caitrin Murphy had been among those urging him off to Topeka. He supposed they would understand the delay.

"There's a doctor's place now," he said, spotting a dripping wooden sign that dangled over the boardwalk. "Doctor Schlissel" it read. "Cures." At least the message was straightforward.

As Lily emerged from the tent, Eli reined the mule to a halt and set the wagon's brake. He realized that the silent baby in her arms looked smaller and weaker than ever before. Was Samuel still alive? How could a human life possibly have endured the days of agony that this child had borne? Eli met Lily's somber gaze.

"I think he's still breathing," she whispered. "Elijah, this doctor had better be sent by your ever-loving God, or I don't know what I'll do."

Lifting the young woman down from the wagon, he noted how thin and fragile she was. Like a sparrow. *Oh, Lord, your eye is on the sparrow. Watch over Lily. Watch over us all.*

Eli knocked on the door of the doctor's office. Grumbling that she never had liked big cities, Mother Margaret chose to remain in the wagon. Lily stood shivering beside Eli, her kidskin boots soaked to the ankle. He slipped his arm around her shoulders and drew her close.

"What?" A bleary-eyed elderly man sporting a two-day growth of gray whiskers and the stub end of a cigar peered out the doorway. "Whatcha want?"

"We're looking for Dr. Schlissel," Eli said.

"He's off duty."

He started to shut the door, but Eli held it open. "Please, sir. We've got to have help for our baby. Would you ask the doctor if he'd just take a look at the boy?"

"Dr. Schlissel, would you like to take a look at the boy?" the man said. He thought for a moment. "No, I wouldn't. I'd like to prop my feet up and drink my tea, thank you very much."

As the door started to shut again, Eli stuck his foot out to block it. "You're the doctor? Please, sir, we've driven all the way from Hope. My son is dying. You've got to help us."

The old man took the cigar stub from his mouth and peered down at the tiny bundle in Lily's arms. "You've got him wrapped up like sausage meat in a pig's gut. Is he still alive?"

"Yes, sir," she said.

"You sure?"

"I think so, sir."

"All right, bring him in." Dr. Schlissel turned around and trundled back into the room. He wore a pair of house slippers that slapped the wooden floor when he walked. A set of bright red suspenders stretched over his ample belly, and a stethoscope dangled from his neck.

"I was having my dinner, if you must know," he said as he sorted through a collection of tools and instruments. "I don't like to be disturbed after a long day. Who would? We had a diphtheria epidemic here not too long ago, and I never worked so hard in my life. I'll tell you folks what. I need a vacation, that's what. I need to go set myself by a river someplace and catch some trout. If it isn't a boy with a broken arm or a mama with a burned hand, it's a baby with whooping cough or a grandpa with pneumonia. You name it, I've seen it all, and I think I've tended to one of every kind of disease there is today. Now, what's wrong with this baby? Great ghosts, do you think wrapping his stomach this tight is doing him any good? You've been *brauching* him, haven't you? *Brauching* is a bunch of hooey, if you ask me. Well, put him on the table, ma'am. Don't just stand there."

Eli took Samuel from Lily's arms and laid him on the long wooden table near the window. At one end stood a ceramic bowl filled with the doctor's tools; at the other end sat his dinner of a half-eaten lamb chop, a mound of potatoes, and a loaf of white bread. The man set his cigar down on his dinner plate, adjusted his suspenders, and peered at Samuel.

"Puny thing," he pronounced. "Looks like he's in bad shape. How many other children do you two have?"

"He's the only one." Elijah held Lily tightly, as though he could protect her from the pronouncement to come.

"Well, you're young yet." The doctor looked Lily up and down. "You'll have more."

Lily started to speak, then fell silent. Eli turned her away from the table and led her across the room to the doctor's horsehair settee. The room smelled of stale cigar smoke, the stench of infection, and the acrid scents of castor oil and ether. Together, the couple sank down onto the settee, and Lily buried her face in Eli's shoulder.

"Father," he murmured, his cheek pressed against her golden hair, "you gave life to Samuel. I know that each of us has a different length of time allotted, but has Sam lived all his days, Lord? Has he spent his whole life in

137

these few short days? Oh, God, could you . . . could you see fit to lend him to us a little longer?"

Unable to continue, he wrapped his arms around Lily and gave himself to his grief. Her hands slipped up his back and clasped him tightly. She shook her head.

"No," she murmured. "This can't happen. God, if you're here, listen to me. If you can hear at all, hear me. If you care about us, reach out to us now. I'm not ready for Samuel to go. I can't bear to lose him."

She stopped and swallowed hard. "God," she went on, "don't do it for me. I know you didn't answer when I begged you for protection from my father. You didn't hear when I pleaded for Abby's life. Do this for Samuel. Please, let him live."

As Eli held the trembling woman, he could feel the agony wracking her. Without thinking, he stroked the side of her face and kissed her cheek. "God's been listening to you, Lily," he said, his hand cupping her head against his neck. "He was with you when your father hurt you so much. And he's holding your baby daughter in his arms right now. He'll bring good out of this sorrow. I know he will. If you'll give him your pain, he'll take it. And he'll give you joy in return. Not only joy, but peace, hope, and love."

"Just like a Mexican tamale," Dr. Schlissel announced. "All wrapped up in fifteen layers and hardly able to breathe. Hot as a tamale, too. You running a fever, little fellow, or are you just trying to stay alive under all those blankets?"

A weak cry from Samuel sent a chill down Eli's spine. He squeezed Lily's shoulders against his chest. The doctor was clanging his tools now, muttering to himself, asking where he'd left his cigar.

"How old is this baby?" he called across the room. "Couple of weeks?"

"I think so," Eli said, lifting his focus to the physician, who was gnawing his lamb chop as he prodded the tiny figure with his free hand. "I found him on the trail. His folks had been murdered."

The doctor gave a grunt and set down the chop. He wiped his fingers on his trousers. "Did you give him any kind of tonic?"

Eli looked at Lily. "We tried everything in the mercantile," she said. "We didn't know what else to do."

"So you gave him a little poison from every bottle. Figures. *Brauching,* tonics, sweating. What else have you tried?"

"Prayer," Eli said.

The doctor lifted Samuel's arm, and the baby let out a whimper of protest. "That's the

139

only thing you did right so far. Did either of you happen to notice what kind of spider bit this baby?"

"Spider?" Lily leapt up from the settee and raced across the room. "A spider bit Samuel?"

"Don't tell me you never looked at the kid."

Eli hurried to Lily's side and stared down at the ugly red welt on Sam's tender skin just beneath his armpit. "We had him wrapped up to sweat out the fever," he explained. "The women in town told us —"

"Next time one of your young'uns gets sick, you look him over before you do anything else. It's real simple. Check his eyes. Open his mouth and look at his tongue. Listen to his heartbeat. See if there's a thorn in his foot or a bean up his nose or a plug of wax in his ear. You know what I mean? *Look* at your child. See what's wrong before you go pouring tonics down his throat and binding his stomach up tight. Now, let's see here. It couldn't have been too bad a bite, or you'd be long gone, little fellow. You're a fighter, though." He looked at Eli. "Your boy's a real fighter, isn't he?"

Eli nodded. "Yes, sir. He sure is."

"I'll have to clean this up and try to draw out the infection." He opened a cupboard that held a collection of dinner plates, wool stockings, raw eggs, and several tubs of ointment. He began to take out one medicine after another. "We'd better try some of this. And he could use a little of that. This ought to help. And this won't do any harm. I figured I wouldn't get through my dinner without interruption. A man sits down with his lamb chop and his tea. . . . Well, now, I forgot about this slice of apple pie I put in here the other day. Mrs. Truman gave it to me after I pulled her husband's teeth out. She swore it was the best apple pie this side of the Mississippi, and she's right. I believe I'll have this last slice for dessert. Yes, sir. We saved the teeth, but I don't think that man will wear the denture she's having me make. No, sir, he'll be gumming down his apple pie from now on. He's a stubborn old cuss. I guess that's why he's lived as long as he has. Well, that ought to do us. I don't suppose you folks are going to be able to pay for this. Dirt farmers never do. All the same, I want you to come back in three days and let me take a look at the boy. We ought to have most of the infection out by then, and the fever will be down."

Eli blinked as the old man slid the plate of apple pie down the table to join his lamb chop, and then he set three small packets of ointment and a bottle of tonic beside the baby. "You mean," Eli said, "you mean,

Sam's not going to die?"

"If you'd kept him wrapped up like a sausage any longer than you did, he would have died. And it's no wonder he couldn't eat with his belly all caved in under that bandage."

"He's going to live?" Lily asked.

"That's what I said, wasn't it?" The doctor adjusted his suspenders and started toward his dinner. "Go on now. You folks did your best to kill him, but he's a fighter. Your prayers helped too. I've been in this business more than fifty years, and I don't understand it to this day — but folks who pray have an edge. So keep it up."

Eli looked at Lily. Then he turned back to the doctor. "Samuel's going to be all right?"

"Are you folks deaf? Take him and go," the old man barked. "I want to eat my apple pie. I'll see you in three days. All of you."

CHAPTER 7

"I want to find Beatrice," Lily said softly. She cuddled the tiny baby beneath her white shawl and shivered with relief that Sam was nursing again. Though she and Elijah had only stepped outside the doctor's office and climbed back into the wagon, somehow a wind of hope had lifted her spirits. The child would live. A future stretched ahead, filled with possibility and promise.

Beside Lily on the wagon bench, the broad-shouldered preacher fiddled with the mule's reins. He hadn't spoken since they told Mother Margaret, who was seated in the rear of the wagon, the good news.

It was clear to Lily that Eli was all but overcome with emotion, knowing the baby would be all right. *A man who truly loves a child. A man who can express something more than rage. A man who can weep. How rare and beautiful,* she thought.

"Beatrice will be able to find us a place to stay," Lily said, laying her hand on Elijah's arm. "She knows Topeka better than I do, and she has acquaintances here."

Though she had no intention of letting Elijah in on her plans, Lily had made up her mind to retrieve her melodeon from Beatrice Waldowski. With the money she had secreted out of her father's vault in Philadelphia exhausted long ago, the small instrument was Lily's only asset. Here in Topeka, she would sell the melodeon. With that money and the wages she was earning from Elijah Book, she could plan what to do next. For the time being, she would return to Hope to see Samuel back to health. After that, she couldn't be sure.

All she knew was that something had touched her during those dark, agonizing minutes in the doctor's office. Desperate, vulnerable, she had allowed the possibility of God to enter her heart. For the first time in her memory, she had let down the walls that barricaded her soul — and she had caught a glimpse of genuine hope, faith . . . and love. Though Lily had no idea which direction her life should take, she now knew she would never continue west with Beatrice and the traveling show.

"There's a hotel here in Topeka," Lily said to Elijah. "It's called the Crescent Moon, and Beatrice knows the owners. If we go there, they'll be able to tell us where she's staying."

Eli swallowed and clenched his hands

around the reins. "God spared Sam's life," he said, his voice rough. "And you want to carry my son into a den of iniquity?"

Lily felt a familiar curl of defiance slide into her chest. "The Crescent Moon is not a den of iniquity. It's a hotel."

"Hotels have saloons."

"I wasn't planning to lead Samuel down the path to strong drink and loose women."

"What were you planning? To find Madame Zahara and tell her to put one of her spells on my son's body? To ask your friend to read the bumps on his skull? *Jesus Christ* saved Sam's life, Lily, and that's all there is to it. I won't bring dishonor to the miracles of almighty God by letting the handiwork of the devil taint my child."

"Beatrice is not a devil!"

"She's no saint."

"Neither are you, Preacher-man." Lily felt the baby squirm with discomfort at the stormy voices around his cocoon of comfort. "I suppose you'd rather camp out on this rain-drenched night, risking pneumonia and who-knows-what diseases on this poor baby, than let anyone catch a glimpse of your holy hide in a saloon."

"My hide's not holy, but it is sanctified by the blood of —"

"Sanctified and saved. Washed in the

blood. Whiter than snow. Glory hallelujah." Lily tried to catch her breath. She suddenly felt ill from the whirlwind that raged inside her. "I seem to recall that Jesus invited himself to the house of Zacchaeus the tax gatherer when he needed lodging and food. And when the disciples questioned Jesus about eating with publicans and sinners, he told them, 'They that be whole need not a physician, but they that are sick —' "

"How do you know that verse?" He turned on her, taking her shoulders in his strong hands. "You know the Bible better than I do, Lily, but you throw the Scriptures at me as though they were stones."

"You deserve it." At his rough touch, she shrank into herself, fearful of the outcome yet determined to have her say. If the man became violent, she would survive as she always had. She would retreat to the protection of the quiet place inside herself, to the golden solace of her music.

"You believe the Bible's words without testing them," she went on. "You put your trust in your own righteousness. You think you know everything, but you know nothing. You don't even know who Jesus Christ was."

"Who was he?" In the sky overhead, the storm clouds had rolled away, and Eli's blue eyes shone in the moonlight. His hands tightened on her shoulders. "Lily, who *is* Jesus Christ?"

She sucked in a breath. "If you don't know —"

"I know. I don't always follow him the way I ought. I make a lot of mistakes. You're right that I judge folks when I shouldn't, and I say things without thinking. But I know Jesus Christ. I know what he's done inside me. I know how he changed my life. If you see a bunch of mistakes being made by a big ol' fool, you can figure it's probably me. If you see love and healing and hope and freedom and peace, that's Jesus."

"I'm sorry," she whispered, lowering her head. "Sorry I lashed out at you. Sometimes you just make me furious."

"You make me so mad I could spit nails."

A smile tickled the corner of Lily's mouth. "At least you're honest about that, Preacher-man."

"I'm honest about everything, even though sometimes it means I put my foot right into my mouth. And the honest truth is, I don't want to look for your friend Beatrice."

"Why not? She knows this town. She can help us."

"What if she lures you back into her —"

"Den of iniquity? You make her sound like a spider."

Elijah studied the reins in his hand, and Lily realized that her description fit the man's opinion of her friend perfectly. To the preacher, Beatrice Waldowski was a spider. A poisonous insect. A venomous instrument of the devil, determined to inflict her evil on the lives of everyone she touched.

"It's because of you, Lily," he said finally. "I don't want to lose you. I know Samuel needs you. But I . . . well, I like having you around, too. We're kind of a team, you know, with the baby. Hearing you sing always lifts my spirits. And I enjoy watching you take care of Sam."

"And she's purtier than a shiny new tin whistle," Mother Margaret finally spoke up from the back of the wagon. "Brother Elijah, I'd sit here all night under this wet tent and listen to you work up to tellin' Miz Lily how you really feel about her. But I figure you might go on for hours before you get it right, and in the meantime, you'll probably make her mad two or three more times. A body can only take so much fussin' and makin' up. Now, I want to get me some supper and some sleep. We gonna head over to the den of iniquity or not?"

Lily chuckled at the old woman's blunt question. Leave it to Mother Margaret to get to the point. Elijah was staring into the back

148

of the wagon as though he'd forgotten they had another rider.

"I'd prefer to camp by the river," he said.

"And sleep under this drippin' ol' tent? On these wet blankets? With nothin' to eat but Eva's soggy biscuits? Please, Brother Elijah, have a heart. Don't you know how old I am? I'm *real* old. Now, I got me a son lives here in Topeka, I recall, but I won't be able to locate him without a good bit of askin' around. We was slaves, don't you know, and all my children but Ben was sold out from under me. When my little Moses was ten years old, he was bought by a man from Topeka, and no tellin' what become of him since. So I reckon I better wait until tomorrow to start lookin'. Meanwhile, I expect the Crescent Moon Hotel has got itself some dry beds and a pot of soup a-boilin' on the stove. Kansas is a free state, so let's see what we can find there."

Elijah tugged on his Stetson brim and gave the reins a flick. "All right, Mother Margaret," he said. "Publicans and sinners, here we come."

Although Topeka, Kansas, had a reputation as a sleepy little cattle town, for Lily the place was steeped in sorrow. It was in Topeka that her daughter had been captured in the deadly grip of diphtheria. It was here that her precious baby had been ripped from her heart and buried in an unmarked grave. It was here that her husband and his employer had died. In Topeka, Lily felt, her own life had ended as well.

Now as she huddled beside Elijah Book, she had the impression that she was traveling in a landscape of hell. One muddy road turned into another. One rickety clapboard house followed another. Hollow-eyed children stared at the wagon through waxed-paper windowpanes. Even though the moon shone overhead, darkness crept around each corner and lurked under every porch. Dogs slinked across the streets, the hair on their spines lifted in wariness. Turn after turn led the wagon down narrow alleys and across vacant, treeless lots.

Now and then, Elijah called out to someone to ask directions to the Crescent Moon Hotel. "Turn left," came one response. "Two streets down," came another. "Turn right and then right again. I think that hotel's near the Boar's Breath Tavern. You'd better check with the night watchman on the corner up ahead."

Lily tried not to shiver, but exhaustion and fear crept into her bones. She wanted to pray again, as she had in the doctor's house. Her heart longed to cry out for help, guidance, and safety. But she was too wary to venture a prayer. She didn't want to trust a God who had let her down so many times before.

Leaning her head on Elijah's shoulder, she gave herself to the swaying, creaking wagon. Why hadn't God helped her when she'd cried out to him all those times when her father's uncontrolled rage poured over her? Why hadn't God saved her? She'd been such a little girl, so thin, so frightened, so helpless.

God will protect you, the preacher had announced in his sermons at church. *God will protect you,* the Sunday school teachers had assured their pupils. Lily had clung to that promise. But God hadn't protected her. Without warning, her father had struck out at his only child, and his fury had blackened her eyes, striped the backs of her legs, jarred her skull, cracked her ribs. Philadelphia's finest doctors puzzled over Lily's series of baffling injuries. Her teachers labeled their precocious student "clumsy." Her friends wondered why so often she could not come out to play — and after a while, they stopped asking.

Until she was sixteen, Lily had thought it was all her fault. She was a bad girl. So naughty. Then one day her father was whipping her after the rehearsal for his orchestra's rendition of Handel's *Messiah* had gone badly. A giant wave of realization washed over her. *No*, she thought, *I do not deserve this beating. My mother will not save me, and God will not protect me. So I'll find a way to take care of myself.* And she had.

"You know," Elijah said suddenly, "I may never find that hotel, but I've had a good chance to do some thinking out here on the streets of Topeka. And here's what I think. You're right, Lily. You're right that I ought to put my trust in the words that come right out of the Bible. Not what some preacher tells me, or what I heard some religious person say, or what I might think sounds right and good. I ought to believe the Bible, nothing else. And that means I need to know the Scriptures as well as I know my own name. I need to learn them — the way you have."

Lily focused on a lamplit building just down the street. "Crescent Moon Hotel and Saloon" a sign read. Almost there, and yet she must know one thing.

"Does the Bible promise that God will protect us?" she asked Elijah. "Because I don't —"

"There it is," he cried out, giving her a brisk hug. "Hey, Mother Margaret, it's the Crescent Moon. We found it." He turned to Lily. "Of course God protects us. Look right there at that sign. He brought us here, didn't he?"

"Did he?" she mouthed, but Elijah was busy reining the tired mule and setting the wagon brake. *Had* God promised to protect her? Did the Bible she had read again and again offer even a single promise of God's abiding shelter at *all* times through *all* things?

Lily sat on the wagon, numb with confusion. Preachers had said it. Teachers had said it. Elijah Book had said it. But had God said it?

And if God didn't promise protection, what good was he? What use was trust in an all-powerful Creator who wouldn't defend his creation?

"Let me have that little fellow," Elijah said, raising his arms toward Lily. "If we're going to walk straight into the valley of the shadow of death, I'd better protect my boy."

Elijah tucked Samuel into his arms as Lily had taught him. *Yea, though I walk through the valley of the shadow of death, I will fear no evil; for thou art with me.* The familiar psalm slipped into Lily's mind. A loving father protects his children, she thought, watching Elijah make a fuss over the little bundle he carried. A loving father keeps his children safe.

But bad things happened to God's children all the time. Did that mean he didn't love them? Or was God like her own father — outwardly perfect as he put on displays of his own brilliance and talent, yet privately inflicting merciless punishment upon the helpless?

Lily realized that Elijah was holding out his free arm to her. She took his hand and slid down into his embrace. The preacher held her for just a moment too long before he moved away. "Mother Margaret," he called. "You planning to come out of that tent?"

"Go check if they let black folks come into the hotel," she returned. " 'Cause if I'm not welcome, I'll take my business somewhere else."

"Serve 'em right, too," Elijah said. "Come on, Lily. Let's go look for your friend."

"I trust you'll restrain your tongue from referring to Beatrice as evil incarnate and this hotel as a den of iniquity."

Eli stopped at the steps to the front porch and took Lily's hand. "Even though I wish you wouldn't walk back into Miss Waldowski's life, I won't try to stop you. You make your own choices. But if you need me, Lily, I'll be right beside you."

As he turned to climb the steps onto the porch, Lily gathered her shawl around her shoulders. The chill of realization filtered down her spine. The preachers and teachers were wrong. Elijah Book was wrong. God had never promised to protect her. He didn't promise to protect anyone.

"Yea, though I walk through the valley . . ."

That's right, Lily, you will walk in paths of danger and places of harm.

"I will fear no evil . . ."

But you don't have to be afraid.

"For thou art with me . . ."

I'll be right beside you. All the way.

Elijah sat on a bench in the lobby of the Crescent Moon the following afternoon and waited for Lily and Mother Margaret to emerge from their room. After hours of searching and questioning strangers, Lily believed she had tracked her friend to a small boardinghouse at the edge of Topeka. When she finished nursing Samuel, she and the others would go in search of Beatrice Waldowski.

With growing discomfort, the preacher watched businessmen and cowboys file into the saloon situated just down the hall from the lobby. His Stetson held loosely in his hands, he turned the brim around and around. Though he tried to calm himself, he could almost hear the thunder of his heartbeat in his chest.

Preach to them, the steady voice inside his soul commanded. *Preach, Elijah Book. Lead the lost to the light of salvation. Guide the wicked onto the path of righteousness.*

How could he just sit idly by and allow these unrepentant and ignorant souls to continue in the darkness of their wicked ways? The men had no idea that Jesus could make a difference in their lives — and they would never hear the message of Christ's sacrifice and love unless somebody told them.

Eli had to do it. He had to preach.

After a quick search for his black leather Bible in the saddlebag beside him, he realized the valued book was missing. Distressed but unwilling to let the moment pass, he climbed onto the bench where he'd been sitting. " 'The Lord is my light and my salvation,' " he cried out in a loud voice, " 'whom shall I fear? The Lord is the strength of my life; of whom shall I be afraid?' "

A passerby stopped and stared. A little boy in a sailor suit ran out of the dining room to see what the commotion was about. His mother quickly followed. The hotel clerk popped up from behind his desk.

"Last night," Eli addressed them, "I wandered the streets of this town without light, without direction, without security. I confess to you that I stumbled in the darkness. I lost my way many times. I shivered in dread of the unknown."

He spotted three men ambling through the

lobby toward the saloon. "Do you gentlemen wander in darkness on this sunny Kansas afternoon?" he called to them. "Do you believe the fleeting pleasure of strong drink will bring you lasting happiness? Do you mistake the passing fancies of a loose woman for the security of true love?"

"Shut yer trap, cowboy!" one of the men called back. "Take yer preachin' to church."

"I used to ride the cattle trails just like you boys," Eli went on, extending his open hand in their direction, "and I worked hard night and day. Long hours, sore muscles, and nothing but a bedroll to call home. I thought I deserved the light refreshments and the sweet-smelling fancies in the towns I went through. But they were empty pleasures. All empty!"

"Sir," the clerk said, approaching from behind his desk. "We have a policy against solicitation in the —"

"Jesus Christ gave my life meaning," Eli continued, searching his mind for a verse he had tried to memorize a few weeks back. " 'Woe unto them that call evil good, and good evil; that put darkness for light, and light for darkness. . . . Woe unto them that are mighty to drink wine, and men of strength to mingle strong drink —' "

"Ain't nothin' wrong with a stiff belt of

whisky, Preacher," one of the men chimed in.

"Let him be," his companion said. "He's a-preachin' the Word of God."

"Sir, would you please step down from the bench?" the hotel clerk pleaded.

"I'm no different from any of you," Eli went on, ignoring the man. Out of the corner of his eye, he saw Lily and Mother Margaret edging warily down the staircase. Their faces registered surprise. "I thought I could be the trail boss of my own life, but I knew I was getting nowhere fast. Then I read the words of truth I'd been looking for: 'Seek ye the Lord while he may be found, call ye upon him while he is near: Let the wicked forsake his way, and the unrighteous man his thoughts: and let him return unto the Lord, and he will have mercy upon him.' "

Eli focused on the gathering crowd, but his thoughts were on Lily. "God loves you," he said, "and he wants to live inside you. He wants to wash away the sins that have stained your soul. He wants to make you as white as snow. If you'll let him, the Lord will lead you onto his path. He'll direct your steps. He'll fill your life with joy and peace. Will you ask him in? Sinners, will you give your heart to Jesus Christ?"

Closing his eyes, Eli began to pray aloud the prayer that filled his heart. Pleading with

God, he begged for the souls of the lost men and women in the saloon down the hall. He prayed for the lost in the lobby. He prayed for the lost on the street outside the hotel. "Open their hearts. Give them strength to stand up. Fill them with love. Amen and amen," he said, lifting his head. The floor around the bench where he stood was filled with kneeling men and women. Some wept. Others clasped their hands in prayer.

For a moment, Eli was stunned. What had happened? He'd only been speaking aloud the words inside his heart — words that demanded an outlet. But God had used his simple, disjointed message to touch these people. He stared in confusion. Again and again, this happened when he preached. People heard the Word of the Lord. People responded. People repented.

Oh, Father, what am I supposed to do now? I'm no good at this part. I don't know how to touch them one by one. I can't . . .

Lily was teaching him how to love. He could do it. Climbing down from the bench, Eli knelt on the floor among the people. Slipping an arm around the man beside him, he instructed all of them to pray with him if they wanted to invite Jesus Christ to become Lord of their lives.

Repeating the words of his own repentance

not so many months before, Eli murmured, "Lord, I know I've walked my own road for too many years. I know I've done wrong to myself and others. My biggest wrong is keeping you out of my heart. Please forgive my sins."

"Yes, Lord," the man beside him said softly.

"I believe Jesus Christ is God," Eli went on. "I believe Jesus came to earth and died in my place to take away my sin. I believe he came to life again after his death, and I know he sent the Holy Spirit to live inside me. Take me now, Father. Take my heart, my soul, my whole life. I give myself to you. Teach me to walk in your path. Amen."

"Mercy, mercy, mercy," Mother Margaret said in a low voice as the crowd rose and gathered around Elijah. "Hallelujah and amen."

Some people shook the preacher's hand; others tried to press money on him. Elijah refused the gifts, giving each person a hug instead. This wasn't half as bad as he'd thought. In fact, he kind of liked touching folks, speaking an encouraging word and seeing their eyes light up.

"Go find yourselves a church tomorrow," he called after the dispersing crowd. "And get a new set of friends, you hear?"

"What have you been up to, Brother Elijah?" the old woman said, folding her arms over her chest. "We can't hardly leave you alone for a minute without the gospel a-comin' right up out of you and a-spillin' over onto everybody."

Eli gave Mother Margaret a sheepish grin. "I hope I didn't keep you ladies waiting too long. I just got to feeling real unhappy about that saloon down the hall."

"They're not feeling too happy about you, either," Lily said, nodding in the direction of a pair of angry men storming down the hall toward them.

"You, sir!" one of them called, pointing at Elijah. "What do you mean by drivin' away our afternoon's trade? We lost half our customers when you went to speechifyin'."

"You have no right to do business in the lobby of this hotel!" the other cried. "I'm George Gibbons, owner of this establishment, and you'd better get your bags and get out of here before we call the law on you."

"Yes, sir," Elijah said, nodding with as much politeness as he could muster. He felt like punching them both in the nose. Clearly, these two men ran the saloon — and probably managed the soiled doves who plied their trade in the back bedrooms, too. But they were right. He hadn't gotten permission to preach.

"I apologize for upsetting you, gentlemen," he said, adjusting his Stetson on his head. "The ladies and I were just leaving."

"For good," one of the men added, sticking a stubby finger in Elijah's chest. "Take these women and your bags, too. We don't need the likes of you folks at the Crescent Moon."

"I'm afraid he's right, sir," the clerk said with an apologetic smile. "The manager just told me that we can't let you stay the next two nights, like you'd planned."

Eli glanced at Lily. With a roll of her eyes, she transferred Samuel into Mother Margaret's arms and headed back up the stairs to fetch the women's baggage. In a moment she returned carrying their few possessions, and the group left the hotel.

As Elijah steered the wagon in the direction of the waning sun, he mused on the disturbance he'd created in the lobby. Truly, he hadn't intended to upset anybody. Something inside him demanded that he speak. He thought of the apostle Paul and his determination to preach in spite of shipwrecks and stonings and prison sentences. That was just how Eli felt. He *had* to tell folks about Jesus — no matter what.

Glancing at Lily seated beside him on the bench, he tried to read the expression on her face. Was she angry? Disgusted? Did she think him a fool?

Becoming aware of his steady gaze, she met his eyes and lifted her determined chin. "You were wrong, Reverend Book," she said.

"I probably should have asked permission," he agreed. "A fellow ought to respect those in authority."

"You were wrong about something you said."

"I was?" He scratched his forehead, trying to remember his own sermon. It wouldn't surprise him a bit if he'd put his foot in his mouth. Maybe he'd even gotten his Scriptures mixed up. Without his Bible, he couldn't be sure. Where had he put that book anyhow?

"Was it the part about being the trail boss of my own life?" he asked her. "I know that didn't make much sense. See, when all us cowhands were driving cattle north to market, we followed a trail boss who —"

"You said God protects us always."

"I did?" He didn't remember that. "I said he loves us. He wants to forgive us and live inside our hearts."

"Last night, right here in this wagon, you told me the Bible said God always protects us. You were wrong."

Eli tugged on the reins and turned the mule

south. He did recall talking with Lily about that. But he couldn't remember exactly what he'd told her.

"I couldn't sleep last night," she said, "so I slipped into your room and borrowed your Bible." She pulled the book from beneath her white shawl and set it on his lap. "Hope you don't mind. Anyhow, I searched all night and I never did find a single verse that promises God's constant protection. You were wrong."

Lifting his focus to the pink-tinged sky, Eli tried to make sense of her statement. Why was she telling him this? What did it mean?

"I guess I *was* wrong," he said finally. "I was thinking about the apostle Paul a couple of minutes ago, and I recollected all those shipwrecks he suffered. Also, folks threw stones at him and tossed him into prison. He wrote down that he figured he'd gone through just about every terrible problem a fellow could face — and you're right, God didn't spare him from any of that."

"Ha!" she said. "Everybody lied to me. God doesn't protect us. He's useless."

"If all you want to do is skip through life on a rainbow, I guess so. But Paul said he was filled with joy in all his sufferings. If you want to grow into someone beautiful and useful to God, Lily, I suspect he's got to do a little molding. I don't know exactly what you've been through, but I do know one thing. You can let your trials turn you bitter and angry, or you can give your heartaches to the Lord. Then he'll use you to reach out to other folks hurting just as bad, and through you, he'll draw them to himself."

Lily sat in silence after that, and Eli didn't know what else to say. He figured he'd probably done enough preaching for one day. Besides that, he was scared he might run Lily off, and Samuel was just beginning to perk up. The baby's cheeks were pink again, and he'd done a fair amount of fussing during the night. Eli had never thought he'd actually look forward to the sound of Sam's squalling.

"There she is," Lily said suddenly, shrinking toward him. "There's Beatrice. Oh, Eli, you've got to help me."

CHAPTER 8

"Lily?" Beatrice Waldowski leaned forward, hands on her hips, and squinted at the approaching wagon. "Lily Nolan, is that you?"

Taking a deep breath and shifting away from Elijah, Lily lifted her hand in greeting. "Hello, Beatrice! We came from Hope yesterday. How are you?"

"I knew you'd come to your senses!" Grabbing her green silk skirts, Bea hurried down the steps of the rickety boardinghouse. "Oh, Lil, just wait till you hear what I've been up to! I've got everything organized. You won't believe the things we can do with —"

She stopped and stared at Elijah. "Who's he?" she said. "Is that the preacher, Lily?"

"Elijah Book," he answered for the woman at his side. Taking off his hat, Eli gave Beatrice a polite nod. "Been awhile."

"Not long enough," she said. "Lily, I hope this man doesn't plan to stay around. You and I have a lot of work to do. We've got plans — plans that *don't* include him."

Lily swallowed. "Mr. Book, Mrs. Hanks, and I came to Topeka to see a doctor about the preacher's baby. A spider bit Samuel." She motioned to Mother Margaret cradling the child in the back of the wagon. "He's better now."

"That's nice," Bea said, her voice flat. "I hope you don't expect me to put them all up here, Lil. This isn't a hotel, you know."

"I was hoping we might be able to stay for a couple of nights. Maybe we could sleep in the show wagon. Bea, you and I need to talk about some things."

The woman pushed her mass of dyed black hair behind her shoulder and gave Lily a sneer. "If you're still choosing to work for that preacher instead of me, Lily Nolan, I don't see that we have much to say to each other. You've made yourself clear."

Hurt that her friend would reject her once again, Lily started to climb down from the wagon. Elijah's hand on her arm stopped her. Turning toward him, she read the plea in his blue eyes. *Don't go. We can find another place to stay. You don't need this woman.*

But Lily did need Beatrice. She needed the melodeon. And she needed . . . perhaps . . . the reassurance that she hadn't completely lost the one true friend she'd ever known. Pulling away from Elijah, Lily stepped down from the wagon and walked toward Beatrice.

"Don't turn me away, Bea," she said softly.

"You saved me from my father once. For so long, you and Ted and Jakov were all the family I had. I trusted you."

"I trusted you, too. You let me down."

"I'm sorry." Lily stopped a pace away. "I chose to take on a job that would put food in our mouths, Bea. I wanted to help you the way you helped me. What's wrong with that?"

Bea's painted eyes flicked to Elijah. Slipping her arm quickly through Lily's, she turned the younger woman away from the wagon. "You scared me so bad, Lil," she whispered when they were far enough away that Elijah couldn't hear. "Can't you see how that preacher is just like your father? I knew he'd fill your head with his pretty lies. What's he been telling you? Does he cast doubt on your certainty that holiness lies inside your very own spirit — that you are the essence of the divine?"

"Well, he does preach from the Bible, but —"

"Does he try to woo you into his confidence and make you believe he's telling you the truth? You know what religious men are like, Lil. Look at your father — how different is that cowboy preacher from the man who told you about God's love and then blackened your eye?"

"But Mr. Book is not —"

"Has he put his arms around you? Has he tried to kiss you? You know what he's after, Lily. He'll tell you he's trying to win your soul, when it's your body he wants. Tell me he hasn't kissed you."

Lily flushed. "Well, he did kiss my cheek —"

"I knew it! He'll use you up, just the way your saintly father did. He'll tell you one thing and treat you the opposite. Oh, Lily, honey, take your things out of that wagon and come with me right this minute. I'll get you into the house where he can't reach you. I'll keep you safe."

Lily took her friend's hands and held them tight. "Elijah Book is not hurting me, Bea. He has no power over me, and I'm sure he doesn't want to use me in the way you think. The truth is, the preacher and I fight all the time, just like a pair of twisters stirring up twice the trouble every time we get near each other. The baby brought us together, that's all. Samuel needed my help — and he still does. Yesterday that poor child was nearly dead, Bea. He's only just beginning to perk up. I can't abandon him now."

"Are you telling me you tracked me all the way through Topeka only to turn away from me all over again?" Bea pursed her trembling lips. "I swear, when I saw you on that wagon,

Lily, I thought this was going to be the best day of my life. You don't know how my spirit rose inside me. It was like all the angels were singing. But now . . . now . . ."

"Beatrice, don't cry." Lily drew her friend close and wrapped both arms around the older woman. The familiar scents of heavy perfume and incense drifted up from Bea's green silk dress. "I'm here now."

"It's just that . . . that the cards told me that today was going to bring a surprise . . . and I was hoping . . . hoping you'd come. Oh, Lil, I've been working so hard to set things up for us. I wanted to tell you everything. It's going to be so wonderful, and I wanted you to share in my joy."

"Why don't you let us stay here with you a short while, Beatrice?" Lily asked gently. "You can tell me all your plans. We'll take Samuel back to the doctor in a couple of days, and once he's completely well, we'll know which way to go."

"Will you let me read your fortune?"

Lily's heart sank. It wasn't that she didn't trust the tarot cards. It was just that . . . well, she didn't want to cloud her thinking with Bea's psychic premonitions and forebodings. For so many years she had put her faith in the words of her ministers and Bible teachers. After rejecting them, she had come to trust

Beatrice's mystic powers.

But now . . . for the first time . . . Lily didn't want to count on anyone. She wanted to search for truth. She wanted to find answers. And she wanted to do it alone.

"Has that preacher turned you against the cards, Lil?" Bea asked, her eyes moist. "Because if he has —"

"The tarot cards let me down, Bea. The cards didn't predict Abigail's sickness. They failed to warn me." Lily looked down at her knotted fingers, fighting the tears that arose every time she thought of her beloved daughter. "But even worse than that, the cards didn't offer any comfort after my baby died. I had nothing but emptiness. No hope, no future, no peace."

"And you think the Bible can do any better?"

"I think I want to sit down and nurse Samuel Book. I want to rest my tired bones. And I want to figure this out for myself."

Beatrice sniffed. "If that's how you feel."

"Do you have room for us?"

"The old woman will have to sleep in the wagon. The preacher can bunk down in the men's quarters. You can stay with me."

"I'll sleep with Mother Margaret," Lily said as she gave her friend a quick hug. "I don't want to leave her alone."

Her sense of relief mingling with uncertainty, Lily returned to the wagon and told the others the news. As Elijah climbed down from the wagon, he assessed her, clearly trying to ascertain the truth in the situation. After he removed his saddlebag, he caught Lily's sleeve and drew her to one side.

"You all right?"

She nodded. "But please don't start preaching in the boardinghouse and get us tossed out. We can't see Dr. Schlissel again for two days, and I won't risk Sam's health over another one of your outbursts."

"Outbursts? Was that what it was?"

"Oh, Elijah, you know you rolled right over those people like a great big thunderstorm. You didn't care a whit about the consequences. You just went right ahead and —"

"The consequences were that ten people came to know Jesus Christ this afternoon. I cared about *that*."

Lily bit her lip and stared into his sparkling blue eyes. Yes, he did care about that. No one could deny the fervor in the man's heart. Beatrice Waldowski embraced her faith in the spirit world, held it tightly, claimed it for herself. But Elijah shared his beliefs with everyone he met, as though he was so full of Jesus Christ that he could do nothing to dam the flood of his joy.

In a way, the two were as opposite as two people could be. Bea trusted her inner spirit to be her guide; Elijah trusted the Spirit of God to lead him. Bea pursued self-fulfillment; Elijah emptied himself to everyone around. Bea made plans that would bring glory to herself; Elijah took on a dying baby and gave away his life's savings to rescue the child.

"Elijah," Lily said, "I wanted to find Beatrice for one reason. She took something valuable of mine. I need to get it back."

The preacher slung his saddlebag over his shoulder. When he spoke, his voice was filled with tenderness. "Oh, Lily, I hope what you're looking to get back from that woman is something more valuable than diamonds or gold. I hope it's your precious soul."

Elijah was getting so good at tracking folks that he thought he might ought to hire on with the Pinkerton Detective Agency. That wouldn't leave much time for preaching, though, and it had been all he could do to keep his mouth shut during the past two days at the boardinghouse. Now, pulling up to a wood-frame shanty on the outskirts of town, Eli reflected on the men he'd come to know in Topeka. Not a single one of them knew the Lord — not as a friend and Savior, anyhow. That burdened him.

"What if Mother Margaret's son doesn't live here?" Lily whispered as the wagon rolled to a stop beside the yard of the little house. "She's going to be so disappointed."

"We'll just keep looking for the man," Eli said. As Samuel had grown steadily better, Elijah and Lily had joined the old woman in her search for her long-lost son. Not many hours before they were to return to Dr. Schlissel's office, a tenant at the boarding-house had told them of a Moses Hanks who lived on the south side of town. Mother Margaret's face spoke of her anxiety and hope.

"I'm afraid he won't remember me," she said, leaning forward on the wagon bench between Eli and Lily. "He was only ten years old when they sold him off. Did I tell you that?"

"Yes, Mother Margaret," Lily said. "You told us."

"He was such a little boy. So skinny and scared. It like to broke my heart."

"I'm sure it did."

"Jack Cornwall's father done it. He was a good master most of the time, but he didn't understand how it felt for a mother to lose her children one by one. Oh, look at that little boy peerin' through the window. You don't suppose that's Moses, do you?"

"Moses will be a grown man, now, Mother Margaret. He's older than Ben, remember?"

"How come I keep forgettin' that? Mercy, somebody's comin' out of the house." She took Lily's hand. "Miz Lily, I'm plumb addled over this. Do I look all right? Is my bonnet tied on straight?"

Lily arranged Mother Margaret's bonnet bow while Elijah jumped down from the wagon and walked toward the approaching man. He was a big fellow, ebony skinned, broad-shouldered, and rawboned. He cradled a rifle under one arm.

"Afternoon, sir," Eli said, taking off his hat. "We're looking for a man by the name of Moses Hanks."

"What for?"

"We'd like to talk with him."

"I'm Mo Hanks. Speak your piece."

"Moses?" Mother Margaret stood up on the wagon. "Moses, child, is that you?"

The big man turned and spotted the little woman. Instantly the hard lines left his face. His caramel eyes lit up with joy. "Mama? Mama, you found me!"

Suddenly a ten-year-old boy again, he dropped his rifle to the ground and sprinted toward the wagon. In one scoop, he lifted the little woman into his arms and engulfed her. Swinging her out of the wagon, he turned her around and around until they were both laughing and crying at the same time.

"Moses, Moses, honey, you're liable to squeeze the stuffin' right outta me!" Mother Margaret squealed.

"I can't believe it's you, Mama. You came for me!"

As he lowered her to the ground, she pressed her face against his chest. "Oh, my precious baby. My sweet child. My darlin' boy. Let Mama hold you now."

"Mama, you found me. You found me."

"I'm here now, baby. I got you."

Elijah stepped back as others began to trickle out of the house. He glanced at the wagon to find Lily dabbing her cheeks. With Samuel propped on her shoulder, she was rocking back and forth and patting the baby's back. His tiny pink fingers curled into her golden hair as she nestled her nose against his neck.

Father, Eli began, and then he didn't know what to say next. At the sight of Lily and Samuel, something welled up like a fountain inside him. He couldn't identify it. Couldn't control it.

Father, I... Lily's hand tucked the thin cotton blanket around the baby's legs. Eli swallowed hard.

Father, I care ... I need ... I think I love Lily.

I love something about her. Help me, Lord. Show me what to do.

"Brother Elijah, this is my son!" Mother Margaret cried, taking the preacher's arm and pulling him close. "This is my sweet Moses. I found my baby!"

The big man pumped Eli's hand. "Thank you for bringin' my mama to me, sir."

"Glad to do it."

"You precious man!" The old woman threw her arms around Eli. "Moses, I want you to know Brother Elijah. He's my preacher from back home. Mercy, can he give a sermon! And that's his little baby over there in the wagon. That's Samuel. There's Miz Lily a-holdin' him, and I do declare, this must be the happiest day of my life. Thank you, Lord! Amen and hallelujah!"

"You haven't changed a bit, Mama," Moses said with a laugh. "Come over here now and meet my wife and all your gran'kids."

"Gran'kids!" Mother Margaret threw up her hands. "Wait till Ben and Eva hear about this! Mercy, I think I'm about to faint."

Grinning, Eli watched the happy pair hurry across the yard to introduce Moses' family to their long-lost matriarch. The preacher strolled back to the wagon and climbed up beside Lily and the baby.

"I think that's the first thing I ever got all the way right in my life," he said. "Have you ever seen so much laughing and crying all at one time?"

Lily blotted her handkerchief across her cheek. "It's wonderful."

"You look about as happy as a tick-fevered calf."

At that, she actually chuckled. "Now you've got *me* laughing and crying at the same time."

Aching to take her in his arms, Eli did the next best thing. He leaned toward Lily and gave Samuel's soft head a light kiss. "What are you sad about?"

"I was thinking of all the other children Mother Margaret lost," she said softly. "She once told me she'd given birth to fourteen. Three of them died, and all but Ben were sold. Now we've found Moses, but nine are still missing."

"You think Mother Margaret's worrying about the nine she's missing — or rejoicing over the one she found?"

He studied the chaotic scene on the front porch of the little frame house. Never in all his days had he heard so much carrying-on. Little children jumped up and down. Dogs barked. Somebody began to sing. A couple of folks were even dancing.

"I think," Lily said, "that she's mourning

the nine, even though she's rejoicing over the one."

"You're missing Abigail, aren't you?" Unable to stop himself, he slipped his arm around her. "I guess you can't ever replace someone you've lost. No matter how hard you try."

Lily leaned against his shoulder, the drowsy baby nestled between them. "No one can take Abby's place."

Eli observed the joyous family on the porch, and his own imminent loss grew sharper. "Nobody can take *your* place, Lily," he said finally, voicing the fear that had troubled him for days. "Am I going to lose you?"

She looked up. "You can't lose something you don't have. Do you have me, Elijah?"

"A little bit, I hope." He tightened his arm around her. "At least you choose to keep feeding my son. You talk to me without shouting. You don't pull away when I touch you."

She shivered. "Elijah, I . . ."

"What is it, Lily?"

"I need to talk to you about something." She drew in a deep breath and began. "Beatrice told me she has the money to build an opera house. Those two men who ran us out of the Crescent Moon Hotel are the ones she had met the last time we were in Topeka.

She asked them if they'd finance a new show house, and they agreed to put up the cash. She's already paid for a shipment of liquor and lined up a bartender. She's planning to hire a cook, a juggler, a magician, and a ventriloquist."

"How about a singer?"

"She wants me to sing," Lily said. "She's offered me good wages."

"Better than I can pay?"

"Yes," she said in a hushed voice. "Much better."

Elijah was pretty sure his heart had sunk to the bottom of his stomach, but he knew he had to keep talking. If Lily got wind of how much he cared about her, she'd hightail it right off.

"Where's Beatrice going to put up her opera house?" he asked.

"Lawrence. A lot of the town was burned during the war, you know. They're eager for people to move in and build."

"Lawrence, Kansas."

He repeated the name, even though he already knew where the city was located. *Oh, Lord, help me. I can't figure out what to say to Lily. I know I'm not supposed to think this way about her. She's not a believer. You don't want the two of us to feel tenderness for each other. But, Father, she's special to me. It's more than the baby, Lord. There's something about Lily.*

"Beatrice took my melodeon with her when she left Hope," she was saying. "It's stored in the show wagon."

"Melodeon?" Eli tried to make sense of her words. "Is that something like an organ?"

Lily nodded. "It's mine. Will you help me get it?"

"Get the melodeon?"

"That's what I said. Are you listening to me?"

"Sure, I'm listening. You said Beatrice is building an opera house in Lawrence, Kansas. She wants you to sing, and you need me to take your melodeon out of the show wagon."

Lily drew back from him and looked into his eyes. "I'm not going with her."

Elijah stiffened up like he'd been shot. "You're not going to Lawrence? You're not going to sing?"

"No." She shifted Samuel to her other shoulder. "I'm going to Philadelphia."

"Philadelphia!" He was sure he'd been shot a second time. "That's in Pennsylvania."

A smile crossed her lips. "You know your states very well."

"I borrowed an atlas one time when my pa and I were living near Albuquerque."

"I see." She squared her shoulders. "Well,

when I sell my melodeon, I'll have some money for my train ticket. So, I'll be going back to my father's house in Philadelphia . . . after I've spent another month or two in Hope."

Hope! Eli didn't need an atlas to know where that was. He felt so light he could have soared right over the wagon. But surely he'd heard her wrong. If Lily had the money for a train ticket to Philadelphia, she wouldn't go back to the prairie. Would she?

"You're going to Hope again?" he asked. "With me and Sam?"

She gave a little laugh. "Are you losing your hearing, Preacher-man? I'll need to earn the rest of the money for my ticket, and I want to make sure this baby is strong and healthy."

"But what about your singing? What about Beatrice?"

Lily lowered her head. "Bea has a good future ahead of her. With an opera house to run, she'll stay busy and make good money. She can find another singer."

"Hallelujah!" Elijah said. "Praise the Lord. Amen and amen."

Lily laughed. "You've been listening to Mother Margaret too long. Oh, Elijah, I need a fresh start. I tried once when I ran away from Philadelphia. I thought I'd found the answers I was looking for. But even before

Abigail died, my life became so . . . so . . . ."

"Mercy, you two, listen to this!" Mother Margaret called as she fairly flew across the yard. "I got me six gran'kids and three great-gran'babies! Three — can you beat that? Brother Elijah, you and Miz Lily better come meet all these folk. There's more kin here than I can shake a stick at. Miz Lily, I want you to know God done blessed me with good measure, pressed down, shaken together, and runnin' over! The Lord is wonderful; praise his holy name!"

"Amen!" Eli said.

"Hallelujah!" Lily added. "Amen and amen."

"This is the fighting-est baby I ever saw," Dr. Schlissel said. "I suspect it's going to take more than a spider and his careless parents to do him in."

The doctor lifted Samuel and turned the baby around in his big hands. Lily had been pleased to discover that during regular office hours, Dr. Schlissel's dinner and smoldering cigar were not in evidence on the long table. Although the physician seemed determined to chide her and Elijah for failing to notice the spider bite, Lily took a measure of pride in the baby's present state of health. After all, she had nursed him faithfully night and day, and his scrawny frame was starting to fill out.

"You say you found this baby in a wagon that was shot full of arrows?" the doctor asked, turning to Elijah.

"Yes, sir."

"Did you happen to notice anything unusual about the folks in the wagon?"

Elijah shook his head. "I mostly prayed over them while I buried them. I couldn't think too clearly just then."

"Did you see which of them was a redskin?"

Lily stared at the dark-haired baby in the doctor's hands. A redskin? An *Indian?*

Elijah rubbed the back of his neck and shifted from one foot to the other. "It was the mother," he said finally. "I couldn't tell what race she was. Maybe Indian or Mexican. She had real black hair."

"Then you got yourself a half-breed here." The doctor laid Samuel back on the table. "You sure you want him? There's a home for orphans and foundlings over in Kansas City. I could put the baby on a mail coach headed that way."

Lily clasped her hands together in disbelief. Put Samuel on a mail coach? Send him to an orphanage? Surely Elijah wouldn't do such a heartless thing.

She didn't care what color the baby's skin was or whether his hair would stay black as he grew older. His heritage didn't matter in the least. Samuel was a beautiful child, a precious little boy. Everyone who saw him would recognize that, wouldn't they? Surely people wouldn't reject Samuel because of the circumstances of his birth or the color of his skin.

"I didn't really give the whole notion much thought before now," the preacher said. "I guess Sam's going to have a hard row to hoe in life."

"He sure is."

"Good thing he's a fighter." Scooping up the baby, Elijah planted a big kiss on the boy's soft forehead. "Come on, little fellow. Let's go home."

Relief flooding through her, Lily grabbed the baby's bag and gave the doctor a final glance. *A hard row to hoe.* Whose life wasn't? Elijah's was. Hers certainly had been.

Perhaps Samuel would face many difficult times ahead — maybe he would even walk through the valley of the shadow of death. No telling what kind of evil and heartbreak might lie in his path. But with Elijah Book as his father, the child would be watched over, tenderly loved, and diligently nurtured. Samuel Book, Lily decided, would grow up to be a strong and courageous man.

"Thank you, Doctor," she said. "For the medicine."

Out in the street, Mother Margaret was lifting Samuel into the wagon. Her face was suffused with the light of the waning sun as she hugged the tiny baby. "Mercy sakes, you're gettin' heavy," she cooed. "Your mama's gonna have to sew you some regular people-clothes. You'll be crawlin' before long."

Your mama, Lily thought as Elijah helped her into the wagon. No, she wasn't Samuel's mother. But if anyone had tried to put that baby into an orphanage, she would have fought tooth and nail to prevent it. Already the thought of abandoning the child in a couple of months seemed unbearable. She had told Elijah that no one could take the place of Abigail — and she had meant it. But Samuel had carved out his own niche in Lily's heart.

Taking Samuel from Mother Margaret and gathering him close, Lily brushed a light kiss across the baby's cheek. "I guess we're ready to go back to Hope now," she said. "After a stop at the boardinghouse to pick up my melodeon."

"There's one more thing," Mother Margaret said from her place in the wagon. "Once we fetch our bags, Brother Elijah, I'd like you to drive by Moses' house one more time. I been considerin' on this matter for a few hours, and I've made up my mind. Moses and his wife asked me to stay with their family as long as I want, and I believe I'll do that. Would you tell Ben and Eva where I am? Would you give them my love?"

Elijah gave the old woman a hug. "I don't know how we'll make it without you, Mother Margaret."

"Well," she said, softly. "You've got the Lord, ain't you?"

CHAPTER 9

Lily handed the baby to Mother Margaret and stepped down into Elijah Book's arms. Though she dreaded the moments to come, she had made up her mind to confront Beatrice Waldowski. Elijah had reminded Lily that it would be a lot simpler just to take the melodeon from the show wagon and then head for Hope. But Bea deserved better.

The flamboyant woman had befriended Lily at a desperate time, and she had continued to support her through the ups and downs that came their way. Most important, Bea had recognized and encouraged Lily's singing ability. For that alone, she must be treated with respect.

"Do you want me to come with you?" Elijah asked as he walked Lily a few paces toward the boardinghouse. "I told you I'd stand by your side. I meant that."

She shook her head. "Bea doesn't trust you. She thinks you're trying to convert me to your religious ways."

"I am."

"You are?"

At her startled look, he gave a chuckle. "I'd be lying if I told you I didn't want you to know Jesus Christ the way I know him. But that's not why I'm choosing to stand by you, Lily."

"It's Samuel, isn't it?"

"God brought the two of us together for Sam's sake, but it's gone way beyond that. In spite of your hard ways, Lily Nolan, I care about you. I've come to know the woman inside you. I'd give my life to protect you."

Lily fingered the fringe on her shawl. She thought about telling Elijah how much he had come to mean to her in the past few days — how she enjoyed the deep sound of his voice, how she looked forward to his laughter, how she treasured watching him hold Samuel. She even liked fighting with the man.

But she didn't want to say too much. Philadelphia would be her destination before long. She couldn't afford to let a man's blue eyes and gentle heart sway her from her own path in life.

"I'll be back soon," she said, touching his arm. "Elijah . . . pray for me."

Without waiting for a response, she hurried up onto the porch of the boardinghouse and knocked on Beatrice's door. In a moment, she heard the sound of chairs scraping and voices murmuring. Lily had rarely known Beatrice to entertain gentlemen callers, but —

"Lily?" The door swung open. Behind Beatrice stood a tall, beefy man with a thin black mustache. His face hardened at the sight of the young woman on the porch.

"Beatrice," Lily said, focusing on her friend, "I've come to tell you that the preacher's baby is well."

"You interrupted me for that?" Bea pushed up the shoulder of her red silk gown. "Can't you see I'm doing business, Lil? This is George Gibbons from the Crescent Moon. He's one of the *owners,* if you catch my drift."

"I'm pleased to meet you, Mr. Gibbons," Lily said. The man looked familiar, and she remembered seeing him at the hotel. "I've decided to go back to Hope, Bea," she went on. "I wanted you to know that. And I'm going to take my melodeon with me."

For a moment, Beatrice stared in silence. Then her black-rimmed eyes narrowed. "You're going with *him?*"

"The baby needs me."

"You've let that preacher bamboozle you." Her lips tightened to a white line. "You're a coward and a weakling. You disgust me, Lily Nolan."

Stung, Lily stood her ground. "I'm sorry you feel that way. I was hoping we could part as friends."

"Who is this gal, Bea?" the man from the

Crescent Moon asked. "I've seen her over at the hotel."

"She's a traitor, that's who she is," Bea said. "I saved her from her pious father, and now she's taken up with a preacher."

"I remember her," George Gibbons said. "She was with the fellow we threw out of the hotel the other day. That preacher just about ruined our saloon business for the whole night."

For some odd reason, Lily felt a surge of pride in Elijah. "Mr. Book speaks from the heart."

"I'd like to punch him in the gut."

Just give it a try, Lily thought. Considering Elijah's years on the cattle trail, she had no doubt the preacher could lay this loser out cold. Of course, Elijah had told her he was trying to turn the other cheek.

"Good-bye, Bea," Lily said, choosing to ignore the man. "Thank you for all you've done for me. I'll never forget you."

She had turned to go when Beatrice burst through the doorway to embrace her. "Don't leave me, Lily!" the woman cried. "I need you. I've counted on you. You've got to help me with the opera house."

"Beatrice, please —"

"You can't go with that man. You're all I have. Oh, Lily, you have to sing for me. How can I have an opera house without a singer? You're not really leaving, are you?" Bea pleaded, clasping Lily tightly. "Everything depends on you! You can't take the melodeon. You can't go."

"Bea, I've made up my mind," Lily said. "I'm going back to Hope."

"You're mad! I've offered you twice what that preacher can pay. Why would you turn me down?"

"I need to help the baby."

"It's not the baby!" Bea's eyes were streaming now, black paint staining her cheeks as her desperation turned to rage. "It's that preacher. He's trapped you with his words. He's snared you in his web of lies."

"This is my choice, Bea. I want to go back to Hope."

"No, Lily! You can't. Tell me you won't do this to me."

"I'm leaving, Bea."

"I'll tell your father where you are!" Bea burst out. "I'll write to him and tell him you've gone insane. He'll come to Hope and find you. He'll beat you black and blue."

Lily grasped the porch post beside her. "Beatrice!"

"I will! I'll tell him you ran off with a show man, and I'll tell him everything you've done.

We'll see what happens then! You'll pay for this, Lily Nolan."

"Bea, please don't tell my father where I am." Lily's lips trembled. "When the time is right, I'm going back to Philadelphia. I'll make peace with him."

"Not after he knows where you've been, how you've lived, the things you've done! You won't live to see the next day after he catches up with you! I'll tell him everything unless you stay with me. This opera house is all the future I've got, Lily. I won't let you ruin me. I'll make you stay."

Lily took a step backward. Her plans to return home hinged on her father's ignorance of her past. She could never tell him about the traveling show, about Ted Nolan and Abigail, about the reckless, desperate choices she had made in her life . . .

"Everything all right here?" Elijah Book stepped onto the porch. "You OK, Mrs. Nolan?"

Lily swung around. "Elijah, I —"

"Don't touch that woman, Preacher," George Gibbons said, stepping into the doorway. "I've had my fill of trouble from you."

"I'm not here for trouble. I just want to make sure Mrs. Nolan is treated right."

"Treated right?" Beatrice exploded. "How

are you treating her, Preacher? Have you managed to get her into your bed yet?"

"Beatrice!" Lily clasped the woman's shoulders. "Bea, please don't say such things. Can't we part as friends? Can't you let me go?"

"I'll never let you go, Lily," Bea snarled. "I made you. I brought you here. I own you."

"Bea —"

"You watch and see, Lily Nolan. I'll tell your father everything you've done. And I'll build my opera house in Hope."

"Hope?"

"I'll put my place of business so close to that church, we'll drown out the preacher and shut down his whole operation. Before summer's out, I'll have you singing for me, Lily. You can count on it."

Lily took a step closer to Elijah. "Bea, what are you saying?"

"I won't let you go, Lily. I have plans, and you're part of them. If you won't help me out of love, you'll do it out of fear."

"But I do love you —"

"You don't know the first thing about love, Lily. You only know fear. Fear drove you out of your father's house. Fear brought you to the traveling show. Fear made you Ted Nolan's wife. And fear's binding you to that preacher and his baby."

"I care about Samuel."

"You're scared he's going to die just like Abigail. That's all you can think about, isn't it? Fear eats you up inside just like a worm in an apple." Bea set her hands on her hips and stared at Lily. "I can't believe you're so ignorant. Can't you see the preacher's onto you just the way your father was? He's playing your fear, Lily. Well, I can play you, too. I'll make you so frightened, you'll do anything I ask. And I'll start by telling your father where you are."

"Don't you dare!" Lily cried.

"Listen here, Madam Whoever-you-are," Elijah said, pointing a finger at Beatrice. "I don't know what kind of hex you're trying to put on Lily, but it isn't going to work. She's a strong woman and a good woman — and what's more, she has a heart. You're not going to scare her into anything, you hear?"

"You shut your trap, Preacher," George Gibbons said, drawing back his coat to reveal a holstered six-shooter. "Now get back in your wagon and head out."

"I'll leave when I'm good and ready. And you'd better cool down that itchy finger. I'm a minister of the Lord, and I'm unarmed."

"As if I care!" Gibbons drew the gun. "Back away nice and slow, Preacher. Bea, grab the singer."

"No!" Lily cried as Bea reached for her. "I won't stay here. Run, Elijah!"

Gathering up her skirts, she leapt off the porch and landed in a bed of peony bushes. As she tumbled forward, Elijah scooped her up in his arms. As Gibbons fired warning shots into the air, the preacher dashed for the wagon. Lily flung her arms around his neck and buried her head against his chest, tensed for the moment when a lead ball would tear into his back.

"Hunker down, Mother Margaret," Eli called as he tossed Lily into the wagon bed and clambered onto the seat. "Come on, ol' mule. Let's go, sweetheart."

As the wheels began to roll, Lily pushed herself up and peered over the side rail. Gibbons was reloading his six-shooter, while Beatrice glared after the retreating wagon. Her heart sick, Lily read the utter hatred on the woman's face.

How many hours had the two women sat together — chatting, laughing, darning socks, or making show costumes? How many times had they dried each other's tears? Oh, Beatrice! What had driven her to such desperation? Why was her voice so filled with hatred? They had shared dreams of a happy future . . . plans for wealth and luxury . . . an opera house . . . music . . .

"Wait!" Lily cried suddenly, clapping her hand on Elijah's shoulder. "Pull the wagon around to the barn. I have to get my melodeon."

Eli's head turned, his hair whipping his cheeks. "Forget the melodeon. We've got to get out of here before that loco-brain blasts us to kingdom come."

"But I need it, Elijah. I can't get home without it."

"Mercy, child," Mother Margaret said, patting Lily's arm as the wagon rolled out onto the main road. "You don't need no melodeon to get home. You're goin' home right now. Home to Hope."

Elijah studied the vast prairie that stretched out on either side of the road and wondered how it compared to China. He didn't know much about that foreign land, only that it was about as far from Kansas as a man could get.

A part of him really wanted to be there.

As the wagon rattled down the rutted trail between seas of bluestem, broom sedge, and switchgrass, Eli searched the horizon for the shingled roof of the little Hope church. He was headed back there to be a pastor again. Not a missionary. Not a traveling evangelist. Just the pastor of a little flock. Lily had warned him that meant weddings, funerals, planned-out sermons, and deacons' meetings.

Oh, Lord, are you sure you wouldn't rather send me to China? he prayed. *Surely they don't have committees in China. Or deacons. Or cemetery funds.*

Eli reached down and picked a stem of purple coneflower from the side of the road and twirled it between his thumb and forefinger. The pale petals fanned out from the dark brown, prickly eye. In a few weeks, the petals would fall and the central black pod would cast its seeds across the fertile prairie sod.

Cast seeds, Elijah, the voice in his soul whispered. *Spread my Word across the prairie. The harvest truly is great, but the laborers are few.*

"Yes, Lord," he murmured in response.

"What?" Lily Nolan straightened on the seat beside him. "Did you say something, Elijah?"

Embarrassed, he shook his head. "Just praying."

"I guess I was dozing. It's such a hot afternoon."

With Mother Margaret at her son's house in Topeka and the baby sleeping in the back of the wagon, Lily and Elijah had been sitting for hours in total silence. He felt uncomfortable alone with her. She was too pretty. She smelled too sweet. His thoughts kept meandering off the main trail and wandering around the notion of what it would feel like to take Lily Nolan in his arms and kiss her pink lips. He wanted to touch her hair too, all that long gold silk. And he wouldn't mind the feel of her soft cheek against his neck or her —

"What were you praying about?" Lily asked.

Eli blanched. Had he been praying?

"Being the pastor in Hope," he said, forcing his thoughts back onto the main trail. "I reckon it's going to be hard work."

"You'll be tending lambs among wolves," she said with quiet assurance. "That's a terrifying responsibility."

Eli shifted the reins from one hand to the other. No, he wanted to tell her. He'd been a pastor in Hope just long enough to realize it would be the tedium of the job that oppressed him. The same people with the same petty arguments and the same complaints day after day. They'd be pulling on him, tracking him down, sucking him dry. The grind of it all would do him in.

Nothing like being a missionary in China — or even a roving evangelist. In Hope there would be no unknown trails to explore, no hordes of unrepentant souls to gather in, no rugged wildernesses and savage tribes to tame. Nothing but Hope, Kansas. Dirt farmers. Broiling sun. Relentless wind. Cows. Chickens. Wheat.

"When I think about the task of a minister," Lily said, "and I mean a *real* minister, someone who's honest and loves his flock and truly has faith in God, I think it must be the highest calling in the world."

"You do?" Eli took his Stetson off, fanned the flies a moment, and put the hat back on. "The highest calling?"

"Mother Margaret could explain what I'm trying to say." She let out a breath. "Oh, I miss her so much. I feel lost without her."

"I'd like to hear your thoughts, Lily. How do you figure a preaching job in an outpost like Hope is a high calling?"

"Because the pastor is the only shepherd the people have. That means he sees to the welfare of the flock — their physical health, their daily needs, their harshest trials, and their sweetest joys. A true minister — if there is such a thing — lays down his life for his flock."

"In Hope?"

"The wolves are all around, Elijah. The hungry lion is on the prowl."

Seeing the call to preach in a different light, Eli squared his shoulders and lifted his chin. "Maybe you're right. I never lived anywhere long enough to have a real pastor, but I sure heard a lot of traveling preachers. That seemed like the best way to get the message across."

"An evangelist came to our church once," Lily said. "He was a mighty man with a hypnotic voice. He left everyone in tears. But the main thing was, *he left.* It was our minister, Reverend Hardcastle, who reached out to all the broken spirits and contrite hearts. He was the one who really made the difference."

"You liked your minister, Lily?"

She shrugged. "Reverend Hardcastle is a loving man — kind to everyone. And that makes him blind."

"Blind to your father."

"I don't want to talk about my father."

"But I do." He took her hand and wove her slender fingers between his. "Tell me about him, Lily."

She looked away, across the prairie, seeing places and events Elijah could only imagine. The thought that anyone could hurt Lily was almost more than he could bear. For one thing, she was so delicate, almost fragile. How could anyone — let alone a father — treat her roughly? Thinking about it made Eli so angry he could taste it.

The man had damaged Lily's tender, childlike trust in God. That sin seemed unforgivable. Had her faith been destroyed completely? Or did Lily still nurture a tiny seed?

"Consider the lilies how they grow." The voice inside Elijah whispered words from Jesus' teaching.

Could Lily still grow? Was there hope for her? Did God have a plan for her life . . . even though her heart was hard and her spirit had been shut away?

"Seek ye the kingdom of God; and all these things shall be added unto you." Eli raised a prayer of thanksgiving as the words of Scripture flooded through him. It was never too late. Never. Not even for Lily.

"My father is a great musician," she said softly, her fingers gripping his. "He conducts the Greater New England Symphony Orchestra, and he directs the choir at the First United Church of St. George, the largest church in Philadelphia."

"People respect him," Elijah said.

"Yes." She nodded, but her focus had left the vast freedom of the prairie and was directed on her lap. "He's a great man. He's always very busy attending meetings and speaking out on behalf of his orchestra. They travel often to perform across the East Coast."

"Has he heard you sing?"

"No," she said, her voice hushed. "No, never."

It was as though the very mention of the

man lapped at Lily's spirit. She began to shrink and wither, her voice growing small and her shoulders drawing together. Elijah rubbed his thumb gently over hers, stroking away the tension.

"I went to the finest schools," she continued. "I always wore expensive clothes. My father liked to show me off to his associates."

"I guess you had a lot of friends."

"Father didn't like children to come to our house. He didn't want me to spend time with anyone but our family, so he kept me inside. He had to protect me from bad influences."

"You must have been pretty lonely."

"Yes, but my father wanted only the best for me. He needed to keep control of things, he said. Everything had to be in order so I would grow up well. He didn't like for me to speak out my own ideas or go places without him. He always kept my mother close, too. She did everything he told her to do, but I . . . I was naughty sometimes. I liked to climb trees, and twice I tore my pinafores. One afternoon I ate half a cherry pie all by myself. Another time I hid under my father's desk because I wanted to make a house there for my dolls. But he found me and —"

She squeezed her eyes shut and shook her head, unable to continue.

Not far ahead, Elijah could see the little

town of Hope, its collection of soddies and timber-framed buildings glazed orange by the setting sun. The glass panes gleamed in the mercantile windows. A drift of pale gray smoke rose from the smithy's chimney. White sheets fluttered on a line. So small and simple the town seemed. A place where children could climb trees and eat cherry pies without fear.

"Your father had no right to hurt you," he said. "You were just a little girl. You were playing."

"Rights? What rights do children have? My father was preparing for an important concert that weekend. I disrupted his . . . his thoughts."

"Did he beat you?"

She bit her lip as she nodded. "His baton made a good whip. Convenient. But Elijah, *most* children are punished when they do wrong. I know that. I realize I was —"

"Most children don't wind up black and blue. A papa or mama might give their child one quick pop on the backside to set him straight. But not a beating. Not pouring out anger on a young'un. That's not right, Lily. Is that what your father did to you?"

"I'm sure he didn't intend to hurt me —"

"Did he bruise you?"

"Yes," she whispered. "He . . . he broke my

ribs once. I remember how hard it was to breathe. My mother told the doctor I had fallen down the stairs."

"She lied."

"She didn't want anyone to think less of my father. He has such a fine standing in the community. He's very —"

"Cruel. Vicious. Mean."

"Talented. He's brilliant and high-strung. They say he's a genius. Sometimes he just can't control everything."

"He can't control himself."

"He couldn't control me. Not completely. I frustrated him."

"You were a little girl. A child, Lily. No one ought to hurt a young'un — no matter what."

She let out a breath, as though the weight of the past had slipped from her shoulders for a moment. "I know," she said finally. "For so many years I took it all inside myself. I defended my father. I blamed myself. I accepted my mother's lies to the doctors. I managed both sides of my world — the glittering parties, fine gowns, soaring music . . . and the shouts of rage, the cruel baton, the bruises and broken bones. And then one day . . . when I was older . . . I stepped outside myself, and I saw it."

"That's when you ran off with the traveling show."

"Beatrice has not had an easy life either, you know. She took me in when she and the others were barely able to feed themselves. At first, Jakov didn't want me, but Bea argued on my behalf. She said she would rescue me, and she did. Ted Nolan became my husband after that. I didn't know him well when we got married, and over time I liked him less and less. But I needed shelter, and he offered it. In return, I worked for the show."

"So now you've run off a second time," Eli said, "and you're feeling just as guilty as when you left your father. You're making up reasons why those people deserve your love and your respect — even though they never loved or respected you."

"Bea loved me," she returned. "I know she did."

"True love doesn't try to control folks." Eli guided the mule off the road, past a grove of shady cottonwood trees, and down the main street of Hope. "I don't know much more on the subject than what you've taught me, Lily, but I know what I've read in the Good Book. If people love you, they're not going to threaten you or make you feel low. And they're sure not going to make a habit of hurting you."

"I think Bea lashed out at me because she's terribly frightened. All her life, she's struggled just to survive. She never had anything to call her own until she joined up with Jakov and the traveling show. She truly needs my help."

"You'd sing in an opera house?"

"You make it sound like another den of iniquity."

"Ever been inside one? There's drinking and gambling and all kinds of carrying on. That's not a place for someone like you."

"Someone like me? Who do you think I am?" she asked, turning her blue eyes on him. "Don't be fooled by my appearance, Elijah. I'm not a porcelain doll. I've made a lot of wrong choices, and I've done things a good woman shouldn't. I've been hard and angry and bitter. I've gone my own way in life, and I've carved out a rough path. An opera house would welcome the likes of me. I'd fit right in."

Eli pulled the mule up to the front of the Hankses' house. "I would have, too, in the old days. I did a lot of things a man couldn't brag about, Lily, and I expect I'll make my share of mistakes in the years to come. But there's one big difference inside me now."

"Please don't start preaching, Elijah."

"I'm not preaching — I'm telling you about *me*. Who I am. Do you care at all?"

"Yes," she said softly.

"I'm walking God's path, not my own, Lily.

I'm following his light, not stumbling around in the dark. I won't choose wrong when he shows me what's right."

"But I'm scared."

"Be scared of your father. Be scared of Beatrice. Be scared of me, if you want. I'm a long way from perfect. But don't be scared of God. All he wants to do is love you, Lily. He wants to love you with the kind of love that never fades."

She clenched his hand. "I can't let go. I've worked too hard to take hold of my own life."

"Are you holding it? Or is Beatrice?" He reached up and touched her cheek. "Lily, don't give your life away anymore. Not to people. We're selfish and greedy and pretty rotten most of the time. And don't try to hold it yourself. You told me you've made a lot of wrong choices, and you're bound to make more mistakes. But God isn't. He won't. You can count on that."

Eli reached down and pulled up the brake lever on the wagon as Ben and Eva Hanks stepped out of their house to greet them. This had been a long road. A wearying path. But it was the right path. He was sure of that.

CHAPTER 10

"My husband built that pew and brung it to church, and that big ol' German feller has took to settin' on it ever' Sunday." Mrs. Hudson's small dark eyes sparked. "That's *our* pew, Preacher, and you better tell him to find another!"

Elijah took the elderly lady's hand in his and regarded her seriously. "I'm sure Rolf Rustemeyer doesn't mean a thing against you folks by sitting on your pew," he said. "This will be my fourth Sunday in Hope, and I've never heard a selfish or harsh word out of the man. In fact, I think he regards your family with the highest esteem."

Mrs. Hudson patted her silver hair. "I reckon he should. We're good people."

"Yes, you are."

"If my son hadn't died, we'da never come to Hope. But we aim to keep helpin' his poor widder with all them young'uns as long as we's needed. Violet and them kids is all we got in the world, Brother Elijah."

"They're good young'uns. And the Widow Hudson is a mighty fine mama to them."

"She sure is, and I don't want that shaggy ol' German to get no designs on her! You hear me?" She shook her finger at Eli. "Him a-settin' on our pew ever' Sunday and makin' big puppy-dog eyes at Violet. It's a downright disgrace."

Bull's-eye! Elijah struggled to hold back a victory grin. He hadn't been at this business of shepherding a flock for long, but he was getting better at it all the time. Maybe he wasn't tracking down the wayward and lost in the wilds of China, but he was working just as hard at rounding up the truth in little old Hope. And he liked the challenge.

"I don't believe Rolf Rustemeyer sitting on your pew is what's really troubling you, Mrs. Hudson," he said in a gentle tone. "I suspect it's the prospect of a man courting your daughter-in-law. You don't want anybody taking your son's place in her heart, do you?"

"I certainly do not." Her righteous indignation began to dissolve into sorrow. "Jim was our only son, don't you know. We didn't have no other kids, Preacher. When we heard about him a-passin' on, well, I just like to have died myself. But now, thanks to the good Lord, we got more young'uns than we know what to do with. Don't you see how it is? We lost our son, but we been given that passel of kids in his place. If that long-haired German feller thinks he can take Violet and them babies away from us —"

"Rolf Rustemeyer would never want to deprive you or your husband," Eli said, patting her hand. "I'm sure he sees you two as part of the family."

"You reckon?"

"I know for a fact that he's a lonely man, and I have a feeling he'd make Violet a fine, hardworking husband. I'm sure he'd welcome all her kin into his home — young and old alike."

She considered this new thought for a moment. "Well, that might not be so bad. He's got hisself a nice place, I hear."

"He's one of the most successful farmers around. Plus he was partners with Seth Hunter and Jimmy O'Toole in building the bridge and founding the town of Hope. That means he's taking in some of the profits from the bridge tolls. Why, he's one of our most prosperous citizens. You never know, Mrs. Hudson. God may have sent Rolf Rustemeyer your way. That hardworking German might be the best thing to come along for your family in a mighty long time."

Her dark eyes lighting up, Mrs. Hudson gave Elijah a smile. "I do declare, Preacher, you might be right."

"Even if nothing comes of his friendship

with Violet, it wouldn't hurt to have such a fine man sharing your pew on Sunday, would it?"

"We'll see that Mr. Rustemeyer has the best seat in the house of the Lord." Standing, she shook out the folds of her patched calico skirt and slipped on her faded bonnet. "Brother Elijah, I do declare, I believe you was the one sent here by God. I heard what you done 'bout fixin' up a town graveyard behind the church. That's gonna be mighty welcome, don't you know. And folks is talkin' over the way you sat with the Rippeto family when their littlest was took sick. You're doin' a good job. Such a good job that I don't even hardly mind givin' my tithe of a Sunday."

Elijah stood and tucked his Bible under his arm. "I appreciate your kind words, Mrs. Hudson."

"I'm a-goin' now, and I thank you for your time."

"Much obliged."

With a smile tickling his mouth, Eli watched the diminutive lady make her way down the aisle between the rows of rickety benches. A little sheep heading back into the safety of the fold. With the Lord's help, he had rescued another lamb from the wolves of jealousy, fear, greed, and covetousness that threatened Christ's body in Hope.

"And one more thing, Brother Elijah," Mrs. Hudson said, turning in the doorway. "We-all think you'd best get yourself a wife. A preacher ought to have a wife. It just ain't right any other way. Especially if he's already got hisself a baby."

"Well, I appreciate your thoughts, Mrs. Hudson."

"We-all like that Lily Nolan pretty good. She's got a nice face and a gentle hand, and she seems to take to your boy."

Eli's humor faded. *We-all.* Who were *we-all* to stick their noses into his personal business anyway? If he wanted their opinion, he'd ask for it.

"She seems to like you real good," Mrs. Hudson went on. "We-all took note of how she laughs at your stories and turns bright pink when you look at her. We-all think you ought to court her formal-like. Make it official, Preacher, and you'll do the town good."

Eli drank in a deep breath to calm himself. "I do care about this town, Mrs. Hudson, but I've got to think about other things, too. I'm sure you'll be the first to know when I make up my mind to go courting."

With a laugh of delight, the old woman stepped out of the church into the afternoon sunshine. Eli gave the bench nearest him a shove with his boot. *Baa, baa, you little sheep,* he thought. *Head back to the fold and gossip with your friends.* If she and her cronies knew what he felt like inside — torn to shreds every time he so much as caught a glimpse of Lily Nolan — they'd think twice about prying.

Truth to tell, he'd been doing all he could to keep away from Lily Nolan. After a week back in Hope, he was hoping that Beatrice Waldowski would fail to make good on her threat of returning to the little town. He could tell that Lily was starting to feel free of her past — freer and lighter and happier than he'd ever seen her. She fairly lit up the whole sky when she walked by. In his effort to avoid the woman whose presence stirred him so deeply, he'd finished the fence around the church, dug and planted a garden, visited everybody in town at least once, and almost read the whole New Testament straight through.

She's not a Christian, he wanted to tell the snoopy Mrs. Hudson. *Lily isn't a believer, and because of that, she wouldn't make me a good wife. A pretty face and gentle hands aren't enough to build the foundation of a good marriage. It takes a shared faith, a joint trust in Jesus Christ, a united front against the destructive forces of the world.*

Not only had his Lord discouraged marriage between a Christian and an unbeliever, but Elijah knew it would never work from a practical standpoint. Whether he was going to be a pastor in Hope or a missionary in China, he needed a full-fledged partner. And Lily Nolan could not be his — not in any way.

Grabbing his hat, Eli stalked toward the room at the back of the church where he made his home. He couldn't understand why Lily had started attending his preaching services. And he wished he'd never asked her to talk so honestly about her father. Now, every time he recollected their conversation in the wagon, he wanted to smash in the man's nose. How dare anyone hurt Lily? She was so sweet, so kind, so tender —

"Hello, Elijah," Lily said as he walked into his living room. She was sitting on the floor playing with Samuel. "Hope you don't mind that I came inside. Eva and I baked some cookies this morning. It's Mother Margaret's recipe. I brought you some."

Eli stopped dead still and stared at her. Her pale blue skirt swirled around her on the floor like a rippled pond. Sunlight danced in the fine strands of her golden hair. As she looked up at him, her eyes sparkled with a blue flame.

"Lily," he managed.

"I trust I'm not interrupting."

"No." He cleared his throat. "I was just . . . just talking things over with Mrs. Hudson."

Had Lily heard their conversation? Did she

know what the townsfolk were saying about the two of them? If Lily thought for a minute that he would ever betray his vow to the Lord by courting a nonbeliever . . . but what if she thought he didn't care for her? What if his words to Mrs. Hudson made her think he didn't appreciate her as a woman? He did. *Lord, help me. I do wish I could take Lily into my heart.*

"I'll bet Mrs. Hudson was complaining about Rolf Rustemeyer sitting on the pew her husband built," Lily said as she wiggled Sam's bare toes. "She wants it reserved for Violet and her children."

"Aren't there any secrets in this town?" he asked, a little more gruffly than he intended. He walked across the room and set his Bible on the table. "I don't know when I've ever met such talkity people."

"The truth is, Mrs. Hudson's afraid Mr. Rustemeyer will marry Violet and move her and all the children away to his farm," Lily said, giving Sam's tummy a soft poke. "Why don't you have a cookie, Elijah? I want to know if you like them."

Eli turned. "What did you just say?"

"Have a cookie. They're oatmeal."

"I mean about Rolf and Violet. How did you know that's what was really troubling Mrs. Hudson?"

"It's just a feeling," she said. "I've watched them all in church, and that's what I suspect."

"You mean you just *know?*"

"Beatrice would say I'm psychic. She'd say the spirits told me. But I think I'm just a woman with two good eyes."

Eli sat down at the table and thumped his fingers on the Bible. "It took me a good bit of tracking to piece together Mrs. Hudson's real trouble with Rolf Rustemeyer. But you figured it out right away. How did you do that?"

"I'm a *woman*, Elijah," she said, giving a shy laugh. "We notice these things."

"Maybe I ought to just take you on rounds with me. Then I wouldn't have to spend half the time beating the bushes to figure out what's really troubling folks. I've learned the problem is never what they tell me to start off with."

"I'll go visiting with you," she said. "I'd like that."

"No." He stood quickly. "That wouldn't be a good idea. Folks might get a wrong notion about us."

"Oh?" She smoothed down the soft cotton gown Sam wore. "What's a right notion about us, Elijah?"

He gave her a wary glance and began to pace. Being cornered like a hunted grizzly was not a good feeling. If he told her he couldn't socialize too much with her because of her lack of faith, she'd be hurt. She'd believe he thought he was too good for her. It might even turn her more against the Lord.

But if he told her how he really felt about her — how much he enjoyed talking to her, listening to her, laughing and even crying with her — well, she'd think he was starting to care about her. He *did* care about her. But he couldn't. Shouldn't.

"You're taking care of Sam," he said finally. "We're like business partners, I reckon. Aren't we?"

"Are we?"

Confound it. He paced across the room and then back again.

"I'm paying you," he said.

"You kissed me."

"Not on purpose."

"On accident?"

"Well, I'm not trying to seduce you the way Beatrice said, if that's what you think."

"No. I never thought that."

"I'm a man of honor."

"I know."

"I'm doing the best I can here."

"You're doing a wonderful job. I heard how you sat up with the Rippeto family when their youngest was sick. Everyone in town speaks well of you."

"There you go! See? I can't do a thing without everybody watching. And I'm trying my best to stay on the right track. But I'm just a man, and you're a woman, and —"

"It's Ted, isn't it?" She looked up at him, her face pale. "You're put off by the fact that I was married before. That I took a husband out of necessity. That I'm not pure."

He frowned for a moment, trying to understand. "What?"

"On the wagon from Topeka, you and I spoke so honestly together. You held my hand. After all we endured with Samuel, I just thought we were . . . we were friends. But since we've been back in Hope, you've hardly looked at me. You won't speak to me more than a moment or two. Do I repulse you?"

"Repulse me?" In disbelief, he knelt on the floor beside her. "Lily, it's all I can do to hold back from you. You're the most beautiful, precious, gentle —" He leaned away. "No, I can't do this."

"Do what? You're not doing anything."

"It's not you, Lily. It's me. I have to focus on being a pastor. There's the Cornwall wedding tomorrow and two sermons the next day. And Seth Hunter asked me to give a little talk at the Independence Day fish fry next week."

"Do I get in the way of your work?"

"All the time." He shook his head. "That's not what I meant to say. It's just that I keep thinking about you. Thinking about . . ." He tried to make himself breathe. "Thinking about what's going to happen to you. You'll be going back to Philadelphia."

"Not until I've earned the money for my ticket. Without my melodeon to sell, I won't be able to leave until fall." She moistened her lips. "Elijah, I wanted you to know that Rolf Rustemeyer has asked me to go with him to the fish fry."

"Rolf Rustemeyer?" Eli slapped his hand on his thigh. "I thought he was after Violet Hudson!"

"I think he's after a wife. Anyone will do."

"You're not anyone. You're *you*. You're . . . you're Sam's . . . Sam's aunt."

"Aunt?" She stared at him. "Is that how you see me? As a sister?"

He raked a hand back through his hair. Confound it, he wasn't about to let Rolf Rustemeyer marry Lily Nolan. If he thought he was in torment now, he could hardly imagine how bad *that* would feel.

But Elijah couldn't court Lily himself. He could never take her as his own wife. And he couldn't tell her why. Or could he? Should he just blurt out the whole thing? *Lord, help me here!*

"I thought Beatrice was wrong about you," Lily said as she tucked the baby's blanket around him. "She insisted you were like my father — concerned only about how the world viewed you. On the way back from Topeka, I was sure she was mistaken. I saw you as a real man, caring and honest. It didn't matter what I'd done wrong. You accepted me and made me think that God would too."

She stood, her blue skirt swirling down to the tips of her black boots. "Now I understand that Beatrice was right about you, Elijah," she went on, her voice taking on that harsh quality he knew too well. "In the watchful eyes of Hope, you're the high-and-mighty preacher. You can't be friendly with a woman from a traveling show. You can't be seen talking to me too often or caring about me too much. I'm not a real person anymore, am I? I'm your business partner. Samuel's aunt. Your sister."

"No, you're wrong —"

"It's all right, Elijah. You warned me you were only human. You told me I couldn't count on you."

"I said I'd stand by you, and I will." Rising, he took her shoulders. "Lily, listen to me."

For a moment he stared down into her blue eyes, trying to make himself speak. What did he want to say? That she was everything he'd

ever wanted in a woman? Spunk and determination mingled with gentleness. Intelligence
and talent softened by a tender heart. Fragile
beauty, a loving spirit —

"Oh, Lily." Without meaning to, he pulled
her into his arms and held her tight. He didn't
have the words he needed to say. So he
pressed his lips against her forehead . . . and
then her cheek . . . and finally her mouth. Her
hands slid tentatively around his back. He
could feel her trembling as he struggled
against the war inside his heart.

"Lily, I —"

"Brother Elijah?" Seth Hunter stepped
through the church door into the little back
room. "Oh, 'scuse me. I didn't mean to interrupt."

Lily jumped like she'd been shot. Elijah
wheeled around to face the visitor. He could
feel the heat creeping up the back of his
neck.

"Seth," he said, jamming his hands into his
pockets. "Come on in. How's the farm? Rosie
feeling OK today?"

The tall farmer eyed the two as Lily scooped
the baby up from the floor. "I was just coming
to tell you the news," he said. "Looks like that
traveling show is back. And they've brought
wagons loaded with lumber. Jack Cornwall
and Ben Hanks went down to see what was

222

up. Turns out those folks have plans to build an opera house."

Lily fled out behind the church with Samuel wriggling unhappily in her arms. She could hardly hold back the tears of dismay as she raced across the rutted main street toward the Hanks house, where she'd been living since her return from Topeka. She needed to talk to someone, to pour out the confusion and agony in her heart. But Mother Margaret was gone. Eva Hanks wouldn't understand. No one would understand.

She hurried into the shadowy depths of the small frame house and laid Samuel in the little crib Elijah had built for his son. Instantly the baby let out a wail that would deafen heaven. Lily set her hands on her hips and stared down at the screaming, frustrated bundle of tiny arms and legs.

"Well, I'd like to cry, too," she told him. "Go ahead and yell for both of us, Sammy. Are you hungry? I just fed you an hour ago, didn't I? Are you wet? Is that it?"

She felt the baby's diaper. "You're dry. You're full. And there's not a pin pinching you or a bug biting you. So what's the matter?"

By now Sam's face was bright red. His little fists pumped the air, and his legs churned as though they were working milk into butter. At her wit's end, Lily stared at the baby's wide mouth, twisting head, and frantic squirms.

"What's wrong?" she asked. *What . . . is . . . wrong?*"

By now tears were streaming down her own cheeks. What was wrong with *her?* Everything. Beatrice had come back to Hope. Samuel was screaming. Rolf wanted to take her to the fish fry. And Elijah . . . oh, Elijah!

"You just want somebody to hold you close," she said, lifting the baby back into her arms and snuggling him against her neck. "That's all you want, isn't it, Sammy? Calm down, now. I'm here. I won't leave you alone, sweet boy. I love you."

As the baby's wails began to subside, Lily rocked him from side to side. "I love you, Samuel," she whispered, feeling the tension slide from her own body. "I can't protect you from every hurt. I can't choose the path you'll take. But I'm here, Sammy. I'm here, and I love you."

Closing her eyes, she swayed alone in the stillness of the little house. Even now, she could feel Elijah's arms around her and his lips against hers. Oh, it had felt so good to kiss him. So right to be held in his warm embrace.

But Elijah had made plain his feelings about her. She shouldn't count on him. No matter what he might feel — what either of them might want — Elijah would not be more to Lily than her employer, her brother . . . her pastor.

As a woman, she sensed the power his male attraction gave her. If she chose, she might be able to tempt him away from his calling. She could lure him into her arms and away from the very purpose of his life, from the work that made him the man he was.

But she would hate herself for it. He would hate her, too, in the end. It would come to nothing but pain. More pain.

No, she thought, brushing her cheek against the baby's downy dark hair, she would not be alone with Elijah again. She would not tempt him. She would not even speak to him. By September she would have enough money to buy her ticket back to Philadelphia. And then she would leave Hope behind.

If only she had someone to talk to. Someone with whom she could share the terrible ache in her heart. Someone she could trust.

"I wish to goodness Mother Margaret was here!" Eva said, racing into the house and throwing her apron onto the table. "Oh, Miz Lily, there you are! It's a terrible thing. Just awful! They've picked out a place right next to the road. The opera-house people, I mean. The lot is not on Mr. Seth's land, so he doesn't have the right to run them off. And they've got a deed for that land! It's all legal, too. You should just see Ben. He's about to have a conniption."

She threw open the oven door and took out two steaming pies. "Some folks are saying that one of 'em's the same wagon you came in on," Eva continued as she set the tins inside the screened pie safe and then began re-arranging every plate on her shelves. "They want you to go down there and talk to them, Lily. Ben says you'll convince those folks to leave. But Mr. Jack thinks maybe you're the one who encouraged them to come back here. And Mr. Seth says he doesn't care why they're here, he's not going to allow that kind of folk in his town. He's thinking of holding an election come the Fourth of July fish fry, and setting up a town government, and a mayor, and all that. And Mr. Rolf says we need a sheriff before we need a mayor. Those folks are unloading their lumber already!"

She restacked her plates and turned all her tins and canning jars label-side out. "Why, you know what an opera house is like," she went on. "It'll be painted some bright color and hung with red curtains. There'll be a saloon in there; I just know it. Anyhow, Ben says they're planning to serve liquor. Just think what kind of undesirables that will attract."

Lily walked across the room to the rocking chair and sat down to nurse the baby again. Maybe if Samuel took a little milk, he'd drift off to sleep. As she rocked, she watched Eva begin to scrub her rough-hewn wooden table.

"Dancing girls," Eva said. "They'll have dancing girls. The men will flock down there — you can count on it. And they'll be too tired to come to church of a Sunday after they've stayed up half the night watching the dancing girls. Oh, mercy, I miss Mother Margaret. Ben's mama could put us all to peace about this."

She wrung out her rag and began to scrub again. "I hear they put on plays in those opera houses. You know what I mean? They act things out. How can that be right?"

"Now, Eva," Lily finally interjected, "some very great and moving dramas have been written. They touch people's hearts."

Eva paused in her scrubbing. "I don't know. I never saw a play. But I can't imagine folks dressing up in costumes and pretending they're something they're not. That's just plain strange, if you ask me. And singing! Ben says they sing the rowdiest songs you ever heard at those opera houses."

"Not all the songs are rowdy. Some of them are beautiful. They often present selections from the great operas of Europe."

"Well, they won't let a black man into an opera house anyhow, so I don't have to worry about my Ben. Thank the Lord for that." Eva hung her rag over the side of the washtub. After straightening her colorful scarf, she sank down onto a stool and pressed her hands together. "You're not going back to them folks, are you, Miz Lily? You wouldn't join up with those actors and dancing girls, would you? Not after all this time with us. And knowing how much Samuel needs you. And seeing how the preacher feels about you."

Lily looked up from the dozing baby. "How does the preacher feel about me, Eva?"

"Why, he loves you," Eva said with surprise. "Can't you see that? He loves you, Miz Lily. Sure enough."

CHAPTER 11

"By the power vested in me by God and the state of Kansas," Elijah said, "I now pronounce you man and wife."

He took Caitrin Murphy's slender hand and placed it on the large callused palm of Jack Cornwall. The young couple, beset by delays ranging from Samuel's illness to a huge order for nails from the nearby military fort, had postponed their wedding date two weeks. Finally, on this sun-warmed Saturday afternoon, they were pulling it off.

The bride wore a white gown trimmed in tiny beads, her flame red hair caught up in a small hat adorned with plumes and a wispy veil. The groom stood tall and handsome in his new black suit and fine store-bought top hat. Roses and prairie wildflowers festooned the church. Ribbons decorated every pew. In all, the Murphy–Cornwall wedding was the most lavish event Eli had ever witnessed.

"May I kiss the bride, Brother Elijah?" Jack Cornwall asked, drawing the preacher from his reverie. "Or are we supposed to stand here all day?"

"Kiss her?" Elijah said. "Sure, go ahead."

No one had told him about *kissing* being part of a wedding ceremony. He'd memorized his part from start to finish, but there wasn't a word in the instruction manual about smooching. As the bridegroom drew his wife into his arms, a collective sigh of delight rose throughout the church.

Eli glanced to the back pews near the door. Lily hadn't come. Everyone in town had been invited to the wedding, but she had chosen not to make an appearance. Disappointment darkened his spirits. The reception would be starting in a few minutes, and he had looked forward to sitting near Lily. Maybe he would ask her to dance. Seth Hunter had evidently kept quiet about seeing their stolen kiss. Speaking of kisses . . .

"Whoa, you two," Eli said, tapping Jack Cornwall on the shoulder. "The guests are all eager to have a slice of wedding cake. Or are we supposed to stand here all day?"

As the crowd chuckled, Jack and Caitrin parted. Her cheeks rosy, the bride gave a musical laugh. Linking her arm through her husband's, she set off beside him down the aisle. The other celebrants clapped as the pair led the way out of the church.

When the building was finally empty, Eli let out a deep breath and slumped onto the chair near the pulpit. He bent over, covering his face with his hands, and prayed for the storm inside his heart to calm.

That opera house was going up faster than a dandelion after a spring rain. In just twenty-four hours, the framework for a large, two-story building had already been erected. Had Lily visited the site or spoken with Beatrice? Was she planning to take a job there? He gritted his teeth.

Why had he kissed her yesterday afternoon? He'd tried so hard to keep himself away from the woman. And now that he had finally run her off, he could hardly bear the distance that stretched between them.

Every morning, Lily sent Eva to fetch Samuel, and Ben returned the baby each night. During the day, Lily stayed busy helping Eva weed the garden, wash and iron laundry, bake bread, and mend shirts and socks. The two women worked side by side, as though they were sisters. And never once did Lily glance in the direction of the church.

Eli was sure he looked her way at least five hundred times a day. Not only was he curious about her relationship with Beatrice and concerned about the welfare of little Sam, but he couldn't make himself stop thinking about Lily herself. Why had she come into his life? Would it really be so wrong for him to court a nonbeliever? Maybe they could just see each other on Sunday afternoons. Eli could borrow a wagon and take Lily for a drive down the main road. Would there be any harm in that?

Eli rubbed his eyes. He hadn't slept much lately. Confusion and turmoil rolled around inside him like thunder.

Of course he couldn't court Lily. If he took her for a drive, he'd want to kiss her again. And if he kissed her, he'd want to tell her how he really felt about her. And if he told her how he felt, he'd want . . .

Well, he'd want to spend the rest of his life with her. That's what he'd want.

He slammed his palms against his thighs and stood. *God, I need your help!* He picked up his Bible. *I need it right now. I don't know what I'm going to do about Lily. I can't change her. I can't unlock her heart. But I care about her. I care about her too much. Lord, you allowed her to come into my life. Please help me now.*

As he cried out his earnest prayer, Eli strode down the aisle to the double-hung front doors. The turmoil inside him felt as though it were raging — a huge twister building up speed, gathering power, and threatening to destroy everything in its path. If he hadn't given his life to Christ, there was no telling what he would do with all this pent-up frustration inside his heart.

Elijah, do you love me? a familiar voice inside him whispered. The preacher stopped, listening.

Feed my lambs.

Eli took a deep breath. The sheep. That was it. He would head over to the reception taking place inside the mercantile, and he'd visit with every member of the church. He'd ask about the health of the Rippetos' youngest, Mrs. Hudson's grandchildren, Mr. LeBlanc's new millstone, and Mrs. Laski's ill sister in Poland. He would inquire after Mrs. Hunter and Mrs. O'Toole and their expected babies, Mr. Rustemeyer's ailing cow, and Miss Lucy Cornwall's latest batch of cinnamon buns.

Elijah, do you love me?

Tend my sheep.

He wouldn't look at the Hanks house. He wouldn't think about Lily. He wouldn't even —

At the sight of a slender figure just down the street, Eli stopped walking. There she was. Her blue skirt fluttered as she hurried along, clutching her white shawl close around her shoulders. Though she wore a cotton bonnet with wide ruching that hid her face, he knew it was Lily. And she was headed for the opera house.

Elijah, do you love me?

233

Eli clenched his fists and squeezed his eyes shut. "Lord," he murmured, "you know I love you. I've given my heart to you. I've turned over my whole life. Of course I love you."

Then feed my sheep.

"What do you mean by that, Lord?" he breathed, bowing his head. "Your sheep are over in the mercantile."

The words of Luke's Gospel came over him like a drenching rain: *"What man of you, having an hundred sheep, if he lose one of them, doth not leave the ninety and nine in the wilderness, and go after that which is lost, until he find it?"*

Eli shook his head. He couldn't go after Lily. He couldn't be her shepherd. He could probably preach to the lost in China. He might even be able to pastor the Lord's flock in Hope. But not Lily. He didn't know how to reach her. Worse than that, he didn't know how to hold back his feelings for her. He didn't know how to be her pastor when he really wanted to be her —

He wanted to be her husband. That was it. That was all there was to it.

Lord, I love Lily Nolan, he prayed. *I love her like a woman, not just another one of the flock. I can't think of her any other way. I know you don't want that. I know you would never want me yoked with an unbeliever, and I'd do any-*

thing to keep from disobeying you, Father.

Eli swallowed hard.

Tend my lamb, Elijah.

The voice was unmistakable. When God spoke to him, the words reflected those of Holy Scripture. Elijah started walking. He trudged past the mercantile, deaf to the laughter and the sounds of fiddles and dancing feet inside. He forced his boots down the rutted main street of Hope, Kansas. And he looked across the prairie toward the frame of a new two-story building.

The opera house.

Lily paused in the shade of a large cottonwood tree near the Hope bridge. She had waited for this moment when the whole town was busy celebrating Caitrin Murphy's wedding to Jack Cornwall. No one would notice a lone woman headed down to the construction site of the new opera house. Lily could slip over to the building, perhaps speak with Beatrice for a few minutes, and then return to the Hankses' home before Sam awoke from his afternoon nap.

There wasn't a thing wrong with her plan. So why did she feel sick inside? Why was her heart as heavy as a piece of Ben Hanks's unforged iron?

Lily laid her hand on the gnarled trunk of

the old tree and studied the framework of the large building. How had it gone up so fast? Determination, that's how. Men swarmed over the frame of the opera house, raising walls and laying floorboards. Within a week or two, the structure would be finished and painted, the roof shingled, and the furniture moved in.

Beatrice's dream would come true. And Lily could join her. All it would take was a step out of the sleepy security of Hope and into the raucous, lively, on-the-edge life of an entertainer. Lily would have the chance to get rich. She would meet travelers with interesting tales to tell. Maybe she would find a husband. And, of course, she could sing.

Lowering her head, Lily considered the lure of the opera house. She had been rich once in her life, but her fine dresses and expensive education had brought her no happiness. She had adventured with the exciting characters the road brought her way, but she had found no joy. She had been married, but it had given her no lasting pleasure.

Singing. How she loved to sing. With Beatrice at her side, Lily could again sing the great arias. She could stir people's hearts and bring a thrill to their weary lives. If she returned to Philadelphia, she would never sing again.

Stepping out, Lily walked across the cleared ground and up to the site of the opera house. This could be her new home. This could be her realm.

"Out of my way, lady," a man called as he shouldered a load of planks past her. "I've got to get this wall up before the sun goes down. Don't want to miss the party, you know. The whisky flows!"

Lily pursed her lips and scanned the construction site. Not far away, George Gibbons from the Crescent Moon Hotel stood deep in conversation with a group of workers. His thin black mustache took on a life of its own as he spoke. At the sight, a light bubble of laughter rose up inside Lily. This could be fun. Parties in the evenings. Lots of men to dance with. She didn't have to feel lonely. She wouldn't even think about Elijah Book across the way in his white clapboard church. She would be the belle of the ball.

"Excuse me," she said as another man hurried by with a load of bricks. "Do you know where I could find Beatrice Waldowski?"

"Who?"

"Madame Zahara?"

"The only madam around here is Mrs. B. You one of her girls?" He gave Lily the once-over and grinned. "I might have to be first in line."

A chill ran down Lily's spine. "Excuse me, please," she said, brushing past him.

It couldn't be true. Surely this building was not going to become a brothel. Beatrice had said it was to be an opera house. There would be plays and ventriloquists, juggling and dog acts, raucous music and lighthearted operas.

Breathless, she strode around the building site until she found Beatrice. The older woman was looking up at the half-constructed second floor, her bright red dress sparkling in the late-afternoon sunlight. She had piled her long black hair high on her head and topped her bun with a crimson silk rose.

"Beatrice," Lily called across the empty space. "I heard you had returned to Hope."

The woman turned, her painted eyebrows arching in momentary surprise. "Lily?" Then she held out her arms in welcome. "You've finally come."

Stepping into the embrace of her friend, Lily was enveloped in the scent of Bea's exotic, spicy perfume. Lily had expected to feel as though she were coming home to the comfortable and familiar, but something about the moment of intimacy repulsed her. Moving back, she slipped her hands into her pockets.

"Your dress is luxurious," Lily said.

"George bought it for me." Bea gave her

hips a toss and then laughed. "He's the most wonderful man. Oh, Lily, I've never been so happy in all my life."

"Are you in love with him?"

"Of course I am! He's the best thing that ever happened to me. So much for Jakov and his traveling show." Her hand made an arc to take in the building. "I'm on my way now!"

"Bea, I'm so happy for you. Has Mr. Gibbons asked for your hand?"

"Why should he want my hand when he's got the rest of me?" With a giggle, Bea slipped her arm around Lily's shoulders. "Oh, Lil, I'm sorry you and I parted with angry words back in Topeka. I was just sick about it for days. All those harsh things we said to one another. It was horrible."

"Let's move forward now, Bea. This is a nice place. You and George must have big plans for it."

"It's going to be a gold mine, honey. We'll have the theater down below, the saloon to one side, and all those rooms upstairs."

"So, it's going to be a hotel?"

Beatrice laughed again, and this time Lily realized her friend's breath smelled strongly of liquor. "In a manner of speaking," she said. "George is going to bring in some girls. Soiled doves, they call them. I hear they're everywhere out West, California especially, and most of them are eager to move to someplace nice."

Lily stiffened at the confirmation of her fears. "A brothel, Bea?"

"Why not? The money is good. Every lonely farmer, merchant, and traveler from the Mississippi to the Rockies can belly up to our bar, have himself a few good laughs at our show, and then buy an evening's pleasure with one of our gals. With that bridge nearby, we'll get them coming and going. Why, we might even lure that pious preacher friend of yours over here for a night of fun. What do you think?"

Hardly able to breathe, Lily reflected on the simple, good-hearted townsfolk celebrating a marriage within sight of this place. Jack Cornwall and his bride. Ben and Eva Hanks. Seth and Rosie Hunter and their growing family. The O'Tooles and their gaggle of red-haired children.

A brothel? A saloon? She felt like she was going to be sick.

"We can make a place for you here, Lily," Beatrice was saying. "There's lots of room."

"Oh, I wouldn't want to —"

"Not with the other gals, silly!" Beatrice laughed and took a small flask from the pocket of her red dress. "You could sing in the theater. We've got a troupe of actors coming from Topeka early next month. They have a bear — can you believe that? A live bear! I know they'd be happy to make room for you in their plays. You could sing, too, Lily. I've told George how wonderful you are. He'd love to hear what you can do. We could make you some costumes. Remember the old days when you and I would sit together in the show wagon and sew ostrich plumes onto our skirts?"

Chuckling, she took a swig from her little bottle and then held it out to Lily. For a moment, Lily hesitated. She had walked this path with Beatrice. They had reveled and laughed and behaved in reckless ways — the best of friends, enjoying the good things in life. Or that's what they had told themselves.

"Don't you want a drink?" Bea asked.

Lily shook her head. "No thanks, Bea. I've got to get back to the baby. He's taking his nap right now, and I —"

"The baby?"

"Samuel."

"Don't tell me you're still tight with that preacher and his brat. I thought you'd come over here to join me, Lily. I thought you wanted to work for me."

Lily swallowed. "I promised to keep feeding Sam for a few more weeks. He's grown a lot, Bea. He's starting to smile at us, and he sleeps all through the night now. Elijah says —"

"Elijah?" Beatrice frowned. "Lily, there's fifteen men right here who can beat the charms of that sour-faced preacher. Why don't you stay with us this evening? Every night we have a party like you wouldn't believe. It's been so much fun, I can hardly believe this is happening to me. It's like a dream. A flat-out dream. George is going to put me in charge here at the opera house; did I tell you? I'll manage the women and schedule the shows and keep the bar stocked in whisky. I'm going to run the whole operation."

"Mr. Gibbons is going back to Topeka?"

"Well, sure. He's got a wife and five kids to feed."

"But, Beatrice, I thought —"

"You thought wrong. Much as I care for the man, he's not free for the taking. We'll see each other now and again, and I don't really mind. I never wanted to marry anyhow. This way I'm still available in case a more interesting offer comes along." She gave Lily a squeeze. "Come on and stay with me tonight, Lil. We'll talk till all hours like we used to. I'll paint your toenails red, and we can have our pick of dancing partners. What do you say?"

Through the window, Lily studied the little town that stretched down the narrow main street of Hope. The celebrants were filtering out of the mercantile now, their laughter carrying to her. She thought of Elijah Book and his warm blue eyes. He had kissed her, but he didn't want her. Eva had been wrong. Elijah didn't love Lily. He couldn't. No matter how her heart ached for the man, no matter how she tempted him, he would keep himself from her. She wasn't good enough. She wasn't pure enough. And he had his reputation to protect.

Just like her father.

"We've got a big pot of stew on the fire," Bea said, turning Lily toward the wagons. "And you should taste the bread that cook of ours can bake. I'll tell you what — if the show, the liquor, and the girls won't draw customers, the food will! Come on, I'll introduce you to Milton. He's the sweetest little fellow you ever met."

Lily walked beside Beatrice toward the show wagon. A place to live, friends to call her own, good wages, the chance to sing — what more could she ask for? In a few weeks, Samuel could start to eat solid food. He could survive without her. Ben and Eva were already making plans to go to Topeka to visit Mother Margaret, Moses, and the rest of their new-found family. Rose Hunter would give birth to her baby. Caitrin Murphy would be busy in her home. After the harvest, everyone in Hope would prepare to settle in for the winter.

Why shouldn't Lily have a place of her own too? Why not here at the opera house?

Beatrice would probably fail her in the long run. Lily knew that. Elijah had warned her not to place her trust in the woman. That was wise advice. But he'd also cautioned Lily not to put her life into his hands . . . or even to rely on herself.

God was the only one to count on. God.

Oh, God! Lily's soul cried out. *Oh, God! God!*

"I can smell that stew from here," Beatrice said. "Bill, where's George? Round up that man of mine, would you? And call Milton over here. I want those fellows to see who's come to join us."

Lily clenched her jaw and pulled away from Beatrice. "I can't stay, Bea," she said quickly. "I won't. I won't do this."

Before Beatrice could stop her, Lily dashed across the cleared ground toward the main street of Hope. The moment she passed the old cottonwood tree, someone moved out of the shadows into the road.

"Lily?"

She swung around. "Mercy, you scared the living daylights out of me, Elijah."

"I'm sorry." He took off his hat as he walked toward her. "I didn't aim to scare you."

"What are you doing out here? I thought you were at the mercantile with the wedding party."

"I told you I'd stand by you." He held his hat in both hands. "I wanted to be nearby in case you needed me."

"You followed me out here?" She didn't know whether to feel flattered or angry.

"I spotted you down on the street right after the wedding. I remembered how things went between you and your friend back in Topeka, and I thought I'd better stay close."

"I'm all right."

"Is there anything I can do for you?"

She glanced across at the opera house and the workers gathering in front of it. A tinny song filtered up, a guitar and a hollow-sounding piano. And then over it all she heard the round, rich notes of Mozart. The song was poorly executed, but she recognized the tune.

"Beatrice is playing my melodeon," she said in a low voice. "She's beckoning me."

"Will you join her?"

"It's going to be a brothel, Elijah."

His nostrils flared as he drank down a deep breath. "Are you sure?"

"I won't be a part of any of it. I've taken enough wrong roads, and I don't want to make more mistakes."

"Lily, I've been needing to —" He reached out to her and then caught himself. Pulling back, he tucked away whatever it was he had almost confessed. Instead, he pulled a small book from the pocket of his black coat.

"I've been needing to ask if you'd sing a special song for us at the fish fry." He handed her the hymnal that had belonged to his mother. "Eva told me you hadn't been looking at this book much, but I thought you might be able to find something in here you'd enjoy singing. Casimir Laski has offered to perform a solo, but I hear he only knows Polish songs. Since this is an Independence Day celebration, I was hoping maybe you could sing something in English."

Lily took the hymnal and held it against her chest. "I have to get back to the house. Samuel will be waking from his nap."

"Lily, about the other day —"

"It doesn't matter."

"It does matter. I was forward with you again, and I shouldn't have been. I'm doing my best to keep back and let you make your own choices. You've had a rough time. I don't have any right to elbow in and try to influence you. No one can decide about your life but you."

He was standing so close now, she could smell the scent of starch in the freshly pressed shirt he'd worn for the wedding. It was all she could do to keep from rushing into his strong arms and burying her head against his shoulder. He would hold her close and shelter her. He would protect her from brothels and saloons and all her poor choices.

He would save her from Beatrice.

But Elijah, too, would fail. He had warned her of that already. He was human, and he would make mistakes. He would let her down. She couldn't trust him. She couldn't trust anyone.

Only God. God!

"Are you all right, Lily?" Elijah was asking. "You look . . . a little off-kilter."

"I'm so confused. I'm being pulled one way and then another. I can't decide on my own. I can't do this by myself."

"Lily." Again he reached out to her — and again he drew back. "Lily, I can't do it for you. Make the choice. Decide now."

She clapped her hands on her head, feeling as though she might explode in the raging storm of torment. Winds of indecision buffeted her from every side. *Go back to Beatrice,* the thunder growled. *Cling to Elijah,* a chill breeze whistled. *Stand on your own,* the lightning flashed.

God! Turn to God! It was a small whisper in the tumult. Small but beautiful. As beautiful and golden as music.

"Lily," Elijah said, touching her arm. "Will you let me lead you to him?"

"No." She shook her head. "Stay away from me, Elijah. You tear me apart inside. When I'm near you I can't think."

"I don't mean to trouble you, Lily. I only want to —"

"I know what you want. You want to be my brother. You want to be my employer. You want to be my pastor."

"I want to be your friend."

"Well, you can't!" she said, grabbing his coat sleeves and gripping them in her fists. "Friends don't kiss each other the way you kissed me. Friends don't hold each other and pray together and look into each other's eyes like you look into mine. Don't try to tell me you just want to be my friend, Elijah. It's a lie."

He studied the ground for a moment, obviously stung. She steeled herself for his wrath. But when he raised his head, she could see that his eyes were rimmed in red.

"You're right, Lily," he said in a rough

voice. "I can't just be your friend."

"You can't be anything to me. No one can be anything to me. I don't trust you. I *won't* trust you."

"I'm a man, and as hard as I try, I can't keep from seeing you as a woman. You're right not to trust me. I don't trust myself." He stuffed his hat onto his head. "But confound it, Lily, you can trust God. You can put your life into his hands and count on him to stand by you every minute of every day."

"Elijah —"

"What in tarnation do you think I am, anyhow? I'm not perfect. I nearly killed Sam feeding him mashed potatoes. And then I let a spider bite him. I got us all run out of the Crescent Moon. I've talked when I should have kept my mouth shut, and I've kept quiet when I should have spoken up. I've preached some of the measliest excuses for sermons you ever heard. And I'll tell you something else. When I was sitting up with the Rippetos and their sick young'un, I was wishing I was home in my own bed. You're right not to trust me. I'm just a man, that's all. I'm weak and foolish and so crazy about you I can't see straight. You'd better not count on me for anything. But you can count on God. That's the only thing I know for sure. You can count on him. There, I've said my piece."

Without another word, he turned on his heel and stalked away down the road, leaving Lily alone in the darkening shadows of evening.

CHAPTER 12

Between the town and the opera house, the old cottonwood tree offered the only hiding place Lily could find. Sinking to her knees in a patch of tall bluestem grass, she pressed her face in her hands. Samuel would be awake and hungry by now. Eva and Ben would wonder where their houseguest had gotten to at this late hour. Even Beatrice might be standing on the porch expecting her to come back. Lily sensed their faint beckoning, but she could not move.

If she returned to the opera house, she would face Beatrice and the lure of her old life — a life she now knew for certain she did not want. If she walked into Hope, she would face Elijah and the call of a man she could never have. Though he cared for her, though his desire was obvious, he would not give in to his passion. His commitment to God controlled his entire life, and Lily knew that no matter what happened, he would never permit himself more than friendship with her.

If she turned inward, relying on herself, she would face the emptiness of her heart. Dependence on her own wits had led her to the traveling show. Led her to Ted Nolan. Led her to Beatrice. Mistakes and more mistakes. She had acted unwisely and made choices out of desperation. Eventually, she had lost her precious Abigail. As strong as she had become in the months since she had left Philadelphia, Lily knew she would never be able to rely on herself.

Fighting tears, she lay down in the grass and pulled her knees up to her chest. She felt so lonely. So hopeless. Everyone had betrayed or abandoned her. And why not? They were all humans, too, fallible and shortsighted.

Why did she feel such a need to turn to someone to fill the emptiness inside her? Why couldn't she do it herself? She was resourceful, intelligent, talented. Surely she didn't need anyone but herself.

Rolling over, Lily swallowed at the gritty lump in her throat. Of course she needed someone else. Like Samuel, she could not exist in this world alone. She would wither, grow frail, and die. No one — not even the most powerful human on earth — could live without sustenance and nourishment.

"Whosoever drinketh of the water that I shall give him shall never thirst."

Lily clenched her teeth as the silent words

filtered into her heart. She had memorized them long ago in Sunday school. Meaningless words. How could Christ quench this burning thirst inside her? How could he become the nourishment that would fill her?

"I am the living bread which came down from heaven: if any man eat of this bread, he shall live for ever."

But her emptiness went too far! It was all-consuming. Her very soul was devoid of hope and life and love.

"Behold, I stand at the door, and knock: if any man hear my voice, and open the door, I will come in to him, and will sup with him, and he with me."

Lily turned until she was lying flat on her stomach, her arms stretched out and her tears wetting the crushed grass. Would Christ really come and dwell inside her as he promised? Could his Spirit really fill the emptiness?

Oh, Lily knew she needed more than filling, though. She needed guidance so she could keep from making such foolish mistakes. She needed direction. She needed a clear path.

"I am the light of the world: he that followeth me shall not walk in darkness, but shall have the light of life."

Unable to move, Lily sobbed out. "God, be my water and my bread. Be my light. Be my friend."

"Ye are my friends, if ye do whatsoever I command you."

But what did God command her to do? She had spent so much time in his presence, yet she had never truly understood him. For many years, she had been able to do nothing but cling to the hope of God's protection from her father. Now she understood that difficulties would come her way. Elijah had explained that God never promised to protect her from all evil — instead, God had vowed to stand beside her and hold her in his loving arms. She could confidently place her trust in his constant presence, light, nourishment, and guidance. But what did he want of her in return?

"Believe on the Lord Jesus Christ, and thou shalt be saved."

Lily let out a deep breath. Believe. Surrender. Give up the anger, the bitterness, the confusion, the doubt. Stop being a child, and become a woman with the courage to place her life in the hands of a living Savior.

"Yes, Lord," she murmured. "I confess my failure. I believe. I surrender. I give you my soul."

For a long time she lay in silence, reveling in the sweet calm that slowly crept through her. Katydids buzzed in the trees overhead. The scent of fresh earth and sun-warmed grass bathed the air. Not far away, the Bluestem Creek gurgled its way toward the Kansas River. When she finally felt fully at peace, she curled up onto her knees. Around her, the darkness of the Kansas night wrapped her in a warm cocoon. It hadn't been hard at all. Just a few words and a release of what she had been trying to carry on her own.

Now she would never walk alone again. Feeling the weight of the little hymnal in her pocket, Lily reached for the book. It was too dark to see, but still she opened it, fingering pages filled with words she knew so well. How odd that she had been brought up to know Christ, and yet she had never given herself to him — until now. She began to sing softly.

"My faith looks up to Thee,
Thou Lamb of Calvary,
Savior divine!
Now hear me while I pray,
Take all my guilt away,
O let me from this day
Be wholly thine!

"While life's dark maze I tread,
And griefs around me spread,
Be Thou my guide;

Bid darkness turn to day,
Wipe sorrow's tears away,
Nor let me ever stray
From Thee aside."

"I don't think I'm cut out for the pastor's job." Elijah sat beside Ben Hanks on a bench near the Bluestem. Despite heavy storm clouds hanging on the horizon, the Independence Day fish fry had gone off without a hitch. Many in the community had come down to the water's edge to eat and have fellowship. Though Eli had been asked to join a game of horseshoes, he didn't have the heart for it.

"I wouldn't agree with that," Ben said. "Folks are still talkin' about the way you sat up with the Rippetos and their sick baby. I think everybody's glad you came to Hope."

"I should have gone to China."

"I bet you don't even know where China is, Brother Elijah."

"I sure do. It's over there on the other side of the world."

Ben took a bite of batter-fried bass and chewed in silence. Finally he shook his head. "What do you want to go all the way over there for anyhow, Preacher?"

"The Chinese people need to know about Christ."

Ben considered this. "I reckon they do.

Somebody ought to go tell 'em the Good News. But what makes you think that 'somebody' is you? There's plenty of folks right here in Hope who don't know the gospel either. And we need you to help us guide our town in the right direction. There's a rumor afoot about that opera house they're puttin' up down the way. Somebody heard those folks are plannin' to bring in whisky."

Elijah plucked a stem of grass and stuck it in his mouth. *That's not all they're bringing in,* he thought. Every time he considered the prospect of a brothel at the edge of town, his gut churned. Half the time he caught himself cooking up ways to demolish the infernal den of iniquity. The other half of the time, he was preaching imaginary sermons that would drop Beatrice and the rest of those wild-living sinners to their knees in repentance before almighty God.

And he knew he couldn't do either. If he preached against the opera house too strongly, he might incite the townsfolk to do something ill advised — like burning it down. That would be just as great a sin as the wickedness taking place inside the building.

In fact, this very afternoon he had led the short worship service with a message on the glory of the Lord — and he was disgusted with himself over it. He had spoken not a single brimstone-laden word about brothels or saloons. He hadn't even extended an invitation to confess sin and be saved. It was just a simple talk about the beauty of the nation — words so lukewarm they would never convict anyone.

"Mr. Jack is thinkin' about starting up a Sunday school," Ben said. "He figures the town ought to get the children off to a good beginnin' in life. They can learn the Bible stories and maybe a little readin' and cipherin', too. And Mr. Seth wants to have a fund-raisin' so's we can put a steeple on the church roof. How about that? A real steeple — and maybe a bell. Wouldn't that be dandy?"

Eli nodded. "It'd be nice, all right."

"Miz Rosie said if we can find us a teacher willing to move to town, we could start a regular school inside the church buildin'. And there's folks talkin' of formin' a cemetery committee. Now that you built us such a nice graveyard, Brother Elijah, why, we want to keep it mowed and maybe even plant some flowers."

"There's not anybody buried in it yet, Ben."

"That don't matter."

"What matters is that I'm no good at leading folks to Christ. Not after they get to know me. It's one thing to preach a sermon to a bunch of strangers and then move on. But here in Hope, people can see I'm just a regular fellow. I don't have much book learning, and I'm not trained to preach. I'm just an old cowhand, Ben."

"Nobody expects you to be God."

Eli considered that for a moment. It was true that he himself could not save a single soul. That was God's business — and in Bible times, God had used some of the most low-down, ornery fellows to do his mighty work. But look at what a mess Eli had made of his talk with Lily Nolan the other night. He cared about that woman so much, but he had only blurted a bunch of outright nonsense and then stormed away. If he couldn't lead Lily to the Lord, who could he lead?

"Take Miz Lily," Ben said. "Now there's one fine lady. I reckon she knows you about as well as anybody does, Brother Elijah, and she don't seem to mind you a bit. She's been comin' to the church services real regular, and of late, she's always singin' hymns out of that little book of yours. You made a difference in her life. Look at her over there right now showin' off that baby to all the womenfolk. Anybody would think Sam was her own young'un. Why don't you make things right with the woman and marry her?"

Eli studied Lily as she stood at the water's edge. Her laughter, musical and light, drifted up the bank. She had pulled her hair into a loose bun at her crown, and it gleamed like a golden halo. Since that night on the road, he had managed to avoid her, but just the sight of her now made his insides hurt.

"I'm not going to marry Lily Nolan," he told Ben. "And I wish you and everybody else would stay out of my business."

Ben fingered a transparent fish bone out of his mouth and tossed it to the ground. A flicker of lightning in the distance led quickly to a low growl of thunder. "Gonna rain," Ben said. "Sure am glad my mama's in Topeka with my big brother. She'd have hung the washin' on the line and took it down again fifty times today already. Mercy, I miss that God-fearin' old woman."

"I'm sorry I was sharp with you," Eli said. "You're not the first who has told me what to do with my life."

"It's all right. I know you're in a pickle. You think God's tellin' you to go to China, when it's clear as daylight to everybody else that he brung you to Hope to do his work right here. And I know you're fit to be tied over Miz Lily. I don't understand what's keepin' the two of you apart when we can all see you belong together."

"She's not a Christian, Ben," Eli said. "I can't marry a woman who doesn't serve my God. I won't do it."

Ben set his tin plate on the ground and nodded in understanding. "I reckon that explains it then. Miz Lily come home late the other night after Mr. Jack's weddin', and she told Eva she'd been out talkin' to you on the road. Did you say somethin' to her?"

"I made it clear we couldn't be anything but friends, that's all."

"She must have took it pretty good, because you ought to see her the past couple of days. She's a new woman, Brother Elijah. It's like a load come right off her back. She's been chipper as a jaybird — singin' and talkin' and scurryin' around till Eva can hardly keep up with her. Maybe you tellin' her where things stood eased her mind so she could get to feelin' better. Look at her right now, climbin' up onto the table to sing. Don't she look a sight?"

Eli groaned. He had asked Lily to perform from the hymnal, but he hadn't really had much hope she would do it. Now how was he going to sit through this? He couldn't, that was all. He just couldn't do it. Grabbing his Bible, he jumped to his feet and headed for the church. With the storm blowing up, he needed to make sure the shutters were latched and that he'd put away the tools for painting the cemetery fence.

As he stepped inside the stuffy building, he could hear Lily's voice lifted in song. She had chosen one of his favorite hymns, "My Faith Looks Up to Thee." Elijah's own mama had sung it to him while he sat on her lap, and he could almost feel her warm arms around him. Almost, but not quite.

Eli quickly fastened the shutters and tried not to think about how lonely he felt all of a sudden. He'd never been lonely on the range. All he'd had out there was a bunch of cowboys and some cattle, but they'd been company enough. Here in the middle of a busy town with people coming and going all around him, he felt a sharp sense of longing.

He'd go find Samuel. That's what he'd do. With Lily spending most of the time with the baby each day, Eli had been free to work on the church and tend to the needs of his flock. But he'd hardly seen the boy except at night, and now the notion of cuddling the little fellow seemed like the best plan he'd thought up in days.

He set the paint bucket and brush inside his back door, and then he walked down to the creek again. Lily was still singing, but Eli walked around the edge of the gathering and found the woven basket in which his son lay.

The moment the child laid eyes on him, Sam's small round face lit up with a toothless grin.

"Hey, Sammy," Eli said, kneeling by the basket. "How are you doing there, little Nubbin?"

Slipping his hands under the baby, he savored the warm, living weight. Sam had grown. He was thriving. If God saw fit, this little boy would one day become a man. Eli settled Sam on his shoulder, patted his small, curved back, and stroked his fingers along the baby's dark hair. It was going to be up to the father to see that the son turned out well.

"You want to take a walk, Sammy?" Eli asked, rising. "Let's go down to the edge of the creek and see if we can find any crawdads. We might even catch us a frog or two. You ever seen a tadpole?"

Suddenly the baby gave a huge leap in Eli's arms. Surprised, the preacher nearly lost his grip. As he struggled to settle Sam, he realized who had caused the child's reaction.

"Tadpoles?" Lily said, stepping up to join them. "Surely you're not going to introduce this sweet, innocent child to tadpoles and crawdads."

Eli breathed up a quick prayer for help. If God had sent down fire from heaven and parted the Red Sea, surely he could perform another miracle now. Eli needed one. Badly.

"I expected you to talk about the opera house in your sermon," Lily said as they made their way to the creek. "I was surprised you didn't mention it."

"This didn't seem like the time or place," he managed.

"Are you resigned to it then?"

He felt the steam rise up his spine and his heart rate increase at the mere mention of the opera house. "You might as well know, I *will* preach out against that place — and soon. I realize the folks running it are your friends, Lily, but drunkenness and adultery are sins. The Bible makes that real clear."

"I know it does," she said softly.

"I won't stand by and watch this little town catch sin like a killing case of influenza. I've been in Hope long enough to see these people struggling against enough kinds of sin — greed, jealousy, covetousness, lies, and faithlessness. Why should I stand around and watch that opera house import a whole new form of evil?"

"You shouldn't."

"I'm the minister of the church," he continued, "and it's up to me to set an example. Either that or I'd better ride off to China and let the whole town burn down like Sodom and Gomorrah."

"I'd hate to see that."

Elijah knew he was walking faster now, but he couldn't make himself slow down. With Lily Nolan, he had always been able to speak his mind. Somehow the woman drew his thoughts right out of his head. If he was planning to denounce her friends and their place of business, well, she had the right to know. Besides, it felt good to talk.

"Seems to me there were two kinds of fellows in the Bible," he said. "Pastors and prophets. Prophets didn't tend flocks; they hollered out for God to send down justice. They called folks to repentance. They showed people their sins. I reckon I'm supposed to be a prophet. In my sermon today, I stayed away from what was really on my heart, and I feel sick about it. So even though you're going over to that opera house to find work, Lily, I'll be preaching out against you every Sunday."

"No, I'm not," she murmured.

"See, I never have been much good at pastoring," he went on. "I get too het up. I have to preach the Word of God, and that means calling folks to look at their lives and make a change." By now they were halfway to the grove of trees where he'd spoken with Lily the other night. Just the memory of his failure there made him sick inside. "I think I'm supposed to be a prophet, not a pastor, and that means —"

"You're supposed to be like Christ, Preacher-man," Lily said.

Eli stopped and looked at her. For the first time, her voice remained gentle when she accosted him. Standing in the road, she gave him a warm smile and lifted her eyebrows.

"Isn't that right?" she said. "Prophets and priests were God's messengers *before* Christ came. After that, our job has been to emulate him."

"Emulate?"

"Copy. And Christ is both prophet and priest, isn't he? What's wrong with shepherding a flock — and pouring God's Word out to the sheep at the same time? Can't you do both?"

"Are you mocking me?" He shifted the baby to his other shoulder, uncomfortable and more than a little confused at her words. "Go ahead and throw Bible verses and religious talk at me like you usually do. I don't mind, Lily. I realize you know the Scriptures better than I do, and you've been to church a lot more years than I ever have. But it doesn't matter. Ever since our talk the other night, I've been doing nothing but thinking and praying. And I've come to see that the only thing I can do is to walk in Christ's footsteps.

That's all. Just follow him. So even if you make fun of me or I mess up a sermon or I give someone lousy advice, nothing matters but that I keep on following Christ the best I can."

By this time, they had come to the shelter of the trees beside the creek. Elijah realized he was patting the baby with such vigor that poor Sam had gotten himself a bad case of hiccups. Every time he "hicked," his whole body wriggled, and every time he "upped," out came a gurgle of white milk onto the shoulder of Eli's black jacket.

"Aw, confound it, Sam," he said, balancing the baby in one arm while he searched his pockets for his handkerchief. "Don't you know I borrowed this coat from Jack Cornwall? It's his wedding jacket, and now it's a mess, sure as shootin'. He's liable to hog-tie and skin me, young'un. Where in tarnation is that handkerchief? Lily, would you . . ." He looked up to find the woman convulsed in giggles, her laughter poorly hidden behind her hand. "What's so funny?"

"Here, give me that baby, would you?" She held out her arms, and Sam eagerly went to her. "It's you, silly. You're so hopeless with babies."

"I am not." He began wiping the wet spot on his shoulder. "What have you been feeding that boy anyhow? The smell is enough to gag a polecat. What am I supposed to tell Jack Cornwall? And would you quit that infernal cackling?"

Lily leaned against a tree and laughed as though she'd never seen anything so funny. He took off the coat and hung it on a tree branch. There. Maybe it would rain soon.

Looking out across the prairie, Eli felt his heart contract at the sight of the sickening green color of the sky. Though rain hadn't begun to fall, the air felt as heavy as a damp dishrag. Lightning licked the horizon like a snake's tongue. Purple and blue mingled with the pea-soup green, a livid bruising of the heavens.

This was going to be worse than a heavy rain, Eli realized. There could be hail. Hail would mean crop damage right in the middle of summer. If the crops were ruined, there'd be no time for replanting before the onset of autumn. The farmers had barely made it through the past winter after last year's grasshopper plague. He ought to get back to the people. Back to his flock . . .

"We've got to go, Lily," he said. "The sky's looking bad."

Sobering, she turned to look in the direction of the oncoming storm. "Oh, Elijah." She took a step toward him. "The sky is green. I've never seen anything like that."

"We'd better find shelter before the hail hits." He let out a breath. "You know, even though you were challenging me again, Lily, you were right. I've got to follow Christ's example — and that means I'll be both a prophet and a priest."

"Elijah," she said, her hand on his arm to stop him. "Before we go, I need to talk to you. I want you to know I wasn't mocking you earlier. I was trying to help you see how important you are to the town. The people need you. Truly they do — and they need you for the man you *are*, not some imaginary ideal of the perfect pastor."

A sudden gust of wind ripped Eli's hat from his head and sent it rolling down the road. He started after it, but Lily tightened her grip on his arm. "Elijah," she went on, "I want you to know what happened to me the other night. I've been waiting for the right time to speak. I want to tell you about my decision."

Eli watched his Stetson tumbling farther across the prairie, and he wanted to go after it. Not because he needed his hat, but because he didn't want to hear Lily's words. She would tell him about her plans to join her friend at the opera house, and that would tear her away from him completely.

The way things were going right now, at

least he could be near her sometimes. He could talk to her. He could listen to her beautiful voice. He could pretend he would be able to hold onto her forever, even though he knew she never would be truly his.

"I'd better get my hat," he said. "We'll talk after the storm passes, Lily. I'll walk over to Ben's, and you and I can sit on the porch."

Disappointment clouded her eyes. "But I'd rather —"

A shrill screaming wind cut off her words. On the horizon a huge black funnel dropped suddenly out of the boiling green clouds. Tearing through trees and fences like a giant plow, the twister churned up dust and kicked sheds out of its path. Haystacks exploded. Brush ripped free from its roots. Birds flew screeching, their wings beating the air in a futile effort to escape.

"Cyclone!" Eli hollered. "Come here, Lily."

Grabbing her arm, he tucked her and the baby against his side and began to run down the road toward the picnic site. He'd seen twisters tear across Texas and New Mexico, and he knew the destruction they could cause. Quicker than a man had time to think, the whirling wind could blast his house to kingdom come, strip the skin off his livestock, and suck his children into the air — never to be seen again. The townsfolk needed to take cover, and Elijah knew the creek bed wasn't deep enough to protect everyone.

"Where are we going?" Lily cried as she struggled to keep up with him. "What will we do?"

"We've got to get everyone into the empty soddy. It's half underground."

As he and Lily reached the site of the fish fry, the crowd had just noticed the black funnel bearing down. Over screams and barking dogs, Elijah bellowed for everyone to run up the slope and take cover in the soddy. Rushing Lily and the baby toward the little house that had once belonged to Seth Hunter, he could hardly believe the chaos. Some people were actually trying to pack up their belongings. Others had elected to race toward the grove of trees. Mr. Rippeto was even hitching his mule to his wagon in hopes of outrunning the cyclone.

"Salvatore!" Eli called to the man. "Run for the soddy!"

By now, stinging hailstones peppered the bare skin of Eli's face. Sam was crying and Lily could barely move against the howling wind. Her long dress tangled around her legs, and her hair streamed back from her face. The cyclone was headed straight for Hope, Eli calculated, and there was not much hope it would avoid the town. His heart sick, fear an acrid taste on his tongue, he swept Lily into his arms and ran the last few paces toward the soddy.

The old door had blown off its hinges, but townspeople were crushed together in a huddled mass on the floor. Children sobbed as husbands called out to their wives, making certain of their presence in the room. Eli worked his way through the throng to the back of the soddy, and he shoved Lily onto the dirt floor beside Caitrin Cornwall and Rosie Hunter. Chipper gripped his dog around the neck. Rolf Rustemeyer hollered at everyone in German. Sheena O'Toole shouted her children's names. Jack's sister, Lucy, began to shriek.

Just as Salvatore Rippeto burst into the soddy and was yanked to the floor by groping hands, the cyclone churned across the sod roof of the little dugout. The sound of ten train locomotives deafened Eli's ears. Praying for protection, he surrounded Lily and Sam with his arms.

Oh, God, dear God, he pleaded as the wire screens ripped off the soddy's windows and the black of night descended. He could feel hands gripping him from every side, as though the whole town was clinging together in one lump of trembling humanity. *Save us, Father! Please save us!*

But God hadn't protected Lily from her

own father, Eli remembered as he held the woman close. His Lord didn't promise shelter from all evil. The buildings would be flattened. The crops ruined. The town devastated. *God, please don't destroy Hope. Please save your people!*

A chair flew out through the open door and vanished into the darkness. A mother clung to her child as the wind lifted the toddler up, pulling, sucking, greedy for ruin. At that moment, a heavy iron plow drove straight through the soddy's front wall, splintering wood, grinding up sod bricks, slamming into the gathered people. Screams mingled with cries for help.

It was no good, Elijah thought as he left Lily's side and crawled toward the injured. The twister had them in its grip. In moments it would devour the whole town. The soddy couldn't hold up under the pressure. It was bound to explode or collapse, and then —

"My faith looks up to thee —"

A beautiful voice lifted over the screams of babies, above the sobs of the wounded, even beyond the growl of the tornado.

"Thou Lamb of Calvary,
Savior divine!"

Amid the storm, other voices one by one joined with Lily's.

> "Now hear me while I pray,
> Take all my guilt away,
> O let me from this day
> Be wholly thine!"

CHAPTER 13

Lily sang, rocking the baby in her arms as howling winds wrapped around the soddy.

> "Bid darkness turn to day,
> Wipe sorrow's tears away,
> Nor let me ever stray
> From Thee aside."

The others in the room had joined in, and as Lily began the fourth verse of the hymn, the roaring, growling tornado suddenly faded into nothing more than shutter-banging gusts. And finally, the tumult transformed into utter silence, eerie in its intensity. The sheer terror gradually ebbed from Lily's body, leaving her trembling and chilled. Next to her, Rosie wept in her husband's arms.

"The cyclone got our house," she cried in an anguished whisper, "I just know it did. All your hard work . . . the new front porch . . . Chipper's toys . . . the baby's room . . ."

"Hey there, sweetheart," her husband said. "We're all alive, aren't we? Even ol' Stubby."

Nearby, the big mutt thumped his tail and

gave a whimper. The little boy lying against him patted the dog's massive head. "It's OK, Stubby. God brought us through, an' now we're all gonna be fine."

"Sure we'll rebuild the mercantile, won't we, Jack?" Caitrin Cornwall asked her new husband, her usually hearty voice carrying a note of uncertainty. "We'll be back in business before the month is out, so we shall. At least, I hope so."

"Caitrin, I'm worried about Lucy," Jack said. Lily knew the man was referring to his sister's fragile mental condition. "She's holding onto Mama for dear life."

"She'll be all right. We'll put Lucy to work cooking for everyone, shall we then?"

"Oh, Caitie, must you always be so cheerful?" her older sister, Sheena, groused. "Next thing we know, you'll be callin' the cyclone naught more than a stiff breeze."

At that, the crowd hunched together in the little soddy began to chuckle and relax. Outlined in the open doorway, Elijah got to his feet and addressed the people.

"Folks, I'd better tell you there's a couple of us injured up here." At the reaction of concern, he motioned for calm. "Salvatore Rippeto was clobbered by the plow that came through the wall. I think his leg is broken, and we may need to get him to Topeka. And one of Violet

Hudson's little boys fell and skinned his knee pretty bad running up here. Other than that, the main thing we need to find out is how many of us made it into the soddy. Before we head outside, we ought to know who we're looking for."

Lily could see dull, gray rain streaming down in a torrent, veiling the destruction left in the wake of the black funnel. Never in her life had she imagined anything so powerful, so all-consuming, so relentless. Never had she felt as small and helpless as she had racing up the hill toward the soddy. Even when her father had been bearing down on her, she had sensed that she would survive the pain. But the cyclone had been a thousand times more frightening than her father, for in its fury, the storm held the potential for death.

Lily had felt terrified, unprotected, panic-stricken. Yet she had not felt alone. Through the growling wind and the grinding dirt, she had sensed a calm fullness within. Not once had she thought to crawl into the secret place inside herself — the place where golden music had blocked the pain of her father's abuses. Instead, in the very midst of the cyclone, a song had erupted from her heart, music both strong and serene. She had known the overwhelming presence of God's Spirit within, for as he promised, Christ had not left her comfortless.

Hugging Sam, she hummed to the baby as Elijah, Seth, and Jack checked on and counted the families crowded into the soddy. Some of the groups elected to brave the rain the moment they were all accounted for — eager to race home and inspect the damage. Others chose to huddle in the security of the thick sod walls until the storm had subsided.

"Are you and Sam all right, Lily?" Elijah asked her as he finally worked his way in the darkness to the back of the room. "I didn't intend to leave you alone, but when that plow —"

"I'm not alone," Lily said.

"I guess not. I never knew so many folks could cram into one house. I reckon we must have looked like a can of oysters all bunched up together. I'm glad nobody got hurt worse."

"Is anyone missing?"

"A couple of the young single farmers took off for the trees near the creek. I sure hope they found some low ground. I'll tell you what; I've seen whirlwinds racing across the desert, tossing around tumbleweeds and darkening the sky, but I've never known anything like that twister."

Lily gathered the baby closer as Elijah sat down beside her. "Thank you for seeing me to safety," she said. "I was frightened."

"Who wasn't? I'll bet that cyclone tore up the whole town." He slipped his arm around her shoulders. "God just barely gave us enough time to get to safety. You sure you're OK?"

"I'm fine." Enjoying the warm comfort of the man's embrace, she leaned her head against his shoulder. "I'm worried about the church."

"It'll be standing. I have no doubt God saw to that. He wants his folks to have a place to worship — especially after something as terrible as that twister. I sure hope the Hunter place is still up. Seth just put on a new front porch, you know, and they've got the baby coming this fall. They need to have things all ready by that time, but this could set them back. Jack Cornwall's smithy is made of sod, so it ought to be all right. But his house and the Hanks place might have gone. I wonder about the opera house."

He fell silent momentarily. Lily stroked Sam's cheek, praying the child would relax enough to sleep. If most of the houses in town had been destroyed, she and the others would be forced to take shelter in the soddy until morning. There wasn't even enough room for everyone to lie down. How had Beatrice, George Gibbons, and their workmen fared in the storm? What if they lay injured even now?

"I'll bet that place is flatter than a hotcake," Elijah said. "A pile of toothpicks."

"Oh, Elijah, that would be terrible."

"Would it? Don't you know the Lord works out his will in this world? If he wanted to get rid of that opera house as badly as I did, he probably smashed it to smithereens."

"But what about the people? What about Bea and the others? You sound as though you'd be glad to find them dead."

Elijah stiffened at her accusation. "I don't want anybody to die, Lily. But I wouldn't object to seeing those folks pull up stakes and head back to Topeka."

Lily busied herself tucking Sam's blanket around him. She had turned from her past and asked Christ to be Lord of her life, but that didn't mean she had stopped caring about Beatrice and the others. Though she had no desire to join them in their business, she would never wish evil upon them either.

"I'm sorry, Lily," Elijah murmured. "What I said just then wasn't really about your friends. It wasn't even about the opera house."

"Well, what was it about then?"

"It was about . . . about not wanting to let you go. I don't want you to leave town, Lily. I don't want you to leave Sam." He was silent for a moment. "I don't want you to leave me."

Lily closed her eyes, soaking up the sound of words she had longed to hear. Could it be possible that now, after all her mistakes and all her pain, she had found a man with whom she could build a future? Would God really allow Elijah to care for her? Did hope for true love really exist for someone like her?

"I know you're angry with me," Elijah said, "and I don't blame you. First I tell you I'm going to do one thing, and then I do the exact opposite. One time I'm walking away from you, and the next time I'm holding and kissing you. Lily, I wish I could explain to you how mixed-up I've been feeling."

"Why don't you try?" Though the darkness around them was alive with people, the pouring rain drowned out all but the sound of his low voice. "Because if you could only tell me how you really feel —"

"I feel two ways." His fingers on her shoulder tightened as he struggled to express himself. "On the one hand, I think you're . . . well, you're a good woman."

"Good?"

"Kind and sweet, you know."

"You're talking about the way I take care of Sam."

"And how you are with Ben and Eva Hanks. They love having you at their house.

Everybody in town really likes you a lot."

"Do you like me, Elijah?"

"Sure I do."

As Eli fell silent, Lily could almost feel the man breaking into a sweat. Why was this so hard for him? What held him away from her? She felt sure it must be her past — her marriage to Ted, her life with the traveling show, her friendship with Beatrice, even the fact that she'd given birth already. How many times had her father told her to stay pure? "Men don't want used goods," he had shouted across the parlor during her first and only courtship.

But she wasn't pure. Not unless Elijah was willing to accept the cleansing she had received from the Lord. *"Though your sins be as scarlet, they shall be as white as snow."* Lily felt sure God viewed her now as whole and pure again. But would Elijah?

"I care about you, Lily," he said finally. "And not just the way a shepherd cares for the sheep."

A smile tilted one corner of her mouth. "I'm glad you're beginning to see yourself as a pastor."

"But not with you. With you, I'm . . . well, I'm flat-out confused." He leaned his head back against the sod wall. "See, I'm a preacher. And that means God has some special work for me to do."

"God has special work for each of us."

"Sure, but I've got to be an example, you know. I can't be a stumbling block to folks. I'm supposed to lead them on the right path."

"And I'm a stumbling block to you?"

"Phew." He shook his head. "You just say whatever you're thinking, don't you?"

"More or less. You said you felt two ways about me. On the one hand, you like me. At least, you like the way I take care of Sam, and you appreciate the fact that I've helped Ben and Eva. Let me guess the other. You see my past life as though it still exists. I'm still that woman who came in with the traveling show, that fortune-teller, that drifter. Am I right?"

"The thing is, Lily, that God might want to send me to China. And if I let myself care about you . . . more than as Sam's helper . . . I'd pretty soon be wanting to cart you off to China."

Lily stroked the sleeping baby's head. Though she was sure she knew why Elijah refused to accept his growing feelings for her, she intended to make him speak plainly. He was hedging. Evading the truth. He didn't want to tell her she was "used goods" and not pure enough for him. If she was to be rejected, she would have the reasons clearly stated.

"You're not worried about whether I'd want to go to China, Elijah," she said. "You know good and well that if God wanted to send me to China, I'd be able and ready to go. And I *would* go to China, because I'd know I was supposed to be there. You're the one who told me we're never alone. Christ's Spirit is always with us — in China or in Kansas. Whether you want to hear it or not, I have the strength to go anywhere and do anything so long as I'm walking the right path and following the light of my salvation. It's true I've made mistakes. I married for the wrong reasons. I ran from my fears. I fell in with tricksters. But you said a life can be changed, made brand-new, made pure again. Because of my faith, I am healed, Elijah."

"What?" His voice was low and filled with disbelief. "What are you telling me, Lily?"

"I'm saying that it's *you* who's veering off the straight and narrow." She set Samuel in his arms, fighting the urge to run out of the stuffy little soddy and breathe freely. "Take your son, Preacher-man. You were so sure God gave him to you. Without doubting the Lord's plan for a moment, you just picked that baby right up out of his dead mother's arms and went on your way. But you've been too blind to see what else God gave you. You don't even know what's right in front of your nose. It's *Hope,* Elijah. The Lord sent you here."

"Well, I —"

"God puts people in places because he has work to do there," she went on, determined to force the man to face the truth. "These townsfolk were hungry for the Word of Christ. They had even gone so far as to build a church. God was already at work in Hope, don't you see? He led you here to be his instrument. It's not just Sam who needs you, Elijah. It's the Hunters, the O'Tooles, the Cornwalls, the Rippetos. It's me. I need you. God brought us together — and it wasn't just so I could feed Sam. It's because he has a plan. Can't you understand that? He has a plan! Now are you just going to veer off the path and live with one foot on the road to China, or are you going to start looking forward into the light of your own salvation and following God's plan for you in Hope?"

Finished, depleted, even angry, Lily pushed to her feet. "I'm going to see what's left of the town," she said. "I'm too tired to talk anymore."

She started off through the huddled figures, most of them now dozing. As she stepped over Stubby, Elijah jerked on the hem of her skirt.

"Hold on there, woman," he said, coming to his feet behind her. "Just one cotton-picking minute."

Wobbling backward, she braced her hand

against the soddy wall.

"I'm going to look for Ben and Eva."

"It's the middle of the night. There'll be critters out. You won't be able to see a thing."

"Would you two be quiet?" someone whispered loudly. "We're trying to get some shut-eye here."

Lily folded her arms and stood as rigid as a fence post in the inky blackness. It was true that she couldn't see. She didn't know which way to turn, which path to take. But she wasn't alone.

Lord, be near me, she prayed silently. Letting out a breath, she sat down on the floor again. *This infuriating, stubborn man is your servant. He knows you and he loves you, but for some reason he won't listen to you. He won't see what you're trying to show him. Speak to Elijah, Father. Please speak to him.*

"Lily," Elijah whispered in the darkness. "Are you there?"

"I'm here," she said. "I'm going to sleep now. Don't bother me."

"Did you say the *Lord* sent me here to Hope?"

"Yes. Be quiet."

He obeyed, but only for a moment. "Did you say *God* brought us together?"

"Shh."

"Did you say you're healed?"

Lily tucked up her knees and rested her head on them. *OK, Lord, he heard that much at least. Thank you.*

"It happened that night under the cotton-wood tree by the road," she said softly. "After you left, I realized what I'd been running from, and I . . . I stopped running."

"Hallelujah!" he shouted suddenly into the silent soddy. "Hallelujah! Thank you, God!"

"Hush, Brother Elijah," someone muttered. "Folks is tryin' to rest."

"Hallelujah!" he said again. He was back on his feet. Lily could just make out his shape as he swung the baby around in a circle. "You hear that, Sam? She did it! She really did it! Hallelujah!"

"What?" the voice grumbled. "What'd she do?"

"Yes!" Elijah cried. "Yes, yes, yes!"

"Preacher, much as we love you," another voice called, "we's gonna have to shove you out on your backside if you won't be quiet."

"Come here, woman!" Elijah said, reaching down into the darkness and grabbing Lily's arm. "I'm free now! Don't you see? You're free! He set us free! I didn't have to do it myself. God did it! We're free."

His arm came around her and pulled her close. Lily felt half sure the poor man had suddenly gone mad. At the same time, his jubilation thrilled her as he hugged her tight. This was how she had been feeling ever since that night under the cottonwood tree. She was free! Free and filled with peace and hope and love. Laughing in spite of herself, she allowed Elijah to move her through the room.

"Sorry!" she called softly as she tripped over someone's foot. "Oh, excuse me! Elijah, not so fast! Slow down."

"Glory to God!" he shouted as they finally burst out of the soddy into the damp night. The rain had stopped falling, but the ground was soaked and littered with debris from the tornado. "Yes, Lily, yes!"

The baby in one arm, he pulled her against his chest. Reeling from the sudden outburst, she slipped her arms around the man and held him close.

"Elijah," she said as Sam caught a clump of her hair in his tiny fingers. "Elijah, what does this mean?"

"Oh, Lily, it means everything." He was breathing hard, his voice ragged with emotion. "You're right; I haven't been looking at the path right in front of my feet. I haven't been trusting God with my life. I've been trying to figure it all out myself, trying to get what I thought I wanted instead of letting God take care of me. But I can see it now — I know why I'm here, what I'm supposed to do. I can see everything. It's all going to work out fine."

"Brother Elijah, that is you there?" Rolf Rustemeyer, lantern in hand, came running through the darkness toward the soddy. "You must hurry. Come quickly!"

"What's wrong?"

"Is the church!" The big German came to a stop, his boots caked in mud. "Is the church!"

"What about the church?"

"Cyclone caused much troubles. Barn of Seth Hunter is blown away. All windows in mercantile broken. Part of Cornwalls' roof is torn off. O'Toole house is missing front porch. But only building completely gone is church."

"The church?"

"No church left. No fence. No cemetery. No benches. All is gone."

Lily covered her mouth with her hand as Elijah let out a cry of disbelief. Taking the baby from him, she stood in a chilly puddle as Rolf handed the preacher his lantern and the two men raced down the street toward the scene of the disaster.

No church!

Lily lifted her head toward heaven as a scrap of doubt fluttered into her heart. "There's no church," she whispered. "I thought you had a plan for him here. He said you wouldn't take it. But you did. You took the church."

As Sam began to whimper, Lily made her way back to the soddy.

Elijah stared at the gaping hole in the ground where Hope Church had stood. Dawn bathed the prairie in a gentle pink glow that softened the edges of the tornado's destruction. Around him, lumber lay scattered on the ground like windblown hay. Shingles hung from tree branches and floated at the edge of Bluestem Creek.

A wagon rested upside down on the roof of the O'Tooles' house, while a length of wet canvas now covered the place where their porch had stood. The Hunters' barn had been lifted, carried to the plot of land behind the mercantile, and dropped with such force that it had flattened like a stomped-on tin can. Caitrin Cornwall's shining plate-glass windows lay on the ground in a thousand knife-sharp shards.

Rolf Rustemeyer's cow had been discovered an hour ago chewing her cud in Ben Hanks's backyard. Three of Rosie Hunter's chickens had landed in Sheena O'Toole's oak tree, barely alive and with only a handful of feathers among them. Jack Cornwall's hog had slid into the creek and drowned. A pair of mongrel dogs no one had ever seen before were found eating sausage in Jimmy's smokehouse.

But not a single person had perished in the storm. Salvatore Rippeto was the only man seriously injured. A couple of young farmers sported bumps and bruises. Will O'Toole had stepped into a hole and twisted his ankle.

And the church was gone.

Elijah swallowed hard as he counted the postholes he had dug with such vigor. Not one of them contained a fence post. Of the hundred rails he had split, not a one lay in sight. His vegetable garden had been stripped bare. Half of a ceramic chamber pot lay where the corner of the cemetery had once stood.

As if in mockery of his fervor to beautify and strengthen the place, the only portion of the church still intact was the door frame to his little room — the cans of white paint and the wide brushes still neatly stored in readiness for the next project he would undertake. He walked over and kicked them skyward. There.

"Elijah?" Lily's voice showered warm rain through him.

He swung around, emotion hanging in his throat like a lump of dry bread. "It's gone, Lily," he said. "The whole thing is gone."

She looked at the ragged, water-filled cavern in the ground, the scattered boards, the empty postholes. Without speaking another word, she walked to him and wrapped her arms around him, holding him close. Elijah rested his head against hers and let the loss wrack through his chest.

"I don't understand it," he said. "We didn't do anything to deserve this. We were trying our hardest to please the Lord. Why did he take the church, Lily?"

She stroked her hand down his back. "You're the man who taught me that bad things can happen to people who don't deserve them. God doesn't protect us from all evil, Elijah."

"But this was his church."

"It was a building."

"It was my work."

"His church is the people of Hope. Your work is the people of Hope. And Christ is right here with us now. He's with us always, remember? Have you lost your faith?"

He gripped her tightly. "Oh, Lily."

"Come on," she said softly. "Eva's watching the baby for me. Let's start cleaning up."

He couldn't let go of her, agony washing over him as the tormented confusion in his mind tumbled forward. Maybe this destruction was a sign for him to leave. Maybe God didn't want him to stay in Hope after all. Lily insisted that the Lord had led him to this town, but hadn't that same Lord just swept away the church building?

Should Elijah gather up the baby and head east? Or should he stay here and rebuild? Did God really have a plan as Lily claimed?

"I don't know," he said. "I've been wandering around here for hours, and I just can't make myself think straight. After the storm, after you told me about your new life, I was so sure I understood what God wanted me to do, Lily. Now I wonder if I was wrong."

"Christ calmed storms and walked on water. Do you think he would allow a single cyclone to change his almighty plan for your life?"

He studied the gentle woman, painfully aware of the trust and hope shining in her blue eyes. She had pulled back her hair into a lump of gold, rolled up her sleeves, and washed her face. Her cheeks glowed pink, her chin tilted upward in confidence, her lips curved into a soft smile.

"We're never alone," she told him. "Not in the midst of the cyclone. And not now. Don't you trust that, Preacher-man?"

He let out a breath. Had the storm blown his faith in God away along with the church building? Was he really that shallow rooted?

No, he lifted up. *Father, I believe you're here*

with me. And I'm going to look into the light of my salvation and step forward on the path you've stretched out in front of me. Amen and amen.

"Well?" she asked, hands on her hips.

"I believe those boards over there belong to Seth Hunter's barn," he said. "Mrs. Hunter told me that's her favorite shade of red."

Lily turned and observed the tangle of painted lumber, long square-headed nails protruding like porcupine quills. "You might be right. If they're his, Seth will be wanting them back. But I'm sure I saw part of your split-rail fence hanging on Eva's clothesline."

"We'd better go fetch it. Jack Cornwall already lost one hog. I don't want him to get the idea he can pen in the rest of those critters with the church's fence." He took Lily's hand and headed for the road. "A church cemetery needs a fence."

"And thank the good Lord no one needs the cemetery."

Elijah laughed as he walked beside her across the street to gather up the fence rails. Eva Hanks spotted them coming and stepped out into the yard, the baby in her arms. "Hey, you two!" she called, giving them a wave. "You look happy as foxes in the chicken house — and that's a mighty good sight after all the troubles we been through."

"God is good," Elijah said, feeling his heart

swell with courage even as the words left his mouth.

"All the time," Eva replied. "I'm going to see if Miz Caitrin will write Mother Margaret a letter for us. If we tell her about the cyclone, maybe she'll come home to check on us."

"That's mighty low-down and conniving, Mrs. Hanks," Elijah said as he tugged the fence rails from the clothesline. "But I sure could use a good dose of her common sense and godly faith."

"So could I," Lily agreed. "Mercy and hallelujah."

Eva laughed. "We're going to be all right. I don't believe this baby of yours even knew what hit him. You should have seen him a minute ago when Ben came home to eat a bite of breakfast. I do believe Sam winked at that big ol' man of mine."

"Winked!" Lily chuckled and began picking up the painted white rails from the yard. "You're seeing things now, Eva."

"Maybe so." The other woman gave the baby on her hip a pat. "Ben said he thought he was seein' a ghost last night when he come upon that opera house a-standin' there by the road."

Elijah stopped and straightened. "The opera house?"

"Perfect as a new penny," Eva said, giving

Lily a glance. "That storm didn't touch it. Not even a lick."

Lily picked up a shingle and dropped it among the others in the hammock she had made of her apron. "The Lord works in mysterious ways," she said, setting off for the church site, "his wonders to perform."

CHAPTER 14

In the late afternoon of the third day, when the sun beat down on the scorched earth and cicadas screeched in the denuded trees beside Bluestem Creek, Elijah finally understood why God had let the cyclone take the church.

From every part of the countryside around the devastated town of Hope, people had come, driving wagons filled with lumber, nails, quilts, benches, window glass, cans of paint, and food. Without being asked, they set about repairing barns, nailing shingles to roofs, and putting up new split-rail fences. Although most of the folks who showed up had never set foot in the Hope Church, they began rebuilding the temple of the Lord with the zeal of King Solomon himself.

Elijah had eaten more apple pie in the last three days than a body could rightly hold. He had hammered so many nails that the smithy could barely turn them out fast enough. He had greeted more newcomers than he'd known lived in the area. And he had never seen people work as hard or as long or with such determination.

"Brother Elijah," an old man called out, hurrying toward the preacher on bandy legs. The fellow lived three miles west of Hope, and he'd been laboring on the church building as though it belonged to him alone. "We got a problem here, Preacher. I say we ought to put a baptistry right up at the front where everybody can see what's a-goin' on. You know, we could haul in water and baptize every new believer the way it should be done. But Simeon over there says we don't need nothing more than a bowl of water to do the baptizin'. He thinks we ought to use the space up front to put in a choir. But everybody with half a brain knows the choir sings at the back of the church, not the front."

Elijah regarded Simeon-the-adversary standing beside the rapidly rising walls of the church. The fellow had his jaw set and his eyes narrowed like a feisty old ram ready to butt the stuffing out of whoever stepped in his way. Aware that the pastor was observing him, he stepped forward.

"At the church where I growed up in Ohio," he said, "we sprinkle babies."

"Sprinkle babies?" the other man bellowed. "In Kentucky, where I come from, we dunk full-grown believers."

"And the choir sets in the front."

"In the back!"

"Now just a minute here, fellows," Elijah said, stepping between them. "We'll work this out —"

"Next thing you'll be wanting to drink grape juice at the Communion!" one of them cut in.

"What else?" the other barked. "You don't reckon we'll be servin' wine, do you?"

"All right, gentlemen," Elijah said, holding up his hands. It was time for the shepherd to come between these two old rams. "We'll use the water God has already provided us for baptizing — and that's Bluestem Creek. If a river was good enough for John the Baptist, it'll be good enough for us."

"What about the choir?" Simeon snapped. "Where's it gonna set?"

"We don't have a choir," Elijah returned. "We don't have a song leader. We don't have a piano. And we won't even have a building if we stand around arguing all day. Now let's get back to work, shall we? Brother Simeon, would you mind helping those fellows frame up that wall back there? And you, sir —"

"Hubert."

"Brother Hubert, I couldn't help but notice what a fine job you do planing down shingles. Would you be willing to supervise the roofing of the new church?"

The old man's chest swelled. "Indeedy-do."

As the fellow hobbled away on his bowed legs, Elijah let out a breath. Shepherding a little flock was turning out to be challenging work. If the sheep weren't butting heads over one doctrinal detail or another, they were bleating that someone was sitting in their pew or not giving a fair share of tithe. Then there were the struggling lambs that needed his tender care — the sick, the lonely, the widowed, the fearful. Just as important, all these new sheep had come to town to help with the rebuilding — and Elijah was bound and determined to round up every last one of them and bring them into the Father's fold.

"Elijah?"

"Hello, Lily," he said without even having to look. The woman's touch on his arm and her sweet voice had become so familiar in the last three days. As he turned to her, Lily's blue eyes lit up. How amazing to see the changes God's love had wrought. When she sang hymns, the words flowed from her heart. When she recited Scripture, the verses poured out like honey. She no longer hurled religion at Elijah like accusing stones. Instead, she used her greater store of biblical knowledge to gently help him find the right pathway.

"Lily, just look at all these good folks," he said, wishing he could tuck her under his arm and hug her warmly. "Instead of sending me out to round up the flock, God used the cyclone to drive the sheep right here to us."

"But the wolves have followed, too," she said. "Some of the builders from the opera house are coming down the road. They've been drinking, Elijah. I think they mean trouble."

This was not the first time the Topeka men had wandered through town calling insults to the laborers and casting lewd suggestions at their wives. Seth Hunter had confronted them once, and they had retreated. This morning Jimmy O'Toole had brought his rifle to town.

"Maybe I should go talk to Beatrice," Lily said. "I'm sure this is partly her doing. She's angry that I haven't returned to the opera house, so she encourages these fellows to come to town and bother people."

"I wish you'd stay clear of that woman," Elijah said. "If you go back to her —"

"What's the worst that could happen? I've made my choice."

He studied the way the rays of late sunlight sent sparks of gold into her eyes and gilded her pale skin. Lily knew the Bible back to front. She'd heard a thousand sermons. But she was a baby in Christ. The woman had no idea of the power of sin to grip a struggling believer, tangle his feet, and try to drag him down. It was true — Lily had made her choice. But Elijah knew from his own experience that the chosen were subject to the devil's sneakiest attacks.

"I'll go talk to that fellow from the Crescent Moon myself," he said. "He's a businessman. He'll understand the town's need to stick to the job of rebuilding. Maybe he'll call off his wolves."

"You can't go over there, Elijah. Beatrice views you as her personal enemy, and Mr. Gibbons doesn't think highly of you either. You ran off his saloon customers, he figures, so why shouldn't he run off your congregation? There's nothing the two of them would like better than to keep the church from going up again."

"We haven't done anything to them."

"They're afraid your preaching will turn the town against the opera house." She shook her head. "I learned a few things in my time with the traveling show, Elijah. Places like the opera house depend on a town's support. They'll rely on the mercantile for mail and supplies. They'll use the local farmers to supply their restaurant with fresh vegetables and butter. They'll hire women from town to clean and cook. In order to function, they need Hope."

"Well, Hope doesn't need them." He

tossed down his hammer. "And they're not going to drive me out of town. I'm here to stay."

The lines of worry between Lily's eyes softened. "Is this the same Elijah Book who was on his way to China?"

"I'll go to China if that's where God sends me. But right now he's sent me to Hope. A shepherd protects his flock, Lily. I'm going to talk to George Gibbons."

"Well, if it ain't the preacher!" The group of five Topeka men swaggered up to the church. Their leader, a fellow in a filthy homespun shirt and a pair of ragged denim trousers, stepped forward. "And there's Miss Lily herself. The flower of the frontier. I do believe you read my palm back in Topeka, Miss Lily. You told me the two of us was gonna have a fine time one of these nights."

"Listen here, buster." Elijah nudged Lily behind him and moved toward the intruder. "I won't have you talk that way to Mrs. Nolan."

"What claim you got on the lady, Preacher?"

"She's a citizen of this town and a member of my congregation. You stand back from her, you hear me?"

"Aw, don't you wanna shake your skirts at me, Miss Lily?" the man said, leering over Elijah's shoulder. "Come on, gal. Let's have us a little dance the way we did back in Topeka."

"Leave the lass be!" Jimmy O'Toole shouted, lifting his rifle as he walked toward the five men. "We don't want your kind of rabble comin' around our town. And you shan't be actin' disrespectful to our ladies."

"Nothin' wrong with a little dancin', is there, Irish?" The man began to sway his hips and wave a half-empty whisky bottle around. His companions laughed and elbowed each other. "Me and Miss Lily's gonna have us a fine time tonight, ain't we, gal? We'll sashay around the town a time or two, maybe stop by the saloon for a sip, and then I'm gonna give you a great big smooch!"

"You better take that back," Elijah growled, grabbing the man by his collar. "Take it back. *Now!*"

As Elijah jerked the man half off his feet, the man's Topeka cohorts drew their six-shooters. The gathering crowd sucked in a collective gasp. Around the circle, Elijah discerned the men who had become his closest friends. Seth Hunter, Jack Cornwall, Rolf Rustemeyer, Jimmy O'Toole, and Ben Hanks — all of them but Jimmy unarmed. He could not let this confrontation turn into a blood-bath, and yet he wouldn't allow anyone to sully Lily's name.

"Set him down, Preacher," another of the Topeka men said, ramming the barrel of his gun into Elijah's side. "Take your hands off'n my cousin, you hear?"

"I'll turn him loose when you fellows put your guns away and head out of town."

"You turn him loose before I blow your guts to glory."

"Elijah, please," Lily said, laying a hand on his arm. "Let me speak to them."

"Stay back, Lily. Rolf, take her out of here."

"No!" she cried as the big German farmer reached for her. "Elijah, please let go of that man. What do you boys want, anyhow? I've already told Beatrice I'm staying here in town to earn my pay. I'm not going to sing for her."

Elijah slowly released the fellow's collar as Lily pushed her way to the center of the crowd. Giving his neck a vigorous rub, the man spat a gob of tobacco juice at Elijah's feet. Then he straightened his shirt and faced Lily.

"Mrs. B says you don't belong with these folks," he told Lily. "She says they've bamboozled you into joinin' them and givin' up your true friends and your callin' as a opera singer. That preacher done suckered you in by gettin' you attached to his baby. Now you're as stuck as you were back in Philadelphia. Mrs. B told us to come down here and remind you of all the fun you're missin' — and all the money."

He took a leather pouch from his back pocket and shook it in her face. The jingle of coins told the crowd he meant what he was saying. Giving his pals a smirk of victory, he pulled a silver dollar from the pouch.

"There's good wages to be had over to the opera house," he told the crowd. "Don't you folks want to get out of the sun? Don't you want to put your plows away for good? We got all kinds of work to be done and steady pay for anybody who'll do his job. Ain't that right, boys?"

The other men let out a roar of agreement, lifting their liquor bottles and stomping their feet. "We're gonna open up for business tomorrow night," their leader shouted. "How many of you want to join us? Come on, Miss Lily, you be the first to step forward. Show these folks you know how to live!"

Elijah clenched his fists in anger as Lily lifted her hands for silence in the midst of the gathering. *Lord, don't let them take her. Protect her, Father! Protect her now!*

"I'm sure you boys have big plans," she said, her voice taking on the worldly bravado Elijah had heard so many times before. "Sounds good, doesn't it, everybody? Big, fat purses filled with coins. Easy work. Cheap liquor. Lots of fun."

"That's right, Miss Lily!" the Topeka man said. "You tell 'em."

"I've been there before. I've done that kind of work, and I'll tell you gentlemen exactly what it's like." She looked into the eyes of each farmer standing around her. "It's sleeping all day and staying awake all night — long, cold, lonely nights. It's a full stomach but an empty heart. It's footloose and fancy-free — but no home to call your own. No family. No true friends. If you want to give up your dreams, your hopes, your very future, join these fellows over at the opera house. But if you want peace, comfort, and an eternal home, you'd better stay with Brother Elijah, this church you're building, and the town of Hope. As for me, boys, I've already made my choice."

Without meeting the preacher's eyes again, she turned and walked back through the crowd toward the Hankses' little house. Eva joined her, and then Caitrin, Rosie, Sheena, and Lucy followed. Elijah's heart swelled as he watched the women of Hope stand united against the opera house.

Spotting the stump of a tree the cyclone had blown down, Elijah jumped up onto it. "Hear the Word of the Lord," he called. " 'Thou shalt love the Lord thy God with all thine heart, and with all thy soul, and with all thy might.' If you love God, you'll keep his commandments, gentlemen! I tell you today, that opera house down the road stands as an enemy of the Lord. I've kept silent until now, but if I keep silent any longer, the stones will cry out."

Allowing the Word of truth to pour out of him, Elijah watched the Topeka men laugh among themselves as they walked off down the road. But the others in the group gathered closer, and he could feel the strong rod of the Shepherd moving through him to draw the flock into the fold.

"A saloon," he said, "is a place with a wicked purpose. I know, because I've spent a lot of time in saloons from Missouri to California and back again. A saloon has three aims. To get you drunk, to help you gamble away your money, and to make you lust after women. Not only does that opera house have a saloon, gentlemen, but they're bringing in women!"

"Lord, have mercy!" old Hubert cried out, his eyes shooting wide open in shock. "Did you hear that, Simeon?"

"That opera house is really a brothel," Elijah told the crowd. "It'll lure the men traveling down our honest roads, and it'll try to lure you fellows, too. The Lord makes plain his commandments about fallen women. 'Let not thine heart decline to her way,' he says, 'go not astray in her paths. For she hath cast down many wounded: yea, many strong men have been slain by her. Her house is the way to hell, going down to the chambers of death.' "

"Amen, Brother Elijah!" Simeon cried.

"Preach the Word of God," Jimmy O'Toole hollered, firing his rifle into the air. "Let's tear down that house of wickedness! Let's drive the sinners out of our midst!"

" 'Vengeance is mine, saith the Lord,' " Elijah countered, recognizing the mood of the restless crowd. These men had labored in the baking sun for three days to rebuild the town of Hope. With the opera house looming as a threat to their hard work, there was no telling what they might do to destroy it.

"The best thing you men can do to stop that place from taking root here in Hope," he told them, "is to steer clear of it. Don't set one foot inside those doors. Don't sell those folks your crops. Don't let your women clean and cook for them. Keep yourselves pure and holy before the Lord, fellows, and he'll drive that place out of our —"

A cry from the Hanks house drew the instant focus of the men. Caitrin Cornwall raced out the front door, followed by Sheena O'Toole and Eva Hanks. "Brother Elijah!"

Sheena cried. "Sure you must come at once!"

"Where's Lily?" He leapt down from the stump and began to push his way through the crowd.

"She's inside," Caitrin called. " 'Tis not her; 'tis the baby! Your baby is gone, Brother Elijah! Sure he's been taken clean away."

Lily lay crumpled at the foot of the cradle, fighting the nausea that had swept over her.

"Lily, what in tarnation is going on?" Elijah dropped to his knees beside her. "Where's Sam?"

"I don't know!" She took his sleeves in her fists. "He was alone for only a few minutes —"

"It's my fault!" Eva wailed. "I left the baby to go watch the opera house men feudin' with the farmers over by the church. I wanted to make sure my Ben didn't get himself into a fix. When all us women came back to the house, we were so busy talkin', we didn't notice for a minute. And then Lily saw the cradle. Mercy, Lord, someone took that child!"

As Eva wept, the other women tried to console her. Lily lifted the blankets and pressed her hand on the soft warm spot where the child had lain. Abigail's little bed had been warm in the minutes after her death. Another child. Another loss. The image of her baby's face drifted into focus, blended with her memory of Samuel's precious smile, and dissolved into tears of disbelief.

It was Lily's fault. She had insisted on helping with the cleanup in town. She had left Eva in charge of Sam, when the baby was truly her own responsibility.

"Oh, Elijah," she said, "I'm so sorry."

"Did an animal drag him off?" He ripped the blankets out of the cradle. "I don't see blood."

"Perhaps 'twas was one of the wild dogs that were in Jimmy's smokehouse after the cyclone," Caitrin cried. "Sure those wicked creatures have been wandering about for three days looking mean and hungry."

Letting out a strangled cry, Lily jumped to her feet and ran to the open back door of the house. "Elijah, you've got to go looking for those dogs!" She grabbed the door frame. "Take Jimmy's rifle. You have to find Samuel."

"I don't think it was a dog," Rose Hunter said. "Stubby's been right here in town all day, and he'd have barked if he caught wind of any strays. I think a person took the baby."

"Who would take him?" Elijah demanded. "Sam's *my* baby. He belongs to me."

"There've been so many strangers in town," Rosie said. "Maybe there's a husband

and wife who've been trying to have a child of their own —"

"What about that peddler who came through selling pots and pans this morning?" someone asked.

"I think it was those opera-house ruffians. I'll bet they took the baby for spite."

"Somebody ought to go look for them stray dogs."

"Maybe it was a coyote."

As the crowd around the Hanks house grew louder and more restless, Lily searched the room for Elijah. They had nearly lost Sam once before. With God's grace the baby had pulled through his illness.

God help us!

Head and shoulders over most of the men in the room, the preacher caught her eye. They communicated in silence for a moment, and Lily felt sure she knew the direction of his thoughts. Who would take Samuel away? Who would be so wicked, so heartless, so cruel?

Without speaking, she walked through the back door as he headed out the front. They met in the yard, and he took her hand. As one, they began to run — out into the yard, down the rutted street, past the half-built church and the mercantile with its new glass windows, and alongside the grove of cottonwood trees.

"Why?" Lily gasped as the opera house came into view. "Elijah, why would she take him?"

"I don't know," he said. "But I aim to find out. That boy is my son. If she's hurt him —"

"She wouldn't do that. Bea's confused, but she's not wicked." Even as she spoke the words, Lily doubted them herself. Beatrice had chosen a path that took her in direct opposition to Christ and his commands. Not so many weeks ago, she had been willing to peddle a useless potion as a healing elixir. She had admitted to making up fortunes and inventing readings from her crystal ball.

Now she had cast herself, body and soul, into the arms of a married man — a conniver willing to lure the unwary with liquor and fallen women. One step down the wrong road had led to another and then another. Lily wondered if Beatrice would stop at anything.

"Let me speak to the woman," Lily said, grabbing Elijah's arm. "I can reason with her."

"I don't trust her. There's no telling what she'll do." His blue eyes bored into her face. "I'm going in alone."

"We'll go together."

"It might be a trap, Lily. She might have taken Sam to lure you over here."

"Or you."

Lily clutched his hands and knew, no matter what the consequences, she was going in after Samuel. He was Elijah's child in name, but he was hers in heart. She had fed and nurtured him, and she treasured the baby as her own.

"I'm not his mother," she said in a low, firm voice, "but I won't let anything happen to Samuel, Elijah. I love him."

"Stay close to me, Lily," he said as he started toward the steps of the opera house.

Climbing onto the shady porch, Lily realized that Elijah couldn't protect her. He was unarmed and outnumbered. But he would do all he could to keep her safe. She could trust him. She could rely on him.

"Well, if it ain't the preacher!" The front door flew open, and the leader of the men who had come to town earlier stepped outside. "You finished up that fancy sermon you was dishin' out, I see. And you brung Miss Lily. Did you come to take me up on my offer of a dance, darlin'?"

"I think you have my son here, buster." Elijah jammed a finger into the man's chest. "I want him back."

"Your son?" A grin crept across the fellow's face, revealing rotted teeth. "I don't believe so."

"Somebody from your camp took my baby

314

while you and your cronies were causing trouble at the church. Now hand him over before I fetch the law."

"The law?" The man laughed. "Well, ain't that a how-de-do? Come on in here, Preacher, and let me introduce you to the law."

"Don't go," Lily whispered. "It's a trick."

"Bring the baby out here, and we'll settle things up," Elijah said.

"What baby are you talkin' about?"

At that moment, Samuel's distinctive cry drifted through the open window of the opera house. Lily caught her breath and dashed past the man into a cavernous foyer trimmed in flocked red wallpaper and hung with gilt chandeliers. "Sam!" she called.

"Lily!" Elijah was at her side in an instant. "Where is he?"

"Sam?"

Again the baby's hungry wail sounded faintly. Lily pointed to a heavy pocket door. Elijah stepped toward it and forced the two sliding panels apart. As they burst into the room, the group gathered there on tufted settees rose as one.

Lily stopped, her heartbeat hammering in her ears.

Beatrice Waldowski and George Gibbons stood beside a massive fireplace. On one side of the room, a crude wooden box held the sobbing baby. Across the thick Oriental carpet stood a short fellow wearing a sweat-stained Stetson and the silver badge of a deputy. Beside him, a giant of a man straightened to his full height, his diamond tie pin and dark frock coat bearing testimony to wealth and importance.

"Lily," the giant said.

Though her every instinct ordered her to rush to the baby, Lily could not make her limbs move. Her blood sank to her knees, and her mouth went dry. Sucking in a breath, she managed one word.

"Father."

CHAPTER 15

"Reverend Book, I assume?" The imposing gentleman stepped forward and extended his hand to Elijah. "You must be the minister of the church in Hope."

"That's right," Elijah said, giving the man's hand a single, quick shake. "And that's my son over there. I don't know how Samuel came to be in this place, but I'm taking him home now."

"Not so fast, Preacher." The sheriff's deputy placed himself between Elijah and the box in which Samuel lay crying. "We had a report in the Topeka office that you found the baby in Indian territory."

"Who sent in that report?" Eli demanded.

The deputy glanced across the room. "Mrs. Waldowski told us about the incident."

"I figured. Listen, mister, I've never kept anything about Samuel a secret. I found the baby when I was passing through Osage land down south. His parents' wagon had been shot full of arrows, and his pa was dead. Right before she died, his mama handed her son over to me and asked me to take care of him. I promised her I would, and that's what I've been doing ever since."

"Do you have any legal papers to show you've adopted the boy, Reverend?"

"Of course I don't. His parents weren't in any shape to sign him over to me."

"All the same, we've got ways of doing things around here. An abandoned baby doesn't just belong to the first fellow that picks him up."

"Well, who does he belong to?"

"The state of Kansas."

"But his mother gave him to me."

"Do you have any witnesses to that?"

Elijah felt like he was about to explode. "My horse."

With a scowl, the deputy scratched the back of his neck. "I guess you noticed that baby's not all white, Reverend Book. He's got some black or Indian blood in him. Maybe Mexican."

"His blood is red, same as yours and mine, Deputy. Now, if you'd please step aside, I'll see to it that he's given some food and put back into his own cradle where he belongs."

"Is this your wife?" The deputy gestured at Lily.

"No, she's not."

"That's a relief." The tall gentleman gave a benign smile as he addressed the deputy.

"This young woman, good sir, is my daughter. Lily, what a surprise to find you here. Your mother and I are very grateful to Mrs. Waldowski for alerting us to your whereabouts."

Lily cast a withering glance at Beatrice before facing her father. "If you gentlemen will excuse me," she said with the barest trace of a tremble in her voice, "I need to tend to the baby."

"I'm sorry, ma'am, but I can't allow you to take the child out of my sight," the deputy said. "He's a ward of the state, and I'm going to have to take him with me back to the state-run orphanage in Topeka."

"Now just a cotton-picking minute —," Elijah began.

"Shall I nurse the child in full view of the public then, sir?" Lily cut in.

"Nurse him?" the deputy and Lily's father said at the same time.

"You don't think he's old enough for meat and potatoes, do you?" She swallowed hard as she walked between the two men. When she lifted the baby, his sobbing began to quiet. "Come on, Samuel, sweetheart," she murmured. "Are you a hungry boy? Wet, too! Oh, poor little fellow."

Turning, she gave the deputy a hard stare. "This baby is in good hands, sir. Better hands than he would be in at an orphanage in Topeka. I'll go and feed the pastor's son now, and when I come back, I trust you'll have seen reason."

As the deputy and her father stood silent, Lily carried the baby out the parlor door. When Elijah turned to follow her, the lawman spoke up.

"You'd better stay here, Reverend. We've got some talking to do."

Elijah took a hard-backed chair as near the door as he could. He felt outnumbered, and that made him uncomfortable. But more than that, he sensed that, although God's presence was inside him, the Spirit was not in this room. An oppressive heaviness hung in the air, sitting on his chest and weighing down his heart. He leaned forward and rested his elbows on his knees.

"Look, what is it you want from me, Deputy?" he asked. "You know I'm a man of God. There are plenty of folks in town who'll testify to my calling as a preacher. I took the baby out of kindness to his dead mother, and I've grown to care about the boy. I'll do whatever I need to do to make him legally mine."

"A warm and godly expression," Lily's father cut in, flipping back his coattails as he sat down on the settee. "You, sir, are a man of righteous intent and pious purpose. I therefore appeal to your reason in the matters at hand. First and foremost, the child's welfare must be addressed. Second, my daughter's future is of great interest to me."

Elijah studied the man's blue eyes, reminiscent of Lily's, yet somehow devoid of the life and spirit that sparkled in hers. So this was the father who had beaten his child black and blue. This was the man who had broken his little girl's ribs and arm. This was the great, respected conductor of the Greater New England Symphony Orchestra — a man in control of everything but his own temper.

"Dr. Richardson has come all the way from back East to fetch his daughter," the deputy said. "And I'm here to take the baby to Topeka. The way I see it, that settles both problems."

"I don't think so," Elijah countered. "Lily has been nursing and tending to Samuel for a long time now. The baby had a rough start in life, and he's still not as strong as he ought to be. If you take him off to Topeka, Deputy, he might die. Does the state of Kansas want to be responsible for the death of an innocent baby?"

"How can we be sure the kid doesn't have relatives on the Osage reservation?" the deputy asked. "It's clear he's part colored. Maybe he's got an Indian grandma or something."

"His folks were dirt farmers," Elijah explained. "They were passing through the reservation."

"How do you know?"

"They were in a wagon filled with belongings — plows and seed and rocking chairs. Look, Deputy, can't you go through your records and search for an account of somebody finding the wagon? I can tell you exactly where it was. That ought to prove me out. I buried the bodies right there by the side of the road."

"Well, I reckon —"

"They were a couple of folks heading west to start a new life — just like thousands of others — when they ran into trouble with some renegade Osage. The wife was Indian, maybe, or Mexican, or even Italian. I don't know, and I don't care. All I do know is, she begged me to take Samuel and raise him up in the Lord. And that's what I intend to do." He turned to Richardson. "As for your daughter, sir, it looks to me like Lily's made up her own mind about her future. She lives with a good family in town, she's got work to do, and she's happy."

"Happy?" Richardson straightened his tie. "Reverend Book, you tell us you care for that baby you found by the roadside. Do you have any *idea* the depth of love a mother and a father have for their natural-born daughter? When Lily vanished from our home, her mother became hysterical. She was inconsolable."

"I'm sorry to hear that, sir. I'm sure Lily didn't mean to upset her mother."

"For more than a year now, we've been forced to accept the conclusion that our only child might be dead," the man went on. "And suddenly, a miracle is sent from heaven! Mrs. Waldowski writes us a letter, informing us that our Lily lives! Though you tell me she is happy, Reverend Book, I cannot accept your judgment. Clearly my daughter is not well. That she would willingly leave our home, the tender care of her mother, a future of comfort and security, illustrates the fragile condition of her mind."

"There's nothing wrong with your daughter's mind," Elijah said.

"But I've been given to understand from Mrs. Waldowski that our Lily has been living with a traveling show, roaming about aimlessly, surviving in the direst of circumstances. I want you to know, this young lady received the finest education money can buy! She is trained in the fine arts of womanly decorum. She has been prepared for a life in the highest echelon of society. And you tell me she chooses to live in abject poverty? Of course she's gone mad!"

Elijah felt like his drawers were crawling right up his back. Lily Nolan wasn't crazy. She'd chosen to run from this very man who claimed to have given her a happy life but in reality had tormented her with his abuses. Everything in Elijah told him to spill the beans on the pompous Dr. Richardson. But why would the deputy trust the word of a down-home preacher with a foundling baby over that of the conductor of the Greater New England Symphony Orchestra — a man with a diamond stuck through his tie?

"Your daughter, sir," Elijah addressed Richardson, "is not only sound of mind, but she's shown herself to be a respectable citizen of Hope. Any number of folks will tell you how she's helped out the Hanks family, taken good care of my son, and even pitched in to rebuild the town after a cyclone hit us. But you ought to let Lily speak for herself. She can tell you what she wants to do with her life."

"My dear man," Richardson said, his mouth pulling into an expression of disbelief, "you of all people should understand a woman's place of submission in Christian society. Surely you've read the scriptural admonition that woman may not be allowed to 'usurp authority over the man, but to be in silence.' I trust you've been trained in a detailed explication of the Bible, and you are aware that the apostle Paul taught the Corinthian church that 'the head of the woman is the man' and that 'it is not permitted unto them to speak; but they are commanded to be under obedience, as also saith the law.' "

Elijah twiddled his thumbs. Well, he'd read the Bible through a few times, but he didn't exactly recall those particular verses. Truth to tell, he'd gotten the impression that Christ loved women as much as men, and that a godly woman could fulfill an important role in the church. Wasn't there somebody named Priscilla who helped her husband hold worship services in their home? And then there was a lady named Lydia —

"You *have* studied at a seminary, have you not?" Richardson asked.

The preacher shifted uncomfortably. "No, sir."

"Then what makes you think you're qualified to preach the gospel?"

"I heard the voice of the Lord calling me to tell other folks about him, so I got on my horse, and I went out and did it."

A triumphant look crossed the conductor's face. "Upon my word, young man, you are completely ignorant! You have no formal training, no religious education, and no experience in matters of family instruction or spiritual guidance — and yet you proclaim yourself a minister of God's Holy Word! You have had the effrontery to place yourself in a position of leadership over the church of Jesus Christ in Hope, Kansas! I am astonished."

Elijah felt about as low as a snake and twice as dumb. The man was right, of course. Elijah had no business pastoring a church or giving anybody advice.

"Young man, you must get yourself to a seminary before the week is out." Richardson adjusted his diamond tie tack. "I cannot, in good conscience, endorse your presence among the people of this warm and earnest little town. Do you not recall the words of St. Paul to young Timothy? 'Give attendance to reading, to exhortation, to doctrine. . . . Take heed unto thyself, and unto the doctrine; continue in them: for in doing this thou shalt both save thyself, and them that hear thee.' "

"I have been reading the Bible, sir, every day. And I'm studying it as well as I can."

"Your sincerity impresses me. In fact, I am quite willing to write a letter of recommendation on your behalf to the dean of the institution of higher learning to which you aspire. I shall personally address myself to this matter in order that your future education is assured.

I am well acquainted with the presidents of various venues of religious instruction, and I shall provide you with a list of recommended schools. You strike me as a man of untrained but sincere caliber. An education will transform you into the model of a minister."

With a nod, he indicated that the subject was closed. Feeling about like he had the night the twister hit Hope, Elijah studied a pair of sparrows building a nest under an eave of the new opera house. Dr. Richardson was right that he didn't know much about pastoring. He was uneducated, too. But he wasn't ignorant. Elijah knew his Savior. And he knew that God had promised to keep his eye on Lily and Sam — just like he was keeping watch over those sparrows.

"As for the foundling child," Richardson went on, "it is abundantly clear that his future lies in the competent hands of the state of Kansas. Do you not recall the admonition of the Lord to Jeremiah the prophet? 'Leave thy fatherless children,' he warns, 'I will preserve them alive.' It is God's work — not yours, Reverend Book — to provide for the orphan. An unmarried, uneducated man in need of schooling cannot hope to rear a helpless baby. The child must be placed in the good hands of the orphanage."

"I reckon you're right," the deputy chimed

in. "Although I've got to tell you —"

"My daughter, of course, will return to Philadelphia with me on the next train from Topeka." Dr. Richardson rose and straightened the tails of his coat. "Obviously her mother and I must attend to the immediate repair of her mental condition and the reconstruction of her reputation. Following that, we shall see that Lily is secured in the good marriage and societal position for which we prepared her."

Elijah stood. Though he knew his boots were on solid ground, he felt a little off-kilter. Richardson was obviously a man who knew God, knew the Bible, and knew the right way of doing things. Educated and wealthy, he cited Scripture as though there could be no arguing. And why would Elijah argue with the Word of the Lord, anyway? But for some reason, the whole thing didn't sit straight.

Could a man like Richardson possibly be wrong in what he said? Even lying? Could someone in a position of leadership in a church and in a city really be speaking in error — especially when he backed up everything he said with verses from the Bible?

As the esteemed gentleman made casual conversation with Beatrice Waldowski, George Gibbons, and the deputy, Elijah thought about Lily. Maybe the woman had deceived him about her father. Maybe Dr. Richardson hadn't hurt her at all, but instead she had chosen a willful and rebellious path away from family and Christ. Maybe Elijah didn't have any business pastoring the Hope church. And maybe Samuel would be better off in an orphanage in Topeka.

"I'm assuming you know the place to which my daughter has taken the child," Richardson said as he walked to the parlor door. "Perhaps you would be so good as to lead us there, Mister Book."

Elijah pictured Lily sitting under the big cottonwood tree beside Bluestem Creek. She would be holding Samuel, singing some little lullaby the way she always did, and stroking his soft dark curls. It was under the cottonwood that Lily claimed to have opened her heart to Christ. Elijah had to believe that much was true. With his own two eyes, he had seen the changes in her.

And he knew a few other facts, too. Lily and Samuel belonged together. Lily and Elijah belonged together. Sam was Eli's son. And Christ had joined the three of them. This image in Elijah's mind of the group of people united for a higher purpose seemed true and quite real. Yet Dr. Richardson's words rang powerfully to dismiss it. Elijah must go to a seminary, the baby to an orphanage, Lily to

Philadelphia. God had ordained their futures.

Unable to see clearly, unable to sort through the whirlwind in his mind, Elijah headed into the foyer of the opera house. "I'll fetch your daughter, Dr. Richardson," he said.

"I don't think it would be wise for you to go alone. 'Be sober, be vigilant,' young man, 'because your adversary the devil, as a roaring lion, walketh about, seeking whom he may devour.' "

Eli stopped, frustration rising to the point of anger inside him. "Now what's that supposed to mean?"

"Ah, ignorance! Ah, bliss!" The conductor clapped him on the back. "How easily you fall prey to the limitations of your own fallible mind. I am telling you that you must stay away from my daughter at this vulnerable time in your life. The powers of the seductress are great, and you — like most men — are hard-pressed to resist them. Come, we'll all seek out my Lily as one party. Deputy, will you join us?"

The lawman was chewing on a wad of tobacco as he studied the inside of the opera house. When Richardson addressed him, he focused again on the matter at hand and nodded his acquiescence. The three men stepped outside, followed by Beatrice and her

330

cohorts, and they all set out for the grove.

With every step Elijah took down the road toward the cottonwood tree, the noose tightened around his neck. If he let Lily go with Dr. Richardson, would she find the happiness God had planned for her, as her father insisted? Or would she fall victim to a man who had no control over himself? At this moment, Dr. Richardson was in control not only of himself but of the whole situation.

And what if Elijah let the deputy take Samuel away? Would the baby really live a better life in an orphanage than in the home of a man who loved him as a son? Of course, love didn't make up for ignorance and inexperience. Eli knew he possessed both of those in abundance.

And what if Eli left the town of Hope and headed east to get himself an education? Would he be turning his back on the call to shepherd that little flock? Or would he be freeing the people of Hope to find themselves a minister who really could meet all their needs?

"There she is," Beatrice Waldowski said. "There's Lil, hiding behind that old tree."

Her voice jerked Eli right out of the cyclone and set him on his feet. The noose around his neck loosened. A peace that passed all understanding filled his heart.

"I'll talk to Lily," he said.

"*I'll* fetch her," Bea insisted.

Eli grabbed the woman's arm. "She left you, Madame Zahara. She chose a new life."

"I suppose you think that means she chose *you*."

"She chose Jesus Christ."

"Oh, please. Lily's as naive and stupid as that baby she's so attached to. She couldn't make a decision on her own if her life depended on it. You tricked her into leaving me. You seduced her away from a good future —"

"In your brothel? I don't think so, Beatrice. Lily doesn't need you, me, or her father. Truth be told, she's given her future to someone she can really count on."

"What's this about a brothel?" the deputy asked.

"Lily!" Beatrice called. "You can come out of hiding now, little girl. Daddy's come for you."

Before anyone else could move, Eli took off through the grove of trees to the place where Lily sat nursing Samuel. As he approached, she tugged her white shawl over the baby's head and looked up at the man, her blue eyes clouded with uncertainty.

Eli hunkered down beside the two of them and let out a breath. This was where he belonged. Right here with Lily and Sam.

"How's my little Nubbin?" he asked, touching one of the baby's bare pink toes.

Lily managed a smile. "He's asleep."

"And how's my Lily?"

"Oh, Elijah!" She leaned her head on his shoulder, and he drew her into his embrace. "I can't believe my father came all this way."

"I can. He's determined."

"Determined to take me back to Philadelphia." She shook her head. "There was a time when I believed I should go home. I knew my life with the traveling show was taking me nowhere. At least in Philadelphia I would have food to eat and a roof over my head. I'd lived so many years under my father's thumb, and I figured I could do it again."

"He wants to take you back today."

"I know."

"He's going to recommend me to a seminary so I can learn how to be a pastor."

"I see."

"He says Sam would be better off in an orphanage."

"Since you'll be in school, and I'll be in Philadelphia."

"That's right." Eli cupped the baby's tiny foot in his palm and stroked his thumb across the puff of soft skin. "He says it's all God's will."

"I'm sure he backed up his position with Scripture."

"Yep." He met Lily's blue eyes. "Your father sure does know the Bible."

"So did I," she said. "Before."

"I remember."

"But I didn't know *him*. I didn't know Christ."

Eli thought for a moment. "You reckon somebody could twist Scripture around? I mean, could a man take verses right out of the Bible and use God's Holy Word for wrong reasons?"

"I was very good at it."

"But a fellow who claims to be a Christian . . . claims to believe in Jesus . . . claims to serve him. Could he be lying?"

Lily lifted the baby away and tucked the shawl around him like a blanket. Elijah leaned over her and kissed Sam's pink cheek. Without speaking, Lily laid the baby in his arms. As Eli gazed down at the pair of long-lashed eyelids, the soft nub of a nose, the tiny rosebud lips, a certainty filled his soul.

" 'Ye shall know them by their fruits,' " he said in a low voice. He had read the verses that morning, and he'd been working all day to memorize them. " 'Every good tree bringeth forth good fruit; but a corrupt tree bringeth forth evil fruit.' Evil fruit. A corrupt tree. 'Beware of false prophets, which come to you in sheep's clothing, but inwardly they are ravening wolves.' "

The verses had slipped unbidden into his mind, but Eli knew who had put them there. Though the Pharisees had appeared holy, Jesus had called them serpents, a generation of vipers.

Yes, it was possible for a man to clothe himself in the sheep's wool of Christ's flock. But in reality, he could be a wolf, a serpent, a predator, distorting truth and preying on the tender lambs. Possible. But was Dr. Richardson a sheep or a wolf? A lamb or a viper?

By their fruits, a small voice whispered to Eli. *By their fruits . . .*

"You've got to go face your father," he told Lily. "You have to talk to him."

She nodded. "I know, but . . . Elijah, would you pray with me first? I need you as my pastor. I need your help."

"I'm right here beside you." He took her hand and bowed his head. "Father, we've got trouble. Lily and I . . . we love Sam, and we believe you gave him to us. We ask you to watch over the little fellow and put him where he needs to be so he can grow up right. As for Lily, Lord, she's your daughter. She belongs to you more than she ever belonged to Dr. Richardson. Please protect her."

"Amen," Lily whispered.

"Listen to me, darlin'," Eli said as they stood. "I won't make your choices for you, and I won't go against God's plan for your life. But I'll stand beside you. I love you, Lily, and that's the truth."

As he spoke the words, her eyes filled with light and a smile lifted her lips. "I love you, too, Elijah Book," she said softly.

Eli nodded as he tucked Sam's small round head into the curve of his neck and gave his little bottom a pat. Yep. That was the truth.

CHAPTER 16

As Lily walked through the trees to the road, she felt herself shrinking inside. She knew Elijah, cradling Samuel in his arms, walked beside her. But each step forward took her back, further and further into her childhood. She was a little girl again, a willful child who had disobeyed her father. What would he do to her? Where could she run to hide? Who could protect her from the coming storm?

"Lily." His voice assumed that tone of disappointment with which he always began. "Lily, Lily, Lily."

She looked up into his face, into ice blue eyes above the stern mouth. "I'm sorry to have troubled you, Father."

"Indeed." Hands behind his back, thank heaven. "Lily, your mother is awaiting your return. I have engaged the services of a coach and driver, and we shall depart for Topeka at once. I assume there is nothing of value here that you wish to retrieve before you go."

Lily studied the tips of her toes. From the corner of her eye, she could see Elijah's scuffed leather boots. Nothing of value? Only the man she loved. Only the child she had come to treasure as her own.

Oh, Father God, is it wrong to disobey my parents? I love Elijah, but I'm so . . . so afraid of this man. Please be with me, Lord.

She lifted her head and spoke. "I'll not be returning to Philadelphia with you, Father. I'm going to stay right here in Hope."

There. She had done it. She steeled herself, drew in her breath, and forced her eyes to meet his. The man's chest swelled. A sneer twisted his mouth.

"I beg your pardon?" he said.

Lily tried to make herself breathe. "I'm staying here," she managed. "I won't go with you."

"You *won't* go with me?"

"No, sir."

"You'd better do as he says, Lil," Beatrice interjected. "He's your father, remember?"

Lily cast a glance at the woman she had once called a friend. "I trusted you, Bea."

"I warned you not to cross me."

"You betrayed me."

She shrugged. "You let me down. I figured if you wouldn't work for me, you might as well go on home to daddy. 'Honour thy father and thy mother,' you know." Smiling smugly, Beatrice swung around. "Come on, boys, let's head back to the opera house. She's going to get exactly what she deserves."

As they walked off down the road, Lily shook her head and turned to the man who had caused her terror, humiliation, torment. *Honour thy father?* she thought. *No, not him. He surrendered his right to wear the name* father.

"I won't go with you," she said. "I'll write a letter to Mother and explain myself. You'll have to go back without me."

"You impudent little fool!" Richardson swung around and addressed the deputy and the preacher. "She presumes to tell me what she'll do. My own daughter refuses to obey me."

It would come now, the black storm. She could feel the pressure building inside her father. First a few raindrops. A slight wind. Then the sky would transform to a sickening green. Hail would begin to fall. And then trees would be ripped from their roots. Barns would topple. Homes would be torn up and dashed to the ground.

"Lily, you will do as I say or suffer the consequences," the thunder rolled. "Are you mad, child? Or are you simply stupid? Can you not see that your life is already settled? I've given you everything. Everything. And you treat me like this? Like I'm nothing? Like I'm dirt under your fingernails?"

"No, sir," she whispered.

"Indeed, you do!" the lightning flashed. "You have the impudence, the absolute gall to dishonor your own father! Ingrate!"

"Now, hold on a minute," Elijah cut in, shifting the baby in his arms.

"You stay out of this, bumpkin." The wind turned, its gale blowing now in a huge circle that encompassed everyone and everything in sight. "You've defiled and dishonored my daughter. You're a disgrace to the calling of the church. What are you? A rube. A rustic. A cowboy."

"No, sir, not any longer. I'm a shepherd, and your daughter is one of my flock."

"Your flock," he snarled, grabbing Lily's arm and jerking her toward him. "This pathetic creature is mine, not yours. She belongs to me, and I'm here to take her back where she belongs. Now, move your feet, Lily. I've had enough of your nonsense."

He pushed her in the direction of the opera house, but she struggled loose. "No," she cried. "I won't do it!"

"You'll obey me, or you'll wish you had."

"I can't obey you."

"Can't?" He drew back his hand, and she ducked, crouching into the fabric of her skirts. "Can't or won't?"

"Stop!" Elijah shouted.

"Can't or won't?" her father bellowed.

Lily covered her head with her arms, and at that very moment, the eye of the storm passed over her. Calm filled her. Security wrapped her in holy arms. She looked up into the red, swollen face hovering over her.

" 'The Lord is my light and my salvation,' " she murmured into the storm, " 'whom shall I fear? the Lord is the strength of my life; of whom shall I be afraid?' "

"What?" her father roared.

Now the final winds would come, Lily knew. She closed her eyes in readiness. " 'Behold, I see the heavens opened, and the Son of man standing on the right hand of God.' "

"Blasphemer!"

" 'Lord, lay not this sin to his charge.' "

"Demon! Witch!"

Lily drank down a breath in preparation for the coming blow, but a loud cry startled her. As her eyes flew open, she saw Elijah Book, baby in one arm and the wrath of God on his face, slam a balled fist into her father's face. The huge man toppled backward onto the road and lay in stunned silence. For the space of a breath, Lily thought it was over. The storm was finished. But then the man scrambled to his feet with a bellow of rage.

"I'll kill you!"

"Stay clear of Lily!" Elijah shouted.

"That's enough, men!" The deputy drew

his pistol and stepped between the two. As Lily's father came at Elijah, the lawman pivoted and aimed the six-shooter at his heart. "Stop right there, mister, or I'm gonna make wolf meat outta you."

Crouched on the road, Lily could see her father hesitate. "Father, please stop this," she called to him. "It won't work anymore. All these years it's been wrong. You can't win this time. Please, Father. Set me free."

The towering man stood heaving for breath, his shirt stained with sweat and his collar sprung from its buttons. His sledgehammer hands clenched and released, clenched and released. A trickle of blood worked its way down the corner of his mouth.

"By your fruit," Elijah said in a low voice, "by your fruit, Dr. Richardson. The fruit of God's Spirit is love. Look at *your* fruit huddled there on the road. What you see is fear. Anger. Sorrow. Confusion. Torment. The Good Book says that folks who sow fruit like that can't inherit the kingdom of God."

Lily watched her father's face as the storm began to die. The red in his cheeks faded. His lips drooped. His blue eyes lost all expression.

"I can't quote the Bible back to front like you do," Elijah went on, giving the baby on his shoulder a pat, "but I've read all about the fruit of the Spirit. That's *love. Joy. Peace. Gen-*

tleness. Are you gentle, Dr. Richardson?"

When the man didn't speak, Elijah continued. "*Longsuffering*. Near as I can figure, that means patient. Are you a patient man, Dr. Richardson?"

Lily watched her father begin to sag as Elijah went on. "*Meekness*. Christ asks us to be servants, not slave masters. *Temperance*. That means we're supposed to control ourselves."

The preacher paused, and his voice was low when he continued. "Maybe some grown-up whipped you when you were a boy. Or maybe somebody told you it was a father's business to beat on his little daughter. It's not. I'll admit, my daddy popped my tail feathers a few times, but he never really hurt me. He never ground me into the dirt or backed me so far into a corner that I didn't have any choice but to run away, fearing for my life."

Lily's father had covered his face with his hands, and she tried to imagine what he was thinking. Was the storm building inside him again? Would he emerge with his fists raised against Elijah? Would he turn on her? In his uncontrollable wrath, would he force the deputy to shoot him?

"I reckon you owe your daughter an apology, Dr. Richardson," Elijah said. "You think you could settle up your unfinished business before you go on your way?"

Lily held her breath as her father took a step toward her. But when he lowered his hands, she realized that his eyes were rimmed with tears. His lip quivered as he dropped to his knees in the dirt in front of her.

"Lily," he said. "My daughter."

Folding in upon himself, he pressed his face into the road as sobs tore from his chest. With a trembling hand, Lily reached out and laid her hand on the man's head. *This* was her father. Not the great conductor, the imperious musician, the overlord of the Richardson household. His hair damp beneath her fingertips, she traced the curve of his head with her palm.

"Father," she whispered.

"Lily, I hurt you. I know what I did."

"Father." She lifted his shoulders and drew him into her arms. "Papa, my papa."

"Oh, Lily," he wept, "I'm so sorry."

As she clung to him, she looked up into Elijah's face. The pastor held his own child close, his large hands stroking the baby's soft curly hair. "I love you, Father," she said. "I forgive you."

"God, have mercy on me," he groaned. "Have mercy on my soul."

"He does," Elijah said.

"I don't deserve —"

"No, but you'll get it anyhow. That's called

grace. Amazing grace." The preacher reached down and took the man's arm. "Dr. Richardson, welcome to Hope."

On the front porch of the Hankses' house, Lily sat in a rocking chair and laid Samuel lengthwise on her lap. As his big brown eyes focused on her face, his mouth broke into a wide grin. With a laugh, she chucked him under the chin. Folds of soft skin testified to his bouncing good health and made Lily think of one of Lucy Cornwall's fresh, doughy cinnamon buns.

"Hello, precious boy," she whispered to him. "How's my little Samuel this afternoon? Did you have a nice nap? You did! Guess what I've been doing? I've been ironing sheets with Auntie Eva, and I'm so hot."

The baby gurgled in response and gave his tiny feet a kick. Lily clasped his pudgy legs and pumped them up and down as the baby cooed with pleasure. Three days had passed since her father's repentance on the road between the opera house and Hope, and he had chosen to stay on for a few days to help rebuild the town. Though father and daughter didn't speak often, he sometimes came to sit with her on the porch while she nursed the baby.

"Look, here comes that big ol' fellow right

now," Lily murmured, spotting Clement Richardson making his way up the street. "Do you want him to hold you today? Shall I ask him if he'd like that?"

She pictured her father's great hands cradling the child. Did she dare allow the man who had hurt her to touch the baby she loved so deeply? Could she trust that he'd changed? Really, truly changed?

"Good afternoon, Lily," her father said, stepping up onto the porch. "Rather hot, don't you think?"

Lily began to rock a little, swaying the baby back and forth. She wished she could get past feeling uneasy around the man, but she'd spent too many years in fear. "Yes, it's quite warm today," she said. "I've been ironing sheets with Eva on the back porch."

Her father took the chair beside her, removed his hat, and mopped his brow with a monogrammed white handkerchief. "It must be difficult for you," he said. "You once led such a pampered life. Now you're reduced to pressing sheets as though you were a slave woman yourself."

Lily swallowed. "Eva's not a slave, Father. She's my good friend. I'm happy to work at her side."

"Of course, of course. I meant no ill will in my comment." He leaned back in the chair.

"Lily, I've been trying to decide how to speak with you. Nothing is simple anymore. I don't know what to tell you of my deepest thoughts. I'm not sure which tone to take with you. But I do know that matters must be addressed. We must talk about the past and the future."

"I prefer the present, Father. I'm happy here."

"Are you?" His face showed the hint of a scowl. "You were brought up with art and music, with gardens and servants, with beautiful gowns and parties every weekend. Now you wash and iron, you cook three meals a day, and you tend that . . . that baby."

"I told you why I care for Samuel, Father."

"Yes, yes." He shook his head. "I'm sorry to be brusque. This is difficult. All of it. I find it so . . . impossible . . . to imagine my daughter, my own flesh and blood, wandering about with that woman, that Beatrice Waldowski. To think that you actually married a stranger in order to escape your home. . . . Well, I find myself both humiliated and enraged by the entire episode. That you bore a child, my grandchild —"

"Abigail."

"Please don't speak the name. I blame myself."

"No, Father —"

"Yes, I do. I am responsible. And yet I am

also determined to make amends. To God, to your mother. To you, Lily. I must try to repair my errors in your upbringing. I must atone for my wrongs."

"Wrongs can be forgiven, Father. I've chosen to put my own past behind me and look ahead to a new day. I'm certain that the Lord has a good plan for my life — and for yours. He is a God of great mercy. When I look at all he's done for me in these past months, I am almost dumbfounded. All this time he's been leading me toward him, waiting for me to open the door and let him into my heart. In spite of everything I did, all the wrong choices, all the willful and irresponsible actions I took, God brought Samuel into my life, and he gave me this home, this town, and Elijah."

"The preacher is a good man, Lily." Her father paused for a moment, as if turning over in his mind the novelty of the man who had led him to the brink of repentance. "I'm thankful that Reverend Book wants to further his education," Richardson went on. "Though he is a bit rough around the edges now, I can envision him in a large church one day. He's good with people. He has intelligence. And he has a way with words."

"Yes," she said softly. The fact that her father admired Elijah pleased Lily. For three days she had pondered her last conversation with the preacher under the cottonwood tree. *"I love you,"* he had said. But what did those words mean to him? Was his affection that of a pastor for one of his flock, or had Lily come to mean something more to Elijah?

"He cares for the townspeople here," her father was saying. "And perhaps he should stay on in Hope for a time. Practical experience is never a bad thing."

"Hope would be poorer for losing him."

"Indeed." He rocked for a moment. "As for you, Lily, I know your mother will be heartbroken should I return to Philadelphia without you. I cannot describe the depths of her agony at your disappearance."

"I'm sorry. Truly I am."

"Then you'll come with me? I've kept the coachman waiting as long as I can. I'm afraid I must leave tomorrow."

Lily lifted her focus to the church. She could see Elijah hammering board-and-batten siding with some of the other men. The deputy, who had stayed on to help with the rebuilding, was handing him nails.

"I can't leave Samuel," Lily said. "Elijah and I . . . we almost lost him once before, Father. He was bitten by a spider. And you know he was terribly weak when Elijah brought him to —"

"The baby will be going to an orphanage tomorrow, Lily." Her father laid his hand on hers. "The deputy has confided in me that he intends to take the child. Without legal grounds for adoption, with no information on the baby's parentage, with no wife or home, the preacher cannot hope to obtain permission to keep an orphan. Everyone knows that you and Reverend Book have become attached to the child, but Lily, you must think in a reasonable manner. This baby needs a stable situation."

"But I —"

"The longer you remain in the picture, Lily, the easier you make it for the preacher to keep the boy around. But for how long? And to what end? This child in your lap is a human being, Lily. Samuel shouldn't be shuffled from one adult to another — neither of whom is truly his guardian. And look at these living conditions! You live with the Hanks family, while Reverend Book resides on a cot in the back of the church. Neither place is suitable for the rearing of a child."

"Father, I'm sure Elijah plans to —"

"Even should there be a proper home one day, Lily, you know that this town has no school, no physician, none of the amenities of polite society. . . . My dear, please set your emotions aside and allow the child to have a

chance at security. Come with me to Philadelphia, to your mother. Allow the deputy to
take the baby to Topeka. And permit God to
have full use of his instrument in this town.
Elijah Book must be set free to grow into the
man God intends. Only you can see that such
a thing happens."

Lily ran her fingertip over the baby's tiny
knuckles. Soft, velvety bumps. But this baby
didn't belong to her. Sam was not Abby's re-
placement. He was a child of God, rescued by
Elijah, and deserving of a good future. Maybe
her father was right. But, oh, how could she
part with this child she loved so much?

And how could she leave Hope?

No, it wasn't the town so much as it was the
preacher. Elijah Book. She loved him. She
couldn't walk away from him. Her heart
would break in two.

But what if she and Samuel truly were
hindrances to God's plan for Elijah? What if
they kept him from doing the work he was intended to do? What if Elijah would be better
off without them?

"Lily," her father said, patting her hand
gently. "Will you come home with me? Will
you restore joy to your mother's face? Most
important, will you allow me to become to
you the father I never was? It would be a gift
greater than anything I have ever received."

Lily gathered Sam into her arms and held him close, fighting the cry that rose up inside her. *No, no!* she wanted to shout. *I want to stay here. I want Elijah. I want this baby. I want my way — my way!*

"Oh, Lily," her father murmured. "Say you'll come home."

"Nevertheless not my will, but thine . . ."

Blinking back the tears that misted her vision, Lily nodded. "Yes, Father. I will."

"This area back here is the cemetery," Elijah explained, nodding toward the expanse of untouched prairie he had just refenced. For three days, Dr. Richardson had been good enough to stay on in town, spending his nights at the Hunters' house and his days helping shingle the church's new roof. A few minutes ago, he had wandered across the street to visit with the preacher.

"I don't see no headstones," the deputy observed. He, too, had elected to remain. He'd been meeting with town leaders to discuss legal problems the citizens of Hope were up against. He had promised to look into helping the town hire a lawman, but so far, he hadn't mentioned carting Sam off to the orphanage in Topeka. Elijah was praying the subject was closed. "How can you call this a cemetery if there's nobody buried in it?"

"I reckon we'll lose one of our people one of these days," Eli said. "In the past couple of years we've had a plague of grasshoppers, a prairie fire, and now a cyclone. There's another winter coming up, and who can tell what that might bring?"

"You're right about that."

"I'm learning that prairie life is hard, real hard. Without a doctor in town, folks don't have any place to turn for healing. I know from experience that sometimes homemade doctoring doesn't work too well. Fact is, I believe a pastor's job is to take care of his flock — and that includes providing a resting place when they go on to be with the Lord. A cemetery kind of helps comfort the family, too, you know, and that's what a church ought to do."

"I'd say you're cut out for the job, Brother Elijah," the deputy commented. "Nobody in town has a bad word to say about you."

"Well, I don't have much training."

"Reverend Book," Richardson said, "would you like to study theology here in Hope?"

The man hadn't said too much to Elijah since that day on the road. In fact, he really didn't talk to anyone. In the evenings, Eli had observed Lily and her father sitting on the front porch of the Hankses' house, but they didn't seem to be speaking to each other.

They just sat and rocked. Eli thought that was OK.

"Hope doesn't even have a grade school, Dr. Richardson," he said. "And I don't know where I'd find the nearest seminary."

"You have a post office, I assume. If you wish, I shall correspond with one of my acquaintances in the East. He's a professor of biblical studies. I believe he would be willing to post a series of his lessons to you."

Eli's heart swelled. "I'd like that very much, sir. Thank you. Thanks a lot."

"You'll be staying in town, then?" the deputy asked him.

"Yes, sir, I will. I promised the Lord I'd go wherever he sent me. And he sent me here."

The deputy grinned. "You preachers are quite a bunch. I wish the Lord would talk to me the way he talks to you."

"He might be. Are you listening?" Eli asked, giving the man a slap on the back. "Listen, has anyone invited you two gentlemen to the all-day singing and fellowship we're going to have? You're both welcome to join us while we dedicate the new church building. Let me tell you, the ladies in this town can bake pies like you wouldn't believe."

The deputy took off his hat. "Thank you

kindly, Brother Elijah, but I'd better head on back to Topeka. Which brings me to the matter I came here for in the first place. We need to talk about that baby you found."

"That baby is my son," Eli replied.

"No he ain't. Not legal, anyhow."

Eli could hear Lily singing to Samuel across the way, and his innards knotted up just thinking about losing either one. "What do I have to do, Deputy?" he asked. "I'll do anything you say. Just don't take my boy away."

The lawman plucked a stem of grass and stuck it in his mouth. "What's a man like you aiming to do with a baby, Preacher? You don't have a wife or a house or even a good-paying job. I'm the father of six, and I've got news for you. Before long here, that little fellow is going to be up on his feet, running everywhere and climbing on everything. I've watched you work this town — visiting with folks day and night, sitting up with the sick, tending to quarrels, building fences and graveyards, reading that Bible of yours at dawn. You don't have time to chase around some snot-nosed kid. Why don't you let me take him to the orphanage in Topeka? I'll admit it's not the best life a child could ask for, but the war brought in a lot of homeless young'uns. He'd have company, food in his belly, maybe even a little schooling. You did your part, Preacher. Now let the state of Kansas do the rest."

Elijah stuck his hands into his pockets and drifted for a minute with Lily's singing. He knew the tune well; it was one of her favorites. Maybe this evening he could carve out a few minutes alone with her.

"I'm going to tell you something else," the deputy added. "That boy's going to have a tough row to hoe, being a half-breed and all. Don't take that on, Preacher. Let him go."

"I know it's going to be rough," Eli began, "but Lily and I —"

"My daughter is going home to Philadelphia with me," Richardson said. "She won't be able to look after the child."

Eli felt the bottom drop out of his stomach. "Lily's leaving Hope?"

"Our reconciliation has opened new doors. My daughter would like to see her mother. We all hope to make a new beginning, thanks to your intervention, Reverend Book."

"Well, I —"

"There's a fine young gentleman, a doctor, whom I have in mind as a husband for my daughter. He's a stable and very honorable man, and he lives and practices medicine not three houses from ours in the city. He comes from a prominent family, his reputation is excellent, and he earns a more than satisfactory income from his profession. Despite my daughter's brief period of indiscretion, I am certain this young man will welcome her into his heart."

Elijah tried to scrape his stomach up off the ground. "So Lily is really leaving town?"

"Indeed. We depart tomorrow morning."

"All the more reason to send that baby on with me, Brother Elijah," the deputy said. "Ain't gonna be nobody to look after him when she goes. You'd better let the orphanage take over."

"I need to do some thinking." Eli paused. "I need to pray."

"I hope it won't take too long, Preacher. The longer I dawdle here, the less my wife is going to like it. Like I said, we've got six young'uns. . . ."

As the man rambled on, Elijah felt his heart stand still in his chest. He had to see Lily. Had to talk to her. Under the cottonwood tree, she had told him she loved him. But loved him how? Like a preacher? Like a brother?

He wanted more from Lily than that. "Excuse me, gentlemen," he said. Then he nodded to the two men and sprinted out of the cemetery toward the Hanks house.

CHAPTER 17

As Lily carried Samuel down the road toward the opera house, she watched a peregrine falcon soar high above in the bright blue sky. Drifting on a current of warm summer air that swirled upward from the prairie, the majestic bird surveyed its territory with an eye that missed nothing. Alone, regal, ever vigilant, the falcon hovered, almost unmoving.

"They that wait upon the Lord shall renew their strength." The words of Isaiah whispered through Lily like a soft breeze. *"They shall mount up with wings as eagles; they shall run, and not be weary; and they shall walk, and not faint."*

Wait upon the Lord. In her awkward, stumbling life, God had revealed himself as the master of time. He had led her, matured her, nurtured her, and finally knocked at a moment when she was willing to open the door of her heart. She had to trust that even now, in the midst of her utter sorrow, God would work his will. In his time.

If she could only be patient, Lily thought as she stepped onto the porch of the gaudy building, he would give her strength. Though right now she felt as worn and ragged as an old dishcloth, she believed that one day God would help her to mount up with wings just like that peregine falcon. She would be able to run and not grow weary, to walk and not faint. Some distant future moment, even without Elijah and Samuel, she would learn to soar.

Oh, Father, guard me now. Please permit me to give Elijah this one gift, something to help him in his work, something from my heart.

She had barely lifted her hand to knock when the door swung open. Beatrice emerged, her purple velvet dress blending with the shadows in the room behind her. A smirk lifted one corner of her red-painted mouth.

"I saw you walking down the road, Lil." She stepped aside and gestured toward the dusky foyer. "Won't you come in?"

Lily tightened her grip on Samuel. "Thanks, Bea. I was hoping you and I could speak for a moment."

"Sure. Old friends, after all."

Entering the room with its red wallpaper and gilt chandeliers, Lily nestled the baby's head against her neck. The sound of laughter and poorly played music drifted through the room from the saloon down the hall. She had hoped to leave Sam with Eva. But the woman's "short trip" to the mercantile had lasted more than an hour when Lily decided to go ahead and finish the matter. Evening approached, and she didn't want to be out after dark.

"How do you like the place?" Bea asked, giving a twirl that sent her velvet gown billowing above her ankles. "The saloon's that way. The girls' rooms are up the stairs. The opera stage is through those doors. Can you believe this is all mine? It's just like the cards foretold, Lil. Grand things are happening to me. And this is the grandest of them all. What more could a woman want?"

True love, Lily thought. *A family. A home. An abiding faith in a saving God.*

"Our girls came in yesterday," Beatrice confided. "We've got five of them, and every one is just gorgeous. We have a singer, too. She's not as good as you, but she'll do. The saloon is fully stocked, and business is good already. George has been counting the wagons and stagecoaches passing this place ever since we started building. He thinks we've got ourselves a regular gold mine."

"Are you happy, Bea?" Lily asked softly.

"Of course I'm happy. I'm ecstatic. Who wouldn't be? This is everything I've ever wanted." With a frown that belied her words, she crossed her arms. "So, what brings you out here? I see the deputy wasn't able to pry you loose from that baby yet. You know, your daddy was fit to be tied when he found out what his little girl had been up to. I guess you two have worked things out. At least, I don't *see* any bruises."

As she laughed, Lily lifted her chin. "I'm going back to Philadelphia with my father tomorrow morning, Beatrice," she said. "I've come for my melodeon."

The woman's face froze. "You've come for what?"

"I want my melodeon."

"What for?"

"Because it's mine. I bought it. Please give it to me."

Bea's face, harsh in the light of the chandelier's oil lamps, twisted into a sneer. "The blasted thing is *here*, isn't it?" she said. "That means it belongs to me."

Lily shook her head. "You know it's mine, Bea."

"I know who's got it, and that's me." She gave a sniff. "You robbed me once already of my biggest asset. You refused to stay with me, even though I'd taken care of you and given you everything I had to give. You left me penniless and hopeless, with nothing to my name but that old show wagon, while you went prancing off after that preacher and his baby. Now you think I'm going to give you the melodeon? Think again, Lily Nolan."

Lily had expected this. She knew Beatrice still wanted to punish her, and she sensed that honor and fairness would never rule in the heart of her false friend. To move Beatrice Waldowski to action, it took money.

"You know the melodeon is mine by rights," Lily said. "If you won't give it to me, I'll buy it from you. Here's everything I've earned working for Elijah Book. You can have all the money in my purse, if you'll let me take my melodeon."

Shifting Sam to her other arm, Lily tugged a cloth pouch from her pocket. The weight of the coins pulled on her arm. Elijah had earned this money by tending to his flock, faithfully ministering to their needs, and laboring day and night on the church. But he had given it willingly to Lily to pay for Samuel's care.

In the beginning, she had felt she deserved every penny. Up most of the night, worn out from washing diapers and helping Eva keep the house, her body depleted by the baby's constant need for nourishment, Lily had taken Elijah's money gladly. Now it meant nothing to her. Nothing but a way to get the melodeon.

"How much is it?" Beatrice asked, giving

the pouch a look of disdain. "Five or six dollars?"

"More than that. You're welcome to count it." Lily handed her the pouch. "It's enough to help pay for a piano. That would suit your needs better anyway."

"What are you planning to do with the melodeon, start your own opera house in Philadelphia?"

"I want the church of Hope to have it."

"A church? You want to put that organ in a church?" She smiled. "Well, too bad, Lil. I'm keeping the melodeon. I like the way it sounds."

She tossed the pouch at Lily before whirling away. Lily strode after her. "You have to give it to me, Bea. It's mine. You have no right to keep it. I need it."

"You can't have it!" Beatrice stormed into the saloon. "Go on back to Philadelphia, little girl. Let your daddy beat on you. You don't need a melodeon for that."

"Where's Mr. Gibbons?" Lily demanded, following on her heels. "I'll speak to him about it. He'll take the money."

"George won't care about your paltry pennies, Lil. He's a rich man." She sashayed across the room toward a table where a group of men were playing cards. "Get rid of this woman for me, would you, George? She's pestering me."

The big man stood up from the table, dropping his cards facedown beside his glass of whisky. "You again?" he said, facing Lily. "What are you doing on my premises? Get out."

"That's my melodeon in the corner," Lily said. "I bought it when I joined the traveling show. I paid for it myself."

"With money she stole from her daddy's vault," Beatrice shouted.

"I've offered to pay for the melodeon," Lily countered, laying the cloth pouch on the table. "There are thirty-two dollars here. Count them if you like, Mr. Gibbons. It's a fair price."

"Get outta here, lady. We don't need your money, do we, Bea?"

"We don't need anything from her."

"Get out, before I send one of my boys to throw you out. You ain't caused me nothing but trouble since the first time I laid eyes on you. You and that infernal preacher. First he drives off my saloon business, and now you try to take my music."

"It's *my* melodeon," Lily repeated firmly. "I have nothing else to leave these people. Nothing to give Elijah. I want the town of Hope to have the melodeon. Please, sir, listen to reason. Take this money and give me my instrument."

"Out!" he roared, grabbing her arm. "Out, out, out!"

As he pushed Lily across the saloon, the customers broke into jeers. The women in their bold silk dresses called out to her. Samuel began to cry. Lily covered his head with her arm and hurried out into the foyer, barely able to stay on her feet as George Gibbons shoved her toward the front door.

As she reached for the brass knob, the door flew open. Elijah, the deputy, and Dr. Richardson — followed by half the town of Hope — poured into the building. George Gibbons and his men drew their pistols.

"Turn the woman loose," Elijah demanded, taking a step toward Gibbons. A half-dozen six-shooters pointed at Elijah's chest clicked to full cock. He held up his hands. "I'm unarmed. I'm the preacher in Hope, and I'm asking you to let Mrs. Nolan go."

"She's trespassing," Gibbons spat. "And so are you, Preacher."

"Well, I'm not," the deputy said, moving into the open circle. "Put your guns away, men. Won't be no bloodshed. We'll settle this peaceable, or I'll haul every one of you off to Topeka."

"We've done nothing wrong," Beatrice said. "We have a deed to this property, and we're just minding our business. It's Mrs.

Nolan you ought to haul off. She came over here to stir up trouble, Deputy — and she brought that poor little baby right into the saloon. If that doesn't show what kind of person she is, I don't know what would. Arrest her, sir, and we'll all be better off."

Lily let out a cry of disbelief. "Beatrice, how can you say such things? I came for the —"

"She came here looking for work," Bea said. "She tells me you're planning to take her back to Philadelphia tomorrow, Dr. Richardson. She was hoping to hide out here at the opera house until you left without her, and then she thought she could get a job singing in our shows. I reminded her of all the trouble she's caused you and everybody else, but she said she didn't care a bit. Look at her standing there with that baby, all sweet and innocent. She knows good and well what she's up to, don't you, Lily?"

"Why would I come here for work, Bea?" Lily said. "You've already got a singer. Don't you, Mr. Gibbons?"

"Well, yes, but —"

"Did you want to join our *other* girls, Lily?" Beatrice asked. "Maybe that was your real reason for coming."

Cornered, Lily spotted one ray of light.

"Maybe so, Bea," she said. "Maybe you'd like to hire me on with the other girls. Why don't you tell the deputy what my duties would be? And while you're at it, you can show him your license to operate a brothel."

Amid the cries and shouts that followed her remark, the deputy hollered for order. "Now what's going on here?" he demanded. "What's this about girls, Mr. Gibbons? I've been hearing rumors ever since I stepped into this town. You operating a brothel here?"

"Absolutely not, sir." Gibbons's face flamed bright red. "We run a legitimate opera show and a saloon."

"What's all this about hired girls?"

"Maids. Cooks."

"And those rooms upstairs? What do you use them for?"

"We rent them out to travelers passing through. Kind of like a hotel."

"I guess you wouldn't mind if I took a look." Without waiting for an answer, the deputy headed for the stairs.

In the ensuing confusion, Lily spotted her opportunity to escape. Hugging Samuel tightly to her chest, she darted through the front door and slipped out onto the porch. Oh, this had been a disaster! How could she have misread the warning signs? How could she have been so naive as to think Bea would agree to her request? She could hardly wait to get back to the quiet security of Eva's house.

"Lily!" Elijah's voice stopped her short. "Lily, can I talk with you a minute?"

She stopped at the edge of the porch and squeezed her eyes shut. She could only pray for strength. At this very moment, she must hand Samuel over to Elijah. She must let them both go, and she had not even the melodeon to give the man she loved. Her father would be coming to get her, and she must leave with him. That was her decision — to do God's will and put her own desires behind her. *God, give me strength!*

"Lily?" Elijah's warm hand covered hers. "I was worried about you. I went looking for you at the Hankses' house. And then Caitrin Cornwall said she saw you walking this direction. Your father and the deputy heard the news, and after that, it seemed like the whole town joined in the parade down to the opera house. Are you all right?"

She drank down a breath, unable to meet his eyes. "I'm sorry to have caused trouble again."

"Lily?" He placed the crook of his finger under her chin and tilted her head. "Lily, I know you're supposed to go to Philadelphia tomorrow morning. I also have a feeling that in some ways you're still scared of your father. Did you come here to get work from Beatrice?"

She couldn't keep the tears from rolling down her cheeks. "No, I came to get my melodeon," she wept. "I wanted you to have it for the church. I wanted to leave the town something. Bea wouldn't give it to me, not even when I offered all the money I've earned working for you. She's keeping the melodeon, and I left the pouch on the table in the saloon, and now the money's all gone, and I don't have anything to give you. . . ."

His arms slipped around her, encompassing both the woman and the baby. "Lily, you already gave me the greatest gift you could give. You gave my son his life. You gave me your music, the sound of your voice, your smile, your words of wisdom, your laughter. You gave yourself to me and to this whole town, Lily. We don't need . . . *I* don't need anything but you."

"No. I've interfered with your work for the Lord. Samuel and I keep you from doing —"

"Keep me from it? You give my ministry meaning, Lily. When I think of you and Sam, I realize why I've got to help folks. I understand how I'd feel if anything ever happened to either of you. I think about what I'd need in a pastor, and that gives me the strength to keep on working for God. It's the thought of seeing you and Sam on the porch every evening that fills my heart with joy and keeps my feet on the servant path. It's you who comes into my mind when I'm praying and planning sermons. What do I want to say to Lily to help her grow? How can I encourage Lily? What words can I offer to make Lily stronger in her walk with God? It's you . . . you and Sam . . . who make this pastor work worth all the hours I spend at it."

He stopped, his breath shallow. "I know you want to go home with your father," he went on. "I know you need to see your mother. And I would never want to put a barrier in the path God has laid out for you. But I meant what I said under the cottonwood tree the other day, Lily Nolan. I love you. I love you the way a man loves a woman. I love you so much, I'm willing to ask you to leave your mother and your father and cleave to me. Which, if I understand Scripture right, means I want you to marry me, Lily. I want you to marry me and live with me every day of my life from here on out. No matter what."

Lily covered her mouth with her hand, unable to believe the words that had tumbled from this man's overflowing heart. "Oh, Elijah, I love you so much!" she cried out. "But I don't want to be a stumbling block —"

"You're my wings, darlin'."

"Wings!" Lily lifted her gaze from the prairie and focused on the falcon still tracing lazy circles in the twilight. "I want you to soar, Elijah. I want God to use you. I'll do all I can to lift you up."

"Then you're saying yes?" He set her away from him, his hands on her shoulders. "Because your father told me —"

"My father can go home to his wife," she said firmly, "and I'll stay here with . . . with my husband. I'll visit my parents soon enough. But then I'll come back here, where I belong."

"Mercy!" Elijah laughed. "Mercy, mercy, mercy."

"Amen," she murmured, slipping into his arms again.

"Brother Elijah!" Seth Hunter dashed out onto the porch. "Brother Elijah, you've got to — oh, I didn't mean to —"

"That's all right," Elijah said. "At least it's you cutting in on us again."

The tall man gave a chuckle. "You two need to make this thing official."

"We are. Just give us a week or two."

"A week!" Lily said, giving Sam a squeeze. "You hear that, Sammy? Your daddy and I —"

Elijah was staring at her. "Lily, do you think Sam would be better off in an orphanage?" he asked in a low voice. "I don't have a house yet. I don't get paid much. And there's no school here in Hope."

"I think you're his God-given father," she said. "He couldn't be better off than that."

"I don't know about that baby of yours," Seth Hunter cut in, "but there's a ruckus going on inside the opera house, Brother Elijah. We could do with a man of God to help sort things out."

"A ruckus?"

"Those ladies came out of their rooms wearing next to nothing, and the deputy was rounding them all up when Jack Cornwall's mother fainted. Then Beatrice Waldowski went to screaming, and all of a sudden she bit the deputy on the arm, and Jack knocked out two of the saloon customers, and George Gibbons fired a bullet into the ceiling, and . . . and, well, I'm just rambling on to beat the band," he said. "I've been living with Rosie too long. You'd better come in and help us, Preacher. It's a mess."

Elijah reluctantly stepped away from Lily. "Go on back to the Hankses' house," he told her, "and start planning our wedding. I want to marry you before anybody gets it in mind to come between us again. You hear?"

"Yes, sir," she said, giving him a mock salute. "And you get in there and round up your sheep, Reverend Book. Don't you know a pastor's work is never done?"

With a laugh, he caught her and gave her a

warm kiss right on the lips. As he turned to go back into the opera house, Lily fairly skipped down the porch steps. *"They shall run, and not be weary,"* she thought as she scampered onto the road, her spirits soaring on eagles' wings.

CHAPTER 18

"That ought to do it for you, Mrs. Nolan," Jack Cornwall said, stepping back from the small stone cross he had set into the ground. "Is it all right?"

Lily held Samuel close as she knelt beside the marker lit with golden sunlight on this bright Sunday morning. "Abigail Nolan" it read. "1866. Rest in peace." She reached out and ran her fingertips over the coarse stone that Elijah had asked the town blacksmith to carve as a memorial to her lost baby.

"Thank you, Mr. Cornwall," Lily said softly. "Elijah was right about the cemetery. It does help."

"Sure the man himself will be back soon enough," Caitrin Cornwall said. She laid her hand on Lily's shoulder. "Perhaps he'll arrive this afternoon before the all-day singing is finished. I know he planned to be here to dedicate the church, but Topeka is a long way."

Lily nodded. "I know."

"If you're sure you'll be all right, then, we'll just pop round the front to help set up tables."

"That would be fine, Caitrin." Lily smiled

at the Irishwoman, whose concern was plainly written in her green eyes. "I'll join you soon."

As the young couple left her alone, Lily sank farther into the lush green grass at the foot of the stone cross. Elijah Book had left town along with the deputy and Dr. Richardson a full ten days before, and no one had heard a word from them since. The three men had planned to escort the entire troupe of opera-house employees to Topeka, where they would have to speak to the authorities about their activities. At the same time, Elijah was hoping to begin the paperwork that would give him the right to call Samuel his son. The deputy had predicted success, but Lily couldn't make herself relax.

What if Beatrice had pulled some kind of trick? What if George Gibbons had gone off half-cocked? What if Elijah had run into legal problems over the adoption? What if . . . what if . . . what if . . . ?

"It's hard to put your whole faith in the Lord, Samuel," she told the baby in her arms. Spreading a small quilt, she laid the child in the grass beside her. "I've always tried to manage things on my own, even though I never did a very good job of it. Sometimes, I'm afraid to trust."

She studied the small stone cross and thought of the wrenching grief she had suffered. "This marker is in memory of Abigail," she told Samuel as the baby took one of his own bare toes in his tiny fist. "Abigail was my daughter. Your sister, in a way. I loved her very much."

Watching the baby through misted eyes, Lily pondered her loss. What if Elijah couldn't get permission to adopt Samuel? What if the baby were taken from them? What if something terrible had happened to Elijah while he was in Topeka? What if . . . what if . . . what if . . . ?

"Here I am worrying again," Lily whispered, giving Sam's nose a gentle pat. "You'll have to learn from your papa rather than me on this matter of letting God take control. I do miss Abby, Samuel. She was my precious daughter. But I'm so grateful to God for putting you into my arms. I want to be your mama, sweet boy. Is that all right?"

"It's all right with me."

Elijah's voice took Lily's breath away.

She swung around to find the man himself standing beside the church's back door. "Elijah!" she cried, getting to her feet. "You came home! You're safe!"

With a laugh, he caught her in his arms. "Where's your faith, darlin'? We tried to make it back last night, but we were just too tired. Spent the night down the river a way, and then got up at dawn to make it here in time for the singing."

"Oh, Elijah, what happened in Topeka? You have to tell me everything."

"The judge shut down the opera house and threw George Gibbons in jail for operating an illegal business. Beatrice hightailed it off someplace before she could even get to court, and nobody could find her. She's long gone. Seems the deed she and Gibbons were so proud of was nothing but a fake. So the judge gave the building to the town of Hope to start up a county school. How about that?"

"But what about Samuel? Can you adopt him? Is it going to be legal?"

"*We* can adopt him," he said. "I found out that Reverend and Mrs. Elijah Book will have an easy time of it — easier than Brother Elijah all by himself, anyhow. So what would you say to taking care of first things first?"

"What do you mean?" Lily asked. She watched in confusion as Elijah took two strides across the grass, scooped up the baby, and headed back to the church. "Where are you going?"

"To get married. Care to join me?"

With a laugh of disbelief, Lily followed the preacher into the church. As they stepped into the crowded room, the round rich notes of Lily's melodeon suddenly filled the air. Everyone rose from the newly built benches and began to clap. Lily covered her mouth with her hand and stared in shock.

"Welcome home, Brother Elijah!" Rolf Rustemeyer called from his accustomed position beside Violet on the Hudson family's pew. "We are waiting for you long time!"

"I had to round up another preacher," Elijah said as everyone laughed and clapped again. "And I needed to find just the right person to play the music for our wedding."

Lily glanced in the direction he pointed. There sat her melodeon. And playing the wedding march was . . . her mother! But how?

"Your father wanted her to come," Elijah explained, "so he sent a wire to Philadelphia. She came on the first train."

With a cry of joy, Lily dashed across the room and threw her arms around her mother. Tears streaming, the older woman lifted her hands from the organ and gathered her daughter close.

"Oh, Lily," she whispered. "Your father told me everything . . . I'm so sorry. So very sorry."

"Mama, you came. You're here. That's all that matters."

The older woman's moist blue eyes crinkled at the corners. "Well, you'd better not interrupt the music any longer, my dear. You know how your father feels about that sort of thing."

Lily lifted her head to see the grand gentleman himself step into the small building along with Dr. Hardcastle, the pastor from the huge stone church in Philadelphia. As the music swelled, the two men marched to the front and took their places near the podium. Lily sat dumbfounded as her father began to sing "Ode to Joy." His magnificent baritone filled the church, rattled the windows, and silenced the birds in the trees.

With a smile as broad as all outdoors, Elijah walked across the room and took Lily's hand. "Will you marry me," he asked, "this morning?"

Unable to speak, Lily nodded. Cradling Samuel in one arm, Elijah encircled Lily with the other as they walked to the altar. Dr. Hardcastle smiled and held out both his hands to her.

"Welcome, Lily," he said gently. "Welcome to the family of Christ."

Lily tried her best to listen to the service, truly she did. But all she really managed was to soar through the heavens on eagles' wings. Her mother had come all the way from Philadelphia. Her father was singing for her wedding. And beside her stood a man more handsome, more kind, more loving than any she could have dreamed possible. In spite of her rebelliousness, her weak faith, her many failings, God had blessed her beyond all imagining.

As she listened to Elijah express his deep love for her, Lily heard herself speak words of the vow she meant with all her heart. For richer, for poorer, in sickness and in health, till death do us part.

"I do," she said as the minister set her hands inside the warm grasp of her new husband. "Oh yes, I do."

"Mercy, mercy, mercy!" The joyous voice at the door to the church drew everyone's attention. Mother Margaret, hands lifted in praise, stepped into the building. As the melodeon began to play, the old woman trundled down the aisle.

"She told me she was ready to come home to Hope," Elijah whispered, leaning close to Lily. "And she didn't want to miss this moment."

As the organ music swelled through the room, Mother Margaret took her place at the front of the church and raised her voice in blessing.

"My faith looks up to Thee,
Thou Lamb of Calvary,
Savior divine!

Now hear me while I pray,
Take all my guilt away,
O let me from this day
Be wholly Thine!"

A NOTE FROM THE AUTHOR

Dear Friend,

In *Prairie Storm* I wanted to capture the pain that I and many others have felt by the betrayal and hypocrisy of some who claim to follow Christ. When storms of hurt, anger, or bitterness threaten to overwhelm us, let's remember that Christ promises to calm the waves if we will keep our eyes on him. We must never place our ultimate faith in other Christians or even in our church leaders. They often are all too human. Jesus alone should be our guide and our hope. His faithfulness is forever!

I pray you've enjoyed *Prairie Storm*. In case you missed the others in this series, be sure to look for both of them: In *Prairie Rose*, Rosie Mills and Seth Hunter overcome doubt and abandonment to build a new family bonded in Christ. In *Prairie Fire*, the flames that threaten to consume the town of Hope are washed away in the flood of love and forgiveness that endures in the hearts of Caitrin Murphy and Jack Cornwall.

My thanks to the many of you who take

382

time to write and express your appreciation for the ministry my books have in your lives. As I personally read and answer your precious letters, your words of love and faith become a ministry to me.

Blessings in Christ,

Catherine Palmer

Catherine Palmer

ABOUT THE AUTHOR

Catherine Palmer lives in Missouri with her husband, Tim, and sons, Geoffrey and Andrei. She is a graduate of Southwest Baptist University and has a master's degree in English from Baylor University. Her first book was published in 1988. Since then she has published more than twenty books and has won numerous awards for her writing, including Most Exotic Historical Romance Novel from *Romantic Times* magazine. Total sales of her novels number close to one million copies.

Her Tyndale House titles include *Prairie Rose*, *Prairie Fire*, *A Kiss of Adventure*, *A Whisper of Danger*, *A Touch of Betrayal*, *Finders Keepers*, and *Hide and Seek*. Her novellas appear in the anthologies *A Victorian Christmas Tea*, *With This Ring*, *A Victorian Christmas Quilt*, *A Victorian Christmas Cottage*, and *Prairie Christmas*.

Catherine welcomes letters written to her in care of Tyndale House Author Relations, P.O. Box 80, Wheaton, IL 60189-0080.